FRIENDS WITH PARTIAL BENEFITS

Friends with Benefits Series
Book 1

LUKE YOUNG

Chapter One

J illian Grayson sat up in bed, typing away on the keyboard of her laptop computer. She wore a nightshirt that wasn't all that sexy, but what she was typing was... or at least it started out that way...

Dallas lay in bed, unable to sleep and wondering if Katrina was suffering the same fate—and for the very same reason. Did she want him as much as he wanted her? Katrina was but a few steps away, yet he dare not go to her, for he was a guest, and then there was Katrina's mother, who was just across the hall. For Dallas, sleep came minutes later, but it would be short- lived, for soon Katrina stood over him, completely nude and pondering how to proceed...

Dallas must have been in a deep sleep, since he didn't feel it when Katrina peeled the sheet carefully off him, exposing his muscular body, six-pack abs, and sizeable manhood. She quivered when his impressiveness sprang into view. For a long time, she kneeled next to the bed, just studying his body and savoring his scent. Taking his sex into her hand, Katrina worked it until it was rigid

1

while she watched him sleep. When Dallas woke, he looked into her eyes, swallowed hard, and whispered, "I've been waiting for you."

Just as fast as his sex expanded, it lost its firmness and flopped against his leg. Katrina looked down at it in disappointment and then moaned in frustration. "What's wrong?"

Dallas said sheepishly, "Sometimes that happens to me. Sorry. Ever since I cheated on my wife with that whore in the pool, I haven't been able to—"

Jillian stopped typing and thought she might be heading in the wrong direction with this. How did her ex-husband get into the story? Then again, most men are assholes, she thought.

Picking up the glass of wine from her nightstand, she took a long sip and then replaced it. She highlighted the last paragraph about Dallas's *problem*, hit one key, and it was gone. Just like his boner. She laughed out loud.

She wasn't exactly in the correct frame of mind to write at the moment, especially on this particular subject. She stared straight ahead and wondered about the likelihood of Dallas slipping in the shower, striking his head, and dying instantly. Or maybe an earthquake could strike, and Dallas's amazingly perfect body would be trapped under a giant beam.

What the hell kind of name was *Dallas* anyway? She thought she might want to give her character a real name like Stewart but figured no one would believe that a guy named Stewart could give you six consecutive orgasms in one night.

What was she doing, anyway, writing novels about people having amazing sex when she'd never had any? Okay, maybe once or twice twenty years ago, but none since then. She had no right. If people knew that she was the one writing these books, they wouldn't buy them. She was a fraud.

Jillian picked up her wineglass and took another long drink. She grinned, wiped those unhelpful thoughts from her mind, and started typing again...

Katrina took his sex in her hand and worked it until it was rigid. As she studied it closely, Katrina noticed two red bumps on the underside of his pathetic excuse for a penis. She recoiled in horror—

Jillian hit the backspace key to erase everything after Dallas's "sex" started expanding. Romance novels about erectile dysfunction and STDs weren't exactly big sellers. She closed the lid on the laptop and tossed it gently onto a pillow at the foot of the bed. After emptying her wineglass with one last sip, she turned on the television.

Jillian Grayson wrote under the pen name of Jaclyn West. She'd written fourteen bestsellers so far and had more money than she needed flowing in, so her next novel could wait. The book royalties had paid for her large, beautiful house in Miami. She still had plenty of money, even after the divorce, which forced her to part with nearly half of her earnings to her bastard ex-husband.

She'd never forget the day she came home early from a book tour and found George performing oral sex on that slut in the pool, the pool she had paid for and an act he rarely, if ever, did for her. Jillian always thought he hated oral sex or, more specifically, he hated the giving part. But there he was, naked, standing in the shallow end of the pool, and going to work on some other woman as she floated in the pool on a ring, which Jillian had also paid for. The pool oral sex thing actually looked like it might be kind of fun, and she often wondered why George had never once tried that on her.

That day, when she spotted them from the second-floor balcony off their bedroom, she had watched for a little longer than she'd care to admit. Maybe that was because all her erotic romance writing had left her desensitized to sex, at least a little. At first, it didn't seem real; it was as if she was visualizing a scene for a book, not watching her husband cheat on her.

When she finally came back to earth, Jillian left the house and went to the side of the pool. She snuck up on the adulterous couple and stood there until the woman noticed they had an audience. The woman tapped George on the shoulder to get his attention. When George turned around, he had a guilty look on his face that Jillian would never forget. Jillian wouldn't let the naked woman back in the house to get her clothes. She simply threw the clothes out the door and forced the woman to get dressed outside, shamefully leaving through the back gate. George went into the house, dressed, and left through the front door. It was the last time he ever set foot inside the house.

Jillian didn't cry that day; instead, she put on a pair of kitchen gloves and retrieved the ring float from the pool. When her attempts to drain the float of air through the valve seemed to be taking too long, she stabbed it ten times with scissors. That could possibly have been overkill, but it did the trick and gave her a much-needed outlet for her rage. She called a company to have the pool drained, scrubbed, and refilled at the cost of fifteen hundred dollars. It was worth it, she thought, because she would never have been able to dip a toe in the pool until she replaced every last drop of that contaminated water.

She imagined what George had been up to all those times she was traveling. What types of women had he explored in and out of the pool? How long had he been screwing around and with how many women? Although Jillian was out of town quite a bit, she had never suspected anything. George never seemed to be sneaking around, nor was he ever evasive about where he was going or what he had planned. Their sex life was certainly not great or very active, but he seemed to be an attentive and loyal husband—at least, most of the time.

Once she discovered the infidelity, she wanted to know if George had left her with any other little surprises. She went to her doctor for a complete STD panel of tests, and luckily for him, she came back clean. Had George left her with something, she would have cut off his balls, or worse.

Jillian could always come up with stories and had never suffered from long bouts of writer's block in the past. But lately, her male characters ended up mangled in some horrible accident, diseased, or unable to perform. Although she had no personal interest in the lifestyle, she even pitched an idea for an all-female, lesbian romance novel, but her publisher declined. She could not focus. Maybe she would try to write in another genre, she thought, but this romance stuff used to come so easily to her.

She was sitting on four unfinished manuscripts. Once Jillian found a story heading down the wrong path, she would start another, but that technique didn't seem to be working for her, either. Since the divorce, she found herself unable to finish a novel, and she was beginning to think that maybe what she needed was a complete break from writing.

She couldn't blame George completely. Ever since her first bestseller, she definitely was less attentive to him than she needed to be. It was probably at least ten percent her fault, although she never admitted that to him. Even so, did he really need to screw other women in their house, especially in their pool? Couldn't he have gotten a divorce first or at the very least done it in a hotel or something? What if their son, Rob, had come home to catch his father with another woman in broad daylight? Rob, currently attending college in Georgia, would have been devastated.

He'd be home for Spring Break in about six weeks, although Jillian was sure he'd spend nearly all his time with his girlfriend, Laura, who was going to school in Miami. They'd been dating since their junior year of high school, and it looked like these two kids were in love and would be married once they graduated from college.

Even though she knew she wouldn't see him much while he was home, Jillian looked forward to his visit. She knew her son was the only truly good thing to come out of the marriage.

Jillian grabbed the remote control and changed the channel just in time to catch the Super Bowl as it was ending. She had forgotten it was on. Not that she would have tuned in anyway. She used the Packers' victory celebration as a distraction from thinking about romance novels, ex-husbands, or even men in general. Although, she did like the way Green Bay's quarterback filled out his tight football pants. She might be bitter, but she wasn't dead.

Staring up at the ceiling, she wondered what had brought her to this place in her life. How had she ended up all alone in this big house? What had she done wrong? She glanced back to the screen. When she saw an image of the Steelers locker room filled with nearly naked men, she thought about her best friend, Victoria Wilde. Jillian wondered what she was doing. She checked the time and saw it was still early. Grinning, she wondered why she bothered checking, since two in the morning would be early for Victoria. She grabbed the phone and dialed. The phone rang three times and just as Jillian was about to hang up, she heard the click. After five seconds of complete silence, the sound of soft moaning spilled through the phone.

Jillian listened for a moment. "Victoria?"

"Hello?" Victoria finally replied in a throaty drawl.

"Hey, what are you doing?"

"Oh, uh... not much. I just have a friend over."

"Sorry, I'll let you go then."

"No, don't worry about it. I can talk for a few minutes."

Only two blocks away, Victoria sat on the sofa in her living room, wearing a skintight cleavage-featuring top. She had just turned thirty-nine but looked much younger. She was in spectacular shape and dressed like a woman in her late twenties. Her 'friend' wasn't currently visible at her eye level, but he was nearby.

"So, what's going on?" Victoria asked.

Jillian sighed and began, "I tried to do some writing tonight, but I'm struggling *again*. I'm just not in a very sexual mood."

"Why don't you try watching some porn? That always gets me in the mood."

"I don't have any... porn," Jillian replied, in a voice clearly indicating to anyone paying the least bit of attention that she was taken aback by the suggestion.

Victoria, however, was preoccupied and slumped down low on the sofa, her miniskirt pulled up to her waist with her twenty-six-year-old friend Austin's head buried between her legs. He was extremely busy.

Victoria moaned slightly, "Yeah," in a low voice.

Back in the Grayson home, Jillian narrowed her eyes and asked pointedly, "You sure this is a good time?"

"I think the ice melted," Victoria said.

"What?" Jillian asked.

7

"Sorry, I was speaking to my friend."

"Oh. You sure you can talk?"

"I have at least five minutes."

"Okay..." Jillian said, a little confused.

"You have no porn? Really? Check Rob's room. I'm sure he has a stash."

"I will not go searching my son's room for porn," Jillian replied, horrified.

Victoria said a little curtly, "Ice."

"What?"

"Again, sorry I was talking to my, uh, oh..." Victoria exhaled deeply. "Come over here, and you can borrow some of mine or I could send you a link to great website that has—"

"No thanks. I think I'll just go to sleep."

Jillian heard rustling over the phone as if it had fallen then she could make out a voice say, "Oh, yeah... that feels good."

"Victoria?" She widened her eyes. "Victoria, are you sure I'm not interrupting anything?"

There was no reply.

"Victoria, are you there?"

"Sorry about that," Victoria finally answered.

"Who's over there? What are you—"

"Oh, yeah. Keep doing exactly that." Victoria moaned. "Jillian, have you ever had anyone perform oral sex on you while sucking an ice cube?"

"What?" Wrinkling her nose, Jillian shook her head. "Ice? No!"

"Well, that would certainly help you write. Oh, my..." After breathing in deeply, Victoria moaned again.

Jillian made a face. "I'm almost afraid to ask. Are you, uh, doing that... right now?"

Victoria exhaled slowly and said languidly, "Yeah, and it's... amazing!"

"And you're talking to me?"

"I can multi-task," Victoria replied, casually.

Jillian's mouth flew open as she thought about how to proceed.

"So, what else is up?" Victoria asked.

"Should you really be talking to me with some guy doing that to you?"

"Well, I figured I'd be returning the favor soon, and..." Victoria paused to exhale deeply again and continued, "I certainly wouldn't be able to talk to you then."

After Jillian nodded, her face registered mild agreement. "Oh, that makes sense... Wait, no it doesn't... I'm going to go."

"Oh... yeah, Austin." Victoria paused for a moment. "Jillian, what I meant was when my mouth is full, it'll be really hard to hold a conver—"

"No, no. That part I got," Jillian interrupted. "I think I'm going to go and let you—"

"You should... totally try this. It would clear up that writer's block issue immediately. When's the last time someone went down on you?"

Jillian made a sour face. "I'm just going to—"

"I mean, like, really got in there and did a good job with it?"

"Okay, I'm really going to hang up now."

As Jillian hung up the phone, her sick expression morphed into a smile. However, it didn't take long for the smile to fade—replaced by something resembling more of a sad longing. She could go for some good oral sex right about now. She stared blankly ahead as she tried to recall the last time anyone did that to her, much less if he did a good job while doing it. She couldn't remember exactly, but she knew it'd been a long, long, long time.

Chapter Two

Rob Grayson was throwing a Super Bowl party in the on-campus suite at Georgia State University that he shared with five other guys. The suite was ordinary, with three bedrooms, two bathrooms, and a common living area. It featured one extraordinary thing—Rob owned the biggest television on campus.

His mother, a bestselling author, had purchased it for him. He never told anyone about the types of books she wrote, because he was totally embarrassed by them. He told people his mother wrote legal thrillers under a pen name. He didn't want to admit that she wrote about perfect-bodied men and gorgeous women with huge, full, bouncing breasts having mind-blowing sex.

Rob and his best friend, Brian Nash, both college seniors, had lived together with most of the same guys in the same suite since sophomore year. Virtual opposites, the two had been best friends almost from the start. They never shared a room, since they were on different sleep schedules. A morning person, Rob preferred early classes, while Brian enjoyed sleeping in and attending afternoon classes. They spent most of their time together at bars and hanging out.

Another probable factor in their close friendship was that neither had been preoccupied with an on-campus girlfriend during the entire time they had known each other. Rob had a longtime girlfriend back in Florida, and Brian... Well, Brian was shy with women. He'd had a few girlfriends over the years, but none were ever serious or lasted more than a few weeks.

At the height of the Super Bowl party, about thirty people crowded into the living area to watch the game on the sixty-inch high-definition screen. Most were Steelers fans, but a few, including Rob and Brian, cheered on the Packers. After the game, the majority left to hit the local bars, but four of the guys and two girls—a junior named Natalie and her roommate, Cindy—stayed behind.

Brian was a little drunk. He sat on the sofa and watched Natalie and Cindy talking to Rob and another guy from the suite. Natalie wore a bulky white sweater and tight gray stretch pants. Her ass looked incredible in those pants. He'd noticed the curve of her backside much earlier, and whenever given the opportunity throughout the night, he stole a quick glance.

Brian had seen Natalie around campus before, but he had never met her. She'd been invited by some of the other guys in the suite and he didn't know much more about her, except that she didn't currently have a boyfriend. He wasn't all that interested since she was a little tall for him and always seemed so full of herself. But now, he was beginning to rethink his initial impressions, after all, she did look spectacular in those pants.

He sipped his beer, alternating between watching the postgame coverage, and the other people in the room trying to coax Natalie into doing something. He wasn't paying close enough attention to know what they were talking about. Natalie rolled her eyes, evidently persuaded, and removed her sweater to reveal a tight camisole underneath. Brian perked up in his seat; this was now much more exciting than the postgame coverage. *Was she going to take off more?*

No more clothing came off, but what she did next would change Brian's life forever, or at least set him on a new course. Standing perfectly still, Natalie took a deep breath and slowly and gracefully lifted one of her legs until it pointed straight at the ceiling. The other remained firmly planted on the floor as she rose onto the ball of her foot. She held her raised leg with one hand, almost effortlessly, as Brian looked her up and down.

He zoomed in on her rear end, trying to see any hint of the underwear she wore under those tight pants, but he could see none. She was either, wearing nothing or some kind of tiny thong. While staring at her, open-mouthed, his beer began to spill on his pants. When he realized it, he simply corrected the bottle without bothering to wipe off, and then quickly looked back at Natalie as she maintained that astonishing pose. He studied her legs and tilted his head slightly to get a better angle. Looking closer, he was convinced that he could see just a hint of the outline of her parts in the crease between her separated legs. He longed to explore that area closer—with his fingers and tongue and hopefully his own *part.*

Like the rest of the group, Natalie's athletic ability impressed him. He hated to admit it, but he was more impressed with the incredible firmness of her body. He supposed that made him shallow, but she looked good. He was young, lonely and a little drunk— all of that played into his fascination with her that night.

Seconds later, Natalie slowly brought her leg down and Brian's eyes followed it the whole way, his mouth still wide open. While her audience clapped, he approached her. He spent the rest of the night talking to her, getting her drinks, and hanging on her every word. Later, he walked both Natalie and her roommate to their dorm.

As he lay in bed that night, unable to sleep, Brian pictured Natalie with her leg in the air, only this time, she was completely naked. It was just the two of them in the living room now, he sitting on the sofa, holding a beer and watching her. While she continued to hold her right leg skyward with a hand near her ankle, she used one finger of that occupied hand to motion for him to come to her. Dropping the beer, he leapt up and went to her. When he reached her, she was somehow able to remove her hand from the leg without it moving at all. He knew it was impossible, but it was his fantasy. He stood next to her with her ankle inches from his head. Natalie looked him in the eye while she used both hands to unzip his pants, extract his equipment, and guide him inside of her. Sighing, Brian rolled over in an attempt to go to sleep, hoping he could coax that thought into his subconscious as a full-length sex dream.

Chapter Three

For the next few weeks, Brian dated Natalie informally. They did homework together, they ate together in the dining hall, and they even made out a few times, but that was all. There was no removal of clothes or touching of parts or even dry humping. Brian would leave her dorm room, usually bent over at a strange angle and very frustrated. He wanted to see her naked, and he wanted to see her strike that ballet pose while she was naked. He was infatuated with her, and the more she held back physically, the more head-over-heels in love he became.

Their relationship took a minor step forward three weeks after they started dating when Rob, Brian, Natalie, and three other friends went to a college party at a university about two hours away. At three in the morning, they left the party and returned in an old station wagon with Brian and Natalie lying next to each other in the cargo area. She reached out to touch his hand, and he took her hand, interlocking his fingers with hers. They held hands for the remainder of the ride home with the back of Natalie's hand resting over Brian's groin. He didn't know if she realized it at first, but as his penis began to expand in his pants, he started to feel her pressing against it a little more firmly, which only made it harder. For the rest of the ride home, he hoped she would unzip and pull him out to relieve the pressure, but she never did. Instead she was either asleep or was pretending to be, as she lay next to him. When they arrived at daybreak, Brian offered to walk her to her room. Natalie declined and told him to come over later that day. Brian went home, jerked off, and quickly fell asleep.

The next morning, Jason, one of the guys who went on the trip, interrogated Brian about the goings on in the back of the wagon as Rob stood near them.

Jason asked, "So did Natalie give you a little tug back there?"

"A tug?"

"A hand job, you idiot!"

"Not exactly," Brian said.

"I heard something going on back there," Jason said.

Rob laughed. "Well, what do you call it when a girl presses the back of her hand into it?"

Brian glared at Rob.

Jason looked wide-eyed at Brian, then his face took on a serious expression, and he asked, "So she never actually touched it?"

"No," Rob answered for his friend.

"Has she never touched it?"

"Outside of clothes?" Brian asked.

"Of course—it's got to be out to count," Jason said.

"Well, then no."

"But last night she put the back of her hand on it?" Jason asked.

"And she pressed on it a little," Brian said before realizing how lame it sounded.

Jason smiled at him. "Well in that case it's called... *nothing!*" He jumped up and announced loudly as he headed into the bedroom area, "Guys, wait till you hear this!"

After catching up with Jason, Brian grabbed him by the shoulder. "Don't be a dick. She said she has a surprise for me tonight."

Jason chuckled. "Yeah, maybe you can put your big toe next to her pussy through her clothes."

He proceeded to tell the rest of the guys the station wagon story. Brian never should have let it slip; his suite mates would never let him live it down. From then on, that particular sex act —or unsex act—was called the BHJ (for "backhand job"), but some preferred to call it "the *un*tug."

Chapter Four

J illian agreed to a blind date with a supposedly great guy who worked with the husband of one of her close friends. Mike had a good job and was a competent tennis player. Years ago, Jillian had put in a tennis court right next to the pool because she loved to play. She played number-one singles on her high school team, and although she wasn't good enough to earn a spot on her college team, she continued to play at least a few times a month for the past twenty years.

Mike arrived and Jillian gave him a quick tour of the house and pool area before leading him to the court. He started their date on the wrong foot, by asking, "What did your ex-husband do for a living to afford all this?"

After glaring at him a moment, Jillian replied, "He didn't pay for any of this. I did."

"You're a writer, correct?"

"Romance novels mainly."

"Huh," Mike said as he returned a look that screamed he couldn't believe writing books could support this type of lifestyle.

"Marci told me you played on your college team," she said.

"I was number one, but don't worry—I'll take it easy on you."

They started hitting the ball around as a warm-up, and Jillian was easily able to keep up with him. She thought he was a good player, but she figured he must have played at a very small school if he'd been number one on its team.

From the first point, it became clear to Jillian that Mike would do whatever was necessary to avoid the embarrassment of losing to a woman. He served first and won his game easily. On her serve, she reached game point against him only to have him call two of her serves, which were clearly in, as out. She didn't take issue with his calls and lost that game on another questionable call. Then he held his serve again, to go up three games to love.

She decided to play more aggressively by coming to the net after each serve in the fourth game. This strategy worked, and she won her next two service games and broke his serve to bring the set even at three. Despite more questionable calls from her immature opponent, both players held serve to six games all, and Mike's frustration seemed to be growing. During the tiebreak, Jillian served first. When she called one of his obviously long shots out, Mike again, questioned the call. She reversed it simply to end the match as soon as possible.

When they reached six points to five in the tiebreak, Jillian came to the net hoping to even the score, but ended up badly out of position. Ignoring his opportunity to go down the line for an easy passing shot, he instead chose to fire a shot into her body. When the ball hit her, Jillian stared at him in disbelief. It didn't hurt all that much, but it did knock the wind out of her. She couldn't believe a grown man would do such a thing.

Grinning widely, he told her she played a good set as she walked to the bench. Still glaring at him, she opened a bottle of water and took a sip as he joined her.

"Best two out of three?" Mike asked, as he opened his hand

for her to pass over the bottle from which she was drinking. After exhaling deeply, she handed him the bottle. He drank from it and attempted to return it.

She waved him off. "I think I'm done."

"Tired?" he asked.

Jillian shot a look at him as if she wanted to kill him and said sarcastically, "Yeah, I'm too tired."

Moments later, they returned to the pool area carrying their racquets, and he asked, "How about one drink before I go?"

She nodded reluctantly, and he asked, "Do you have a beer?"

Jillian went into the house, and when she returned with the beer, she found him swimming in the pool. Standing at the edge, she glared at him. "What are you doing?"

"I was hot," he answered as he stood in the pool, looking at her. "This feels great. Why don't you join me?"

He appeared to be naked, except for a huge black patch around his groin. Squinting, she thought he was wearing a black bathing suit, or he had the most unkempt pubic hair ever on a human being. When she looked closer, she realized it was the latter but asked anyway with a sick expression, "Did you bring a bathing suit?"

"No," he replied and then repeated, "Why don't you join me?"

"Who gets into someone's pool naked on a first date?"

"I was picking up these signals from you on the court. You had this angry, sexy look on your face."

"Because I was in pain after you hit me with the ball."

"You're not mad about that, are you?"

"No, but you acted like a complete ass on the court, and then somehow think that's an invitation for you to dunk your naked, sweaty ass in my clean pool. Get out!"

He looked at her with a grin, and when she didn't smile back he asked, "Seriously?"

"Yes. Please, get out and go."

"All right," he said as he unashamedly climbed from the pool with his huge thicket of wet black pubic hair matted down around his unattractive groin. His sizeable gut was protruding enough to add to the overall look. He stood dripping with his hands on his hips as he asked curtly, "A towel?"

After grunting, she took a sip of his beer and glanced once more at his train wreck of a body before grabbing a towel and tossing it to him. He proceeded to dry his groin first while she stood ten feet from him. She continued to drink the beer, alternating a sip with a grimace, as he lifted his hairy parts while drying off in some obviously misguided attempt to impress her.

He said, "Maybe that beer will loosen you up a little."

"No, it's merely keeping me from calling the police."

Jillian nearly vomited in her mouth when she noticed that after he dried his pubic area, it appeared even hairier than before. She looked away for a moment but then back, to confirm that some of the strands of hair were about six inches long. Then he used the towel to over dry his ass, appearing to shove it in there a whole lot more than was actually necessary.

"You really don't want me to stay?" he asked, standing naked and holding the towel.

After staring at him in disbelief, she placed the beer on the table, pulled her cell phone from her pocket, and pointed it at him with her finger poised on the screen.

"What are you doing?" he asked with a smile.

"If you don't get out of here right now, your Don King super-bush is going viral."

"Okay. Okay. Relax! You successful women can be so bitchy."

As he dried the hair on his head while standing in full view of her, she pushed the button on the cell phone to snap a picture. He didn't notice. She needed proof of this to show her friends. He extended the towel to her while she shook her head and made a face as if he were offering her a biohazard.

"Keep it," Jillian said. She strolled over, picked up his racquet and all his clothes, calmly walked to the back of the yard, and threw them over the fence.

"Geez, what's your deal?" He wrapped the towel around his waist.

"Oh, *now* you cover up," she said sarcastically. Then she pointed to the gate, and he headed for it with her following close behind. She said, "Believe me when I say that I hate to be the one to tell you this, but you are in desperate need of a trim."

After shooting her an evil look, he went through the gate. Jillian locked it and headed back to the house while thinking that would be the last blind date she'd allow her friends to arrange. It would also be several days before the image of his nether regions would leave her brain, although she would save the picture for a long time.

Chapter Five

That evening, Natalie's roommate was away for the night, so she and Brian lay in her bed making out. She allowed him to remove her shirt and bra but not her jeans. He spent a lot of time enjoying her newly unveiled breasts as she ran her fingers through his hair. He tried repeatedly to unbutton her jeans and she stopped him each time. While his hands were all over her body, her hands never went below his shoulders, much to his growing frustration.

"God, you feel amazing," he said.

"Oh, so do you," she said breathlessly.

"I'm so hot for you right now."

"So am I."

"Well, why..." he began before thinking better of it.

"'Why what?" she asked.

Aching for her, Brian looked down at his straining groin before glancing up at her face. "Why, uh, aren't you touching me?"

"I *am* touching you."

"Why aren't you touching me... anywhere else?"

She looked innocently at him. "Oh, I can't do that."

"Why not?"

"I can't. I just can't touch it right now, because..."

Natalie stared at the ceiling a moment, sat up in bed, and pulled her legs to her chest. Sitting up next to her, he looked sympathetically at her. "You can tell me. Really, what is it?"

She paused and then looked at him. "I, uh, when I was younger, there was this thing that happened, and now I just can't."

He wrapped his arm around her shoulder and looked devastated. "Jesus, I'm so sorry. I didn't know. Do you want to talk about it?"

"No, I, uh..."

"Is there anything I can do?"

"I just need time. Will you wait for me?" Natalie asked as she looked away from him toward the door.

"As long as it takes."

She turned back at him with a smile. "You mean it?"

"Yes, I'm crazy about you," Brian said.

"Will you stay and just hold me all night?"

Nodding, he gave her a compassionate smile.

Chapter Six

Jillian had a date that night with James. It would be their third date together, and this guy seemed like long-term boyfriend material. They met through an Internet dating site. The plan was for James to pick her up and take her to dinner. They left the remainder of the night open to other possibilities. She was attracted to him so Jillian thought she'd invite him in afterward, but probably not go all the way. It had been eight months since her last sexual encounter, if you could even call it that, and she was starting to long for the touch of a man. She didn't want to sleep with just anyone; she was waiting for the right guy.

James arrived with a bag full of Chinese food and carrying a soft briefcase. She was surprised with the change of plans but was a fan of Chinese, so she didn't object. She brought out some plates, and they ate in the dining room. As she spooned out the food, James pulled three books from his bag and set them on the chair next to him. Jillian couldn't see the titles and didn't ask about the books as she poured them each a glass of wine. She figured he'd talk about the books when he was ready. They conversed about the usual stuff, and she forgot all about the books. When she returned to the table after clearing the plates, she found he had the titles arranged neatly in front of him.

She could see the spines of each book, and she read the titles of the first two in horror. They were all relationship books. One was *How to Strengthen Your Relationship*, another was *Relationship Secrets*, and she didn't bother reading the third. James looked at her as he held his folded hands over the books. "Where do you want to do this?"

"Do what?" she asked, confused.

"Work on our relationship," he snapped.

Jillian wondered exactly what relationship he was referring to. *We've been on two dates and this thing tonight, whatever the hell this is.*

He asked, "Want to do it here or on the sofa?"

"Sofa." She filled her wine glass to the top and slowly walked into the great room and sat down. James sat next to her—right next to her—and placed two books by his leg. He opened the third to a page he had marked with a Post-it note.

She took a long sip of her wine. "What do you think we need to work on?"

He announced, "I think all relationships need work. Don't you agree?"

"Well, yes. I guess," she replied hesitantly.

She sat speechless, drinking wine as he proceeded to go through the pages marked with Post-its. After five pages, she refilled her glass, and after five more, she brought the bottle over. By the time they had finished the bottle, James had reviewed what seemed like forty pages of lists, charts, and relationship secrets. She desperately wanted to strangle him. Instead, she hoped for a house fire, so she wouldn't have to get her hands dirty. While he droned on, she resorted to thinking about how she'd like to remodel the room. During his presentation, when he looked to her for confirmation, she politely nodded and said, "Uh-huh."

After two more grueling pages, she checked the time. Feeling as if they had been going at it for at least an hour, she was shocked to discover that they were only about thirty minutes in at that point. When he picked up the second book, and she saw what looked to be about a hundred Post-it-marked pages, she sprang to her feet. "I'll be right back. I have to go to the bathroom."

She stayed in the bathroom, which was just off the hallway between the great room and the kitchen, for about five minutes. Then it hit her and her lips curled up into a smile. She returned to him, clutching her stomach, but he was glued to book number two and didn't seem to notice.

As James began to review the highlights of the first page, he glanced over at Jillian then eyed her with concern. "Are you okay?"

"I have a little stomach ache."

He gave her a sympathetic smile. "Oh, I had explosive diarrhea last week. It was horrible. You don't have that, do you?"

She looked at him, a little horrified. "Well, no, but I—"

"That's good," James interrupted. "You should take half an Imodium and a tablespoon of Pepto. I think I have Imodium in the car if you—"

"No, thanks. I'll be okay," she said in a tired voice.

"Let's finish going through the text later then."

Jillian let a tiny smile escape from her lips. "I think that would be best."

"Let's do just one more thing tonight, though," James said as he reached into his briefcase and pulled out a stack of papers. Separating two stapled documents, he handed her a copy and kept one for himself.

"What's this?" she asked hesitantly.

"A relationship quiz that I put together from the books and some Internet sites."

"Quiz?" she asked, flipping the pages as her eyes widened.

"It's mostly multiple choice, but there are a few short-answer questions," James said, paging along with her. He flipped to the back page, and she continued to review the document while breaking into a sweat. James added, "The last page is focused mostly on religion. We've never really discussed—"

"No, we haven't," Jillian interrupted before leaping up from the sofa. "I really need to go to the bathroom again. Be right back."

Rushing to the hallway, she continued into the kitchen and quietly opened the freezer. There, she pulled out a bag of frozen vegetables and grabbed the milk carton, along with a large plastic cup. Carrying her items, she slipped quietly into the bathroom and closed the door. She placed the cup on the counter and rushed to open the frozen vegetables. The bag ripped, and vegetables shot all over the sink. She cursed, scooped up some vegetables to fill the cup halfway, and then added milk. She opened the bathroom door slightly, lifted the toilet seat, and poured one-third of the contents from about two feet above the bowl. For the next ten seconds, the frozen soupy mixture splashed loudly into the toilet, and Jillian added a groan before repeating the process twice more.

"Jillian?"

"Yes," she replied in a pained voice.

"Would you bring in a couple of pencils?" he yelled out loudly.

She frowned. After scooping the rest of vegetables into the cup, she added milk and opened the door a little more, repeating the process a fourth time. This time, she held the cup about four feet above the bowl and provided a louder groan, which she directed out the door. Then she rushed to the door, inching out into the hallway just enough so she could see if her theatrics were getting a reaction.

When she left him, James had been slumped back against the sofa, leafing through his relationship material. Now, he was sitting straight up, looking horrified, and staring straight ahead with his eyes bugging out.

Satisfied, Jillian returned to the bathroom, flushed twice, and ran the water while she collected the few vegetables that remained scattered over the sink. She splashed some water on her face, turned off the faucet, and returned to the great room, holding her stomach. James wore an odd expression.

"Are you okay?" he asked.

"You didn't hear any of that, did you?"

His eyes darted back and forth, as he said, "No, I, uh, well—"

"Wow. That was... Sorry. I had to open the door. I was dying," she said while waving her hand in front of her face. "There's no window in there."

Standing, he shoved his books into his briefcase. "Uh, maybe we should do this another time."

"I'm so sorry about this," Jillian said. "Why don't you leave the quiz with me, and I'll e-mail it back to you?"

"Uh, okay." He handed her the papers then rushed to the front door.

Stepping out onto the porch, she watched with a guilty grin as he hurried to his car, never looking back. Then she closed the door, walked into the kitchen, grabbed the phone, and sat at the island. Reviewing the quiz and shaking her head, a big smile appeared on her face as she dialed Victoria's number.

Chapter Seven

Brian sat with Natalie on her bed. They were making out once again. On this visit, there was no removal of Natalie's shirt and bra, or anything else intimate. Brian still enjoyed being with her and wanted to give her some time. There was a knock at the door. Natalie got out of bed, walked over, and opened it just enough to see who was there. From his angle, he couldn't tell who it was. She whispered something through the tiny opening as he looked on curiously. She closed the door, told him she'd be back in a few minutes, and said he should read something while she was gone. Before he could say a word, she slipped out the door.

After forty minutes, she still had not yet returned. Brian kept himself occupied by reading a few magazines and looking at her books. He checked the clock again. When he put his hands back to lean against the wall, he noticed an opened book face down on the bed. Picking it up, he scanned the page. Once he realized it was her diary, he quickly put it back down. He placed it back where he found it and glanced over at it a few times. He considered the phrase that had caught his eye; it was something about being in love with him or thinking she was in love with him. He stared at the book, desperate to know, but hesitant to invade her privacy. He also thought about her leaving him in that room for so long with the diary right out in the open. Remembering she told him to read something, he was convinced that she intended for him to read it. Maybe it held the secret to why she could not get close to him, and this was her way of telling him. After glancing once more at the clock, he grabbed the diary. He read the important entry, which was:

I think I'm falling in love with him, but I just can't give myself to him yet because of you know. There's too much pressure. I need some space now, but I hope he will wait for me because I know I will get there soon.

He read the entry a couple of times with a smile on his face, assuming that he was the "him" being referenced. Brian went to return the book exactly as he'd found it, but stopped when a realization hit him—from what he'd read, there was no real evidence that he was actually the "him" in question. Reading the book again, he got what he needed from the first entry on the previous page:

Brian is coming over tonight... can't wait to see him.

He quickly flipped through the diary and so far, there was writing only on the first four pages. Quickly skimming the entries, he found no mention of any previous life-altering event. Maybe the new diary meant she was starting fresh—fresh with him. He smiled, replaced the book exactly where he had found it, and quickly picked up a magazine.

Minutes later, Natalie entered, looking a little flustered. Brian smiled and barely looked at her as he climbed off the bed and set the magazine down.

She said, "I'm so sorry, but I, uh, had to—"

"I just realized that I've got to go."

"Really?"

"Yeah, I've got this paper due and I'm really behind."

"Oh, okay."

He put his hand on her shoulder then kissed her. "Call me some time, but no pressure... I mean, you know or I'll call you."

"Yes." Her brow furrowed. "Sure."

"Cool." Beaming, he walked out the door.

Chapter Eight

Brian played on the intramural tennis league on campus, and he'd asked Natalie a few times to watch him play a match, but she never went to one. He hadn't seen her in a week—not since the diary incident. He didn't tell her about this particular match as he was trying to give her space, and he was playing horribly, probably because he was so preoccupied with thoughts about her.

He lost the first set, and during the second, he noticed someone in the empty stands. When he looked over, he realized it was Natalie, watching him with a bright, encouraging smile on her face. She waved, and his face lit up. He was down three games to one and facing break point on his serve. If he lost the game, he would be down a devastating four games to one, with little chance to come back and win the match.

From that moment on, Brian was in the zone—blasting aces and hitting blistering passing shots. He won that set six games to four, and his excellent play continued into the third set, until he looked to the stands and saw that she was gone. He scanned the surrounding area and spotted Natalie walking quickly away with some guy next to her.

Devastated, Brian couldn't regain his focus and lost the final set. Walking back to his dorm, he found Natalie, sitting alone on a bench near the center of campus. She looked depressed. He walked over and sat down next to her.

"Where did you go?" he asked.

"I don't know how he found me, but my high school boyfriend showed up at your match and said he wanted to talk," Natalie admitted.

"What high school boyfriend?"

"His name is Soros."

"Are you still dating?" he asked.

"Sort of."

Brian stared straight ahead, pausing for a moment. The sting of losing the match, combined with this news, sent his head spinning. He turned to her. "But what about what I read in your diary?"

"You read my diary?"

"I, uh, did."

"*You* read my diary! Why?"

"Um, well," he stammered then his confused look was replaced with a sneer. "Oh you *wanted* me to read it. You left me in your room for forty-five minutes, telling me you'd be right back, and you told me to read something. It was right on the bed next to me."

"I most certainly did not want you to read it. It's private."

"What I read was about me, wasn't it? It said you thought you were falling in love with him, but you just couldn't get close to him yet, and you hoped he would wait."

Speechless, Natalie just looked back at him.

"Am I *him*?" he asked.

"Yes... Maybe. I don't know."

"Exactly how many *hims* are you dating right now?" he asked sarcastically.

Rising from the bench, she looked at him. "I don't want to talk about this. You're scaring me."

"I'm *scaring* you? *How* am I scaring you? I'm just sitting here, asking how many guys you're seeing."

"I don't like you when you're like this." Natalie backed away from him as if he had a knife pointed her way.

"What are you talking about?" He looked at her as if she was crazy. "Like what?"

"I just can't talk about it now." Turning, she walked quickly away.

He stood and said sarcastically, "Thanks for coming to my match!"

Returning to his room, Brian collapsed on the bed. He looked over at the John McEnroe poster on his wall. Brian's father had given him the poster when he was ten, after introducing him to tennis. His father, a big McEnroe fan, had shown Brian tapes of the classic Borg–McEnroe matches of the early eighties. McEnroe was the reason Brian played tennis. The poster showed the tennis great with his hands in the air and his fists clenched in celebration of his first Wimbledon championship. Most of Brian's friends made fun of his 1980 poster, but he didn't care. McEnroe changed tennis forever, and that image was the one he tried to picture in his head when he was feeling down. McEnroe's Grand Slam victory after being an unranked amateur only one year before proved that if you work hard enough and really want something, you can achieve just about anything. As he looked at the poster, he thought, Johnny Mac would never put up with this kind of crap from a girl, and he could hear John's iconic phrase playing over and over in his head:

. . .

"You cannot be serious!"

He could hear John saying it to him about Natalie. How could he seriously be putting up with her shit? Either she wanted to be with him now or not. It was as simple as that. But Brian was too scared to give her an ultimatum, because he feared what the answer might be. At least this way, he felt there was still a chance.

Chapter Nine

Two weeks had passed since the tennis match, and Brian hadn't spoken to Natalie once. When Rob entered the suite, Brian was standing in front of the window in the living area, staring out at the landscape. Rob walked over. "What the hell are you doing?"

"Nothing," Brian said as he stood there, pretending to enjoy the scenery and weather on that early spring day. They both watched as students walked quickly by on the sidewalks below.

Rob glanced at Brian. "Don't I see you right here when I get back from my ten o'clock class every Monday, Wednesday, and Friday?"

"I don't think so," Brian said nervously.

Below them, Natalie appeared on the sidewalk, wearing one of her standard outfits, her long, blonde hair flowing down to her ass. Brian spotted her on schedule, and his expression changed to one of confused longing.

Rob glanced down to Natalie then back at Brian. "Man, you have a serious problem."

"What are you talking about?"

"She has a ten o'clock, too, but it's across campus," Rob said with a knowing look that screamed he had solved the case.

"Who?" Brian scoffed.

Rob walked away and then sat on the sofa. "You're obsessed with her."

Brian turned toward him. He sighed and raked his fingers through his hair.

"Admit it—you're stalking her," Rob added.

"I'm not obsessed," Brian replied defensively. "It's not like I'm hanging outside her window, watching her change or anything. And yes, maybe I rush my little sorry ass up here every fucking Monday, Wednesday, and fucking Friday at exactly 10:57 a.m. to watch as she walks by." Brian closed his eyes with his hands on his cheeks. "The earliest she's ever walked by was at 10:59 and the latest was 11:07."

"Oh, well, I take it back then. You are not obsessed," Rob said sarcastically.

Pulling his hands away from his face, Brian looked to Rob, desperate for understanding. "I think she's just trying to mess with me. She likes me. She doesn't like me. She has this thing from her past that prevents her from getting close to anyone. Then there's this Greek guy, this high school boyfriend—Poros or Milos or Dildos. One of those freaking oses."

"Greek boyfriend?" Rob asked.

"I didn't tell you?"

Rob shook his head no.

"All I saw of him was the back of his big, fat Greek head as he was leading her away from the court."

Rob stood up and walked to the window. After pausing for a moment, he turned back to Brian. "What are you doing for Spring Break?"

"I'm staying here. I can't afford to go anywhere."

"Come home with me," Rob said.

"I can't."

"If you stay here, you'll pine away for her all week. You'll be here all alone, you know. Everyone in the suite is leaving. You'll drive yourself so nuts thinking about her that you'll stalk the entire campus until you find a girl who looks like her. Then you'll kidnap her, skin her, and be caught wearing her skin."

Brian looked at him as if he was insane. "Isn't that from *Silence of the Lambs?*"

"Probably. Look, my mom's place is in Miami. It's only about ten hours from here. We have a pool and a tennis court and—"

"You have a tennis court, and you don't play?"

"I only play *real* sports."

"It's a real sport."

"I don't consider any activity where a skirt is an appropriate uniform a sport."

Brian scoffed. "Only the women wear the skirts."

"Okay, the men might as well, with all that skipping around after the ball in their little white shorts. A real sport involves men getting dirty while smashing into each other, and getting hurt while playing. Unless it's got that—it's not a real sport."

"I've seen players get hurt playing tennis," Brian added defensively.

Rob chuckled. "What, like a guy got hit in the nuts once?"

"No, I saw a guy sprain his ankle," Brian began but quickly realized how lame it sounded. "It was, uh, really... incredibly swollen."

Rob exhaled. "Wow, that sounds painful, but unless there's a strong possibility of a compound fracture, I don't want to play, and I certainly don't want to watch."

"Okay, so it's not as violent and dangerous as your precious rugby."

"That's right. It's not even close."

Brian shot Rob a confused look. "Why the hell are we talking about this?"

Rob shook his head. "I'm not sure."

"Wait. I remember, so if you're not going to play me, what am I going to do—just stand on the court for hours and practice my serve?"

"My mother plays—really well, in fact. I'm sure she would play you," Rob said.

Brian rolled his eyes. "Dude, there is no way I'm playing tennis with your mother. Maybe we should go to my house instead, and you can go bowling with mine."

"So, don't play with her. We'll go down there. The weather will be warm. The women will be wearing practically nothing. I can get Laura to hook you up with a friend, and if you get the hell out of your funk, maybe you could actually get *laid* for once."

"You can get me laid?" Brian said, beginning to warm to the idea.

"I said *maybe*. It's not like I have hookers lined up, or anything. You need to actually have a personality and talk with them about something other than tennis."

Brian's mind raced, and he looked Rob in the eye. "The tennis court—what's the surface?"

"You see *that's* what I'm talking about. Surface? It's a fucking tennis court."

"No, I mean is it asphalt, Har-tru, concrete, or one of those, uh, awesome Decoturf courts?"

After exhaling deeply, Rob gave Brian a tired look. "If I knew the answer to that question, I'd be dead. I would have killed myself already. You know, there's more to life than tennis. You really should—"

"Okay... Jesus," Brian interrupted.

"So... Miami?" Rob asked as he put his fist out for a bump.

Brian exhaled, smiled, and finally gave him one.

Chapter Ten

Rob drove his nearly new black BMW south with Brian in the passenger seat. As Brian looked out the window, he decided to try to put Natalie out of his mind while on break. He might even try to talk to women about something other than tennis, as Rob had suggested. He struggled to think of some sample topics.

Rob said, "Like I told you, Laura will want me to stay over with her a couple nights, at least. We haven't seen each other since Christmas Break, and the last time I spoke to her on the phone, she sounded really freaking horny... like I've never heard her before, you know?"

Brian nodded. "Good for you. I'll find something to do, and I've got a test to study for anyway."

"Oh, we'll definitely hang out some. I'm not going to dump you down there and take off. Anyway, I cleared it with my mom, and she's totally cool with it... Look she's still going through a hard time right now—divorce. My dad's basically a dick who cheated on her. So, if she's, kinda, depressed or just staring at the pool like a zombie or something, it's because of that."

As they crossed the state line into Florida, Rob said, "And no thinking about Natalie. You are missing the prime *get laid* time in your life by waiting for her, only because she can do that thing with her leg over her head. It's stupid. You'll look back in a few years on all the opportunities you missed and hit yourself in the nuts over it."

Brian shook his head, slightly offended. "It's not stupid. The leg thing is really awesome, dude. Have you pictured in your mind what she'd look like doing that... completely naked? She can hold her leg up there for like thirty minutes." Brian glanced at Rob.

Rob scoffed. "Dude, you need help."

"Seriously, you've never thought about it?" Brian turned and stared out the window with his eyes glazing over, mumbling, "Wow... her body and that, uh... I mean, she's so..." He exhaled loudly and a peculiar groan escaped from his lips.

"Okay, that was creepy." Rob's eyes bugged out of his head. "Yeah, she's really flexible, and that could have its advantages in certain areas, but if *your thing* never gets anywhere near *the leg thing,* then you're just some douchebag who wasted his best college years pining away over some female version of Gumby."

After sighing, Brian rubbed his chin. "You're right. I know you're right."

Chapter Eleven

As they pulled into the driveway, Brian's eyes lit up. The house was a huge stucco mansion with a palm tree-lined driveway and beautiful landscaping. They arrived just after four in the afternoon and were a few hours early. The front of the house featured a huge two-story archway that led to double-beveled glass front doors, accented with a large fanlight that stretched nearly to the top of the arch. Large travertine tiles adorned the foyer, and the rest of the house featured 10-foot ceilings, 8-foot doors, large moldings, and built-ins. He thought it must be at least three or four times the size of his family's modest 2,000-square-foot home.

Awestruck, Brian walked through the foyer, toward the kitchen, as Rob tossed his duffle bag carelessly on the wide-planked dark hardwood floors of the great room. Rob called for his mother, and when she didn't answer, he directed Brian through the patio doors for a look at the pool and tennis court while he went upstairs to find her.

Brian walked out to the backyard. The pool was large and free form in shape, with lagoon-like landscaping and detailed hardscaping. Big, comfortable-looking lounge chairs dotted the patio area, which also featured an outdoor kitchen with a fireplace. To the right of the pool, Brian spotted the tennis court. Smiling, he headed that way.

As he got closer, Brian stopped in his tracks at the sight of a woman lying face down on one of the lounge chairs. He stood speechless while taking in the scene. She wore a white micro-bikini bottom that must have only provided about four inches of coverage at its widest point, near the top of her perfectly shaped rear end. Lower down, the suit's coverage quickly dwindled to nearly nothing. The woman's skin was evenly tanned—not dark and leathery, but lusciously golden. Her dark brown hair fell just past her shoulders. Brian's eyes took one more trip down her supple body, lingering briefly along her trim waist and long, toned legs. Then, as her arm slipped off the chaise to the patio, he noticed the sides of her breasts were showing just enough to reveal that her top was probably just as skimpy as her bikini bottom.

His first thought was that this was Rob's girlfriend, but he remembered that she was supposed to be a blonde. Then he figured she must be Rob's sister, although he couldn't remember him ever mentioning he had one. After staring at the woman for about thirty seconds, he said, "Sorry to bother you. I'm Brian." When she didn't move, he noticed the wires leading up to the woman's ears and realized she must be listening to music. Rob came up quietly behind him and stood there shaking his head with disapproval.

"Jesus, Mom," he said loudly.

Rising quickly, Jillian looked a little frightened. When she turned her head, she found Rob standing there with an angry look on his face. Smiling, Jillian pushed herself up, turned on her side, stood, and rushed over to hug her son. Brian's guess about the modesty of the bikini top was right on the money, and Rob's face seemingly confirmed it. Brian tore his eyes away from her chest to avoid being rude and to see if her face was worthy of that body. He found that it was more than worthy. Jillian looked young; she was in her late thirties or early forties, he thought, worst case, forty-two.

Rob asked, "What the hell are you wearing?"

Jillian ignored the question as she grabbed hold of him and squeezed tightly while he reciprocated halfheartedly. Brian looked on, amazed. This was not your average mother of a college-aged son, he thought. For some reason, he pictured his mother wearing Jillian's tiny bikini, but he quickly shook off the image. His mother's bikini days were well behind her.

"You look good," she said. "Looks like you're eating."

"Is that one of Victoria's bikinis?" Rob asked with a sneer.

Jillian glanced down, cringed then folded her arms quickly over her chest. Then she turned to retrieve a large beach towel from the chair. She wrapped it around her shoulders so it draped over her breasts and the tiny bikini bottom front. "Sorry. I forgot I had on my tanning suit. Oh, and it *is* one of Victoria's. It's too conservative for her now, if you can believe that."

Rob said, "Mom, this is Brian Nash. Brian, this is my mother, Jillian Grayson."

Looking at Brian, she smiled. "I've heard a lot about you. We're glad to have you here."

Brian replied, "Nice to meet you, Mrs. Grayson. Your house is incredible."

"Thank you. Please, call me Jillian."

Rob mumbled something which sounded a lot like, "Please cover up." Obviously, his mother was wearing way too little for his taste and the towel was only working to shield the front of her.

"What's that?" Jillian asked.

Turning away, Rob waved his hand dismissively at her.

Rolling her eyes at her son, she turned away from them

both, which re-exposed her shapely backside to Brian. Then she removed the towel and wrapped a sheer sarong around her bikini bottom. Brian's jaw dropped. She draped the towel around her shoulders and turned back toward them, fully covered. Brian shot Rob an evil look.

"What time is it?" she asked.

"About four," Rob replied.

"You guys are really early. I didn't expect to be greeting you wearing this. As I said, this is my not-so-family-friendly suit." Jillian gave them a smile.

"I like the bikini," Brian said, casually, as he looked back toward the tennis court and began walking toward it.

"Thanks," she said as she turned to follow his gaze.

As he approached the court, Brian said, "You've got Decoturf."

She trailed after him, and they stood at the entrance to the court. Rob walked over to join them.

Brian looked at her. "Did you put this in or was it here when you bought the house?"

"I put it in," she replied. "How'd you know it's called Decoturf?"

"It's what they play on at the Open," Brian replied as he knelt down to touch it.

"That's one of the reasons I chose it."

"What else did you consider?"

Jillian smiled at Brian as he remained on the ground, touching it and looking back up at her. She said, "It was between the Har-tru and this."

Standing, Brian looked over the court, nodding. "You definitely made the right choice."

Rob groaned loudly then turned to look toward the pool.

She said, "I was worried about the fact that it might be harder on your knees."

Brian said, "From what I've read, I think the only advantage of the Har-tru surface over the Decoturf is that it dries a little faster when it rains. Both provide the player equal cushioning, but the Decoturf wins, hands-down, with its truer bounce and surer footing."

Jillian gazed at Brian, seemingly captivated by his court surface analysis. Rob turned back toward them gape-mouthed and shaking his head.

"What do you think of the color? I went with the spring green on the inner and the Olympic blue on the outer."

Rob breathed in deeply. "Excuse me, guys, but I'm going to go in, turn on the gas, wait five minutes, and then light a match."

Neither Jillian nor Brian looked Rob's way.

"All right," Brian said, absently toward Rob and looked Jillian in the eye. "I think it looks great, and there's just enough contrast between the blue and the lines, to make it easier to call those baseline shots. Yet the blue's not so overpowering, you know?"

"I think you're right," Jillian replied.

As his mother and best friend continued discussing their shared interest with even more intensity, Rob sighed. Heading toward the house, he raked his hands through his hair and mumbled under his breath.

Chapter Twelve

Jillian prepared steaks and baked potatoes on the grill and added a salad for dinner, which she and the guys ate at the outdoor table. She had a glass of wine, and Brian and Rob drank beer. Luckily, for Rob, there was no talk of tennis surfaces at dinner, that subject was exhausted ad nauseam for at least twenty more minutes after he left the tennis-obsessed nerds alone on the court. However, there was a discussion of the current state of men's and women's tennis. They also discussed how, on the men's side, the U.S. players had been such a disappointment during the last decade with no dominant champions. Rob sat through it all looking bored while the two of them eagerly exchanged opinions.

Jillian noticed the look on her son's face. "That's probably enough tennis chat for the night. Brian do you have a job lined up after graduation?"

"I do, actually. It's with America Bank at their headquarters in Delaware. I interned there last summer, and they offered me a position in their management program."

"That sounds like a good opportunity," she said.

"It's not my dream job, but the job market stinks right now," Brian replied. "Rob tells me you're a writer."

"Mostly romance novels. Somehow, they sell really well. Thankfully, I have a large group of loyal readers."

Rob said, "Women love her books. Once, I tried reading one and couldn't make it through. No offense, Mom."

She waved him off as if she agreed.

Jillian looked at Brian. "Rob told me he'll be with Laura for part of the week. So even when Rob's not here, feel free to use the pool and the workout room, and eat whatever food you want. Make yourself at home."

"I appreciate that."

Rob said, "I spoke to Laura—I think the three of us are going out tomorrow night."

"I usually wake up early, Brian," Jillian said. "So, I'll try to keep it down in the morning, if you're a light sleeper."

Rob scoffed. "He's not a light sleeper at all. He's the heaviest sleeper on the planet."

Brian said, "Noise doesn't bother me at all. I have to set my alarm to the loudest volume for it to wake me."

"His alarm wakes up the entire building," Rob said with a grin.

"I turn it off quickly, so it's not that bad. Besides, I only have an early class one day a week, so most days I wake up before it goes off anyway. But I never get up before eleven otherwise. My eyes just don't open."

Rob began, "Once he was dating this girl—"

"She doesn't need to hear about that," Brian interrupted, shaking his head.

Rob added, "She was trying to wake him up and tried all the normal stuff, you know, but nothing would work. So she finally sat on top of him and bounced up and down. We all watched. It was hilarious. And he still didn't get up. Wait... I have a picture."

Pulling out his phone, Rob began searching. Brian said, "She doesn't want to see that."

"I do," Jillian said smiling.

Rob handed Jillian the phone. She looked at the picture and laughed.

"Wow, that didn't wake you up? She's a big girl. How tall is she?" she asked as she handed back the phone.

"She's five-eleven and on the volleyball team," Brian said. "I remember, that night I couldn't sleep so I took Tylenol PM. When I do that, I'm out cold."

"I have trouble falling asleep, too, but sometimes an Ambien helps. But no matter what time I go to bed, I get up about six hours later. I wish I could sleep late. You still dating the volleyball girl?" Jillian asked.

"No, I'm kind of dating this girl, Natalie, sort of..." Brian said.

Sighing, Rob shook his head.

"What?"

"I thought we weren't going to talk about her."

"She asked," Brian said defensively.

"She really didn't. She only asked about the tall girl," Rob shot back.

Brian exhaled. "Would you rather we talk about tennis?"

"God, no! Tell her the whole story, then. Continue torturing yourself," Rob added as he sat back in his chair and took a sip of beer.

Jillian looked at one and then the other. "Relationships can be hard work."

Sitting up, Rob frowned. "Some are way more than others. This girl is messing with his head. He fell in love with her simply because she can do this ballet move where she keeps one leg on the ground and points the other toward the ceiling. She can hold it there for, like, an hour."

"She's really talented," Brian announced proudly.

"Talented, yeah," Rob muttered.

Jillian smiled. "A ballet dancer, huh? I used to take gymnastics back in middle school. It's similar, with the balancing and all. That sounds like a very advanced position."

"You see," Brian said, looking pointedly at Rob.

Rob sneered. "He's obsessed with her, and she's telling him to wait for her, while she's running around with other guys."

"I just want to give her a little more time because she asked me to wait, so—"

"Wait? Wait for what?"

Brian looked down at his plate for a moment, then back to Rob as he opened his mouth to speak, but he had nothing.

After looking around uncomfortably, Jillian's eyes brightened. "Let's have dessert."

She got up, went into the house, and returned a few minutes later with a small birthday cake with twenty-one lit candles. She placed it on the table in front of her son as he rubbed his forehead, fighting back a smile

"I know your birthday isn't until tomorrow, and you didn't want me making a big deal, but I figured you'd be with Laura, so..."

"Just no singing, okay?" Rob said before he blew out the candles.

"Happy birthday," Jillian said with a proud smile.

"Happy birthday, dude. No more fake ID for you," Brian said.

Jillian gave Brian a mock-angry look and then smiled. "Yeah, Brian, weren't you the one corrupting my young son? You got him that ID when he was only a sophomore."

"Mom, knock it off."

"He said I got it?" Brian looked at her confused. "He's the one with the connections."

Raising her eyebrows, Jillian looked at Rob.

"So, I lied. I didn't want you to think I was going crazy at college," Rob explained sheepishly.

She said, "I'm scared to ask what other connections you had back then."

"*My* connections? What about your connection—Victoria?"

Jillian shook her head as if she didn't want to go there.

Brian sat on the edge of his seat. "What do you mean?"

Rob chimed in, "Victoria is my mother's crazy friend. If you need *anything*, see her."

Jillian laughed. "She's not that crazy. She's just..." She caught Rob making a face and added, "Okay, she's a little fun—yeah *fun* is the word."

Rob nodded. "I'll say."

"I forgot the plates," Jillian said. "I'll be right back."

As she headed toward the house, Rob picked up his beer, smiling. "Let me tell you a *fun* Victoria story..."

Chapter Thirteen

The next morning in the kitchen, Jillian prepared scrambled eggs while wearing a bikini under a beach cover-up. Rob entered the room, selected a banana from the bowl on the table and grabbed a bottle of water.

"Happy birthday!" Jillian gave him a smile.

"Thanks, Mom."

"You want some eggs?"

"No, I'm late and I've got to meet Laura." Rob moved to the back door and looked out. "Holy shit!"

"What is it?"

"He must have slept out there."

She turned off the burner, moved the pan off the heat then headed over to join him at the door.

"We were both pretty drunk last night. I don't remember all of it, but we were out there late doing shots and sorta celebrating my birthday then somehow, we got on the Natalie subject." Rob exhaled deeply, shaking his head. "We were unpacking that again."

Brian appeared to be sleeping soundly on the chaise lounge

chair wearing gym shorts and a T-shirt. He was lying flat on his back with his mouth open slightly.

"Oh, no." Jillian raised her brows in shock. "You just left him out there!"

"He said he was going to be right behind me. Like I said, I was sorta out of it."

"We need to get him in the house."

"Remember we aren't going to be able to wake him up easily. So, unless we're both carrying him in here like dead weight, he ain't moving."

"Okay." She sighed.

Rob flipped his hand dismissively as he moved away from the door. "It's like perfect weather out. Just let him sleep."

"Are you sure?"

"I've slept out there. You've slept out there. He'll be fine."

"I haven't slept out there all night."

"Well, I have."

Her mouth dropped open. "When did you do that?"

"Mom, I really have to go." He exhaled deeply. "Can we do this police interview thing later?"

"All right. Sorry." Jillian headed back toward the stove. "What about the girl? Did you work anything out?"

"Not really, but he'll be fine... well, maybe at some point he will be." He peeled the banana, took a huge bite and mumbled with his mouth full, "I've got to run."

"Drive carefully."

He took another bite, gave her a half-wave, grabbed his keys and headed for the front door.

Jillian sat at the table eating breakfast and from her vantage point she could still see Brian as he slept out near the pool. As the morning sun rose in the sky it was slowly creeping toward him.

She flipped on the television and sipped her coffee, occasionally glancing from the screen to her sleeping guest. About twenty minutes later, she rose to her feet and moved to the back door to check on him. The sun was now blazing on his feet and the bottom of his legs as he lay on his side. Her concern was growing by the minute.

She headed outside for a closer look. Standing about ten feet from him, she pondered her options. Should she try to wake him? Should she cover his legs with a towel or try to drag the large umbrella stand over to shade him? He was sleeping so peacefully, breathing slowly in and out. She hated to disturb him.

Slowly Brian rolled onto his back. He was sporting an unmistakable erection which tented at an angle, snaking down his silky shorts. Upon seeing this, she gasped. She looked to his face and found he was still unconscious then turned away and closed her eyes. Her mind drifted to her unfinished novel, *Lover's Slumber,* realizing she was in the midst of a sort of *life-imitating-art* moment. She began rewriting her scene. What if Dallas was lying poolside instead of in bed? Would that make the story hotter—sexier—more realistic? What if Katrina thought Dallas was in pain with his penis being trapped like that? Would she wake him? Would they make love out there by the pool?

As her gaze traveled up Brian's muscular legs, her lips parted slightly. She was half immersed in rewriting her story and half there enjoying this slightly voyeuristic and naughty experience with this attractive younger man.

Pulling herself back to reality, she headed toward the house then stopped in her tracks remembering why she came out there in the first place. She needed to protect her guest from the very strong Miami sun. Unguarded, it didn't take long for a serious sunburn to develop, and his legs had been exposed for quite some time already.

Turning back, she looked to the umbrella stand. It was too far from him and very heavy to slide over to where it could offer him any shade. Not to mention the racket all that might make if she attempted to relocate it. When her gaze returned to Brian, she was shocked to notice the tip of his erection just barely poking out through the bottom of his shorts. He shifted slightly, smacking his lips together groggily. He ran a sleepy hand down his body to tug at his shorts, causing even more of his length to be exposed to the open air. Her heartbeat quickened and she swallowed hard.

Suddenly, she felt guilt and shame even though this was her house—her pool and she was doing nothing wrong. He was out there revealing himself for all the world to see. She turned away and centered herself, deciding she would simply retrieve a towel from the house and lay it over him. Rushing to the door, she slipped inside and headed toward the bathroom.

When she returned outside, she stepped onto the patio to find Brian lying flat on his back. His strong erection appeared even larger now, standing at a ninety-degree angle, straight, tall and thick. She stopped in her tracks, dropping the towel. Momentarily stunned, she found herself unable to move. Her thoughts were all over the place as she considered what to do.

She turned away then shook her head. She took a deep calming breath, her pulse raced, and her body tingled. She whispered softly to herself, "You're just helping him. You need to pull yourself together and simply cover him." Picking the towel up, she spun back toward him and closed the distance between them, unfolding the towel to drape over his exposed skin.

When she was a mere few feet away, she stopped once again to take in the sight of him. Tilting her head, she stared at his erection, mesmerized. Now fully free of its confines, it expanded even more, the fabric slipping down his shaft and exposing nearly all of his impressive length. Her mouth shot open with a soft gasp as she looked at it, first in shock, then in awe. She hadn't been this close to a real live erection in longer than she cared to remember. She froze with her eyes locked on it and unable to breathe until she finally blinked then slowly exhaled. Moving closer, she readied the towel.

Suddenly, the cell phone in her pocket rang loudly, scaring the hell out of her. Leaping backward and almost out of her skin, she dropped the towel and quickly pulled the phone out. She hit the button to answer the call and the phone slipped from her hand. She quickly tried to snatch it in midair, but instead of securing it, she knocked it toward the pool. It landed on a chair, bouncing off then it skidded across the concrete before coming to rest under another chair.

"Shit." She gasped. Her gaze shot to his face, and he was somehow still sleeping just as the second ringtone blared. Falling to her knees, she scrambled after the phone, reaching under the chair to scoop it up.

Slowly she turned and discovered she was in line with his groin—only inches away from his erection. As her eyes widened, she lost her balance, falling backward and catching herself with her hands. Suddenly remembering the call, she rose to her feet and headed toward the house. Once safely inside, she leaned against the wall, putting the phone to her ear as she whispered, "Hello."

"What the hell's going on there?" Victoria snapped.

"What do you mean?"

"I mean, what was all that noise and what took you so long?"

"Oh, nothing," Jillian continued to whisper as she turned then peered outside to check on her guest's condition. There was no movement from his body, but his penis was still standing at attention. "I just dropped the phone." Sighing in relief, she moved toward the table. "This really isn't a good time."

"Is there a man with a gun in your house?"

"No! What are you talking about?"

"I just saw the movie, *Taken*, and this so reminded me of that. Why are you whispering?"

"Whispering?"

"Yes, why are you whispering?"

"I wasn't whispering," Jillian said a little louder but still not at a normal volume.

"Uh-huh," Victoria said. "I know when something's not right with you. Now, what is it?"

"Rob's friend, Brian, is here."

"Oh, so that's it. What's he like? Is he a nice guy?"

"He's nice, all right."

"What's he look like?"

"Look like?"

"It's a simple question. What does he look like? Is he tall or short or skinny or what?"

Returning to the doorway, Jillian studied Brian's body with an odd look on her face before breaking into a slight giggle. "He's not skinny."

"What are you doing?" Victoria asked.

"Crap!" Jillian exclaimed as she noticed he was still unprotected from the sun. "Jesus Christ."

"What is it now?"

"Hold on." Placing the phone on the table, Jillian headed back outside, picked up the towel and walked with purpose toward him, avoiding looking directly at the problem area. She carefully placed the towel over his feet and legs, sliding it up over his groin as well. She smiled in satisfaction until she noticed it had slipped off his feet. The towel was just slightly shorter than needed. Closing her eyes, she sighed. She checked his face to find he was still sleeping then quietly moved toward the foot of the chair. Kneeling down to take hold of the ends of the towel, she gingerly slid it up over his feet which caused it to fall off his massive erection, revealing it once again.

"Crap," she muttered.

Brian moaned softly, sliding his hand down toward his groin and shifting slightly. Jillian froze. What would this look like if he suddenly opened his eyes and spotted her there with him in this condition?

She'd be mortified.

She had to escape.

Nearly losing her balance, she raised her arms to steady herself. Remaining still, she watched until his breathing returned to normal, and his movement stopped. Taking one small step backward, she moved away slowly then tiptoed toward the house mumbling under her breath. Once inside she was partially satisfied that he was now safe from the sun. She pondered retrieving a second towel to fully cover him, but she'd had enough mission impossible work for one morning.

When she picked up the phone she heard, "Jillian! Jillian! I want to know what the hell is going on there."

"Okay, he's sleeping out by the pool."

"Who's sleeping?"

"Rob's friend, Brian."

"Where are you?"

"In the house now. I was out there and—"

"He slept through you dropping the phone and all that?"

"He's a really, really sound sleeper."

"Did you drug him, or something?" Victoria asked.

"No!"

"Why are you watching him sleep?" Victoria asked incredulously.

"I'm not."

"It sure sounds like you are."

"He, um..." Closing her eyes to recall the vivid memory,

Jillian took a deep breath. "I forgot what a man's body looked like. You know, one that's really in great shape."

"I know exactly what you mean. I was with one last night." Victoria let out a creepy purring sound. "Let me tell you about it."

"Please, don't," Jillian said.

"So, does he have great abs?" Victoria asked.

"Abs?" Dazed, Jillian sat at the table and could once again spot him sleeping.

"Yes, his abs. Are they amazing? Young guys have—"

"Look, I really need to go."

"Just tell me about his abs and then you can go."

"Really?"

"Yes, really." Victoria said in a tired voice, "I'm a little bored over here and I'm on the fence about pulling out my vibrator. I could use some inspiration to push me over. It's a lot of work you know."

"I can imagine." Jillian sighed. "So, if I tell you about his abs, you'll let me go?"

"I will."

Jillian moved to the doorway, glancing out to her sleeping guest. It was an odd sight for sure. His lower body was covered by the towel with his erection still standing proudly just above that. His upper body was covered by a T-shirt which had ridden up a little exposing his belly button and just a bit of his flat stomach. "He's wearing a shirt so I can't see much of his abs, but what I can see is nice. He's in shape for sure. There is one other thing. No, I shouldn't say."

"What is it?"

"Um."

"Tell me."

"You know how when men sleep, they get..."

"A boner!" Victoria exclaimed with a loud squeal.

"Yes."

"You can tell?"

"Oh, I can tell." Jillian nodded. "I can definitely tell."

"What does that mean?"

"Um, it means that I can just... tell."

"What aren't you telling me?"

"Nothing," Jillian lied.

"I want to know exactly what you're doing right now."

"I write about..." Jillian paused with a smile on her face as she placed her hand on the glass. "I mean, I *used to* write about gorgeous penises every day, but until now, I've never actually seen a real one."

"The gorgeous ones are wonderful," Victoria said.

"Yeah."

"You shouldn't have gotten knocked up at prom. You might have seen a few."

"Uh-huh," Jillian added, barely listening and unable to look away. "Well, I'm seeing one now and it's, it's... out."

"What do you mean out?"

"I mean, it's out."

"Like out, out?"

"Yes, I don't know how else to say it." Jillian took in a sharp breath.

"So, you're looking at his dick right now?" Victoria asked.

"Yeah, but from in the house. I tried to cover it, but it didn't work."

"What does that mean?"

Jillian turned away from the door. "Look, he's outside and the sun is rising. It was starting to burn his feet and then before I knew it his, you know, slipped out of his shorts and—"

"Are you drunk?"

"No, but I have to tell you that it's completely... incredibly... super-hard."

"Seriously? Have you been smoking that pot I left you?"

"No."

"Send me a picture," Victoria demanded.

"I'm not taking a picture of him," Jillian said, horrified.

"No, not him," Victoria grumbled. "Just it."

"No way."

"Why not?"

"That's totally creepy."

"That's creepy!" Victoria choked out a laugh. "But it's not creepy for you to be hovering over an unconscious naked guy with a boner?"

"I'm not hovering! But yeah, maybe this is a little creepy, but I... I just couldn't look away. It's like a big, beautiful car wreck, or something."

"Is the sun hitting his cock?"

Jillian checked him again. "Not yet."

"Well, don't you think you need to protect it too?"

"If it comes to that, I'll get another towel."

"I have a better idea." Victoria said.

Jillian leaned against the door frame, shaking her head. "I know I'll regret it, but what's that?"

"Grab some sunscreen and lotion it up."

"I don't think so."

"Believe me you don't want to see a sunburned penis. That skin is very sensitive and damages easily."

"I take it you know this from personal experience."

"I do. Do you have sunscreen handy?"

"No, I'm not doing that." Jillian scoffed. "I'm not jerking him off with lotion under the guises of protecting him from the sun."

"Fine, if you won't do it, I will. I'll be there in ten minutes."

"Don't! Really, why don't you—" Jillian pulled the phone from her ear and saw the call had ended. Glancing once more outside, she discovered Brian's erection had subsided a bit, but was still out in the open now flopped against his leg. Turning on her heels, she headed toward the bathroom to grab another towel. When she returned to the kitchen, she spotted him through the window now sitting up in the chair, rubbing his hands over his face. Before he could see her, she quickly changed course and headed toward the stove, grabbing a sponge to look busy and wipe the already clean appliance.

Glancing over her shoulder, she discovered him standing and facing the pool. When he started to turn toward the house, she returned to cleaning.

Seconds later she heard the door open and his footsteps behind her. He said, "I must have fallen asleep out here."

Spinning around, she put on surprised expression, clutching her chest. "You scared me."

"Sorry."

"Were you out there all night?"

"Yeah." He tilted his head from side to side, stretching. "We drank too much, and I guess I just passed out."

"Oh, really," she tried to reply in a casual tone, but her voice was cracking.

"Those chairs are so comfortable."

"They are." Jillian swallowed hard. She glanced to his midsection and all evidence of his previous state had now disappeared.

"Is Rob gone?"

"He just left. Would you like some breakfast."

"No, thanks. I'm going to try to get some more sleep."

"Okay, you can heat it up when you're ready."

"Thanks." He gave her a groggy smile as he walked past her toward the stairs.

After he disappeared down the hall, she tossed the sponge in the sink and breathed a sigh of relief.

Chapter Fourteen

When Victoria arrived, Jillian was already lounging by the pool. Wearing a sheer bikini cover-up, Victoria entered through the back fence, frowning with her palms raised. "Where is he?"

"He went up to the guest room."

"Damn. So did you take care of his problem?"

"I'm going to pretend you didn't just ask me that."

"Did you?"

Jillian sighed. "If you must know, it seemed to take care of itself."

"Another missed opportunity." Victoria rolled her eyes.

"I won't even dignify that with a response."

"You're no fun," Victoria said, as she removed her cover-up and proudly displayed her bathing suit. It was a sheer white bikini; the top barely covered her nipples and the tiny rectangular bottom struggled to conceal much of anything else.

Jillian's mouth opened wide. "What is this?"

"You like it?"

"Where's the rest of it?"

"Wait till you see the back." Victoria spun around, revealing nothing but a string, which ran up the crack of her ass.

"Jesus, this isn't St. Barts," Jillian said, a little shocked.

"Oh, it's not that revealing."

"I guess your nipples could actually be showing, and I think I can only see part of your vagina."

Laughing, Victoria headed to the pool and slipped into the water. When she returned, her suit, now wet, was completely see-through. Her nipples were hard and definitely showing, along with the clear, clear, clear outline of all her lower womanly parts.

Jillian stared at her friend, shaking her head as she approached. "I stand corrected I *can* see your nipples and your *vag.*"

Victoria smiled brightly. "Great because it's supposed to be see-through when it gets wet."

"Well, mission accomplished then."

After struggling to look down to check it out, Victoria said, "From this angle, I can't really see my pussy."

"Believe me, from mine, you can," Jillian said while rolling her eyes.

"Well, I like this suit." Victoria moved to a lounge chair, dried herself with the towel then sat. She looked down at her chest and added, "Look, it's already starting to dry a little, and you can hardly see my nipples now."

Looking over to her, Jillian nodded in agreement. "Nobody wants to see your nipples."

"There are plenty of people who want to see them."

"Okay, you're right. *I* don't want to see your nipples," Jillian said with a slight grin.

"You probably really do, but you just can't admit it."

"You are to stay out of the pool when you're here wearing that bikini." Jillian scolded. "And when Rob or Brian is out here, you stay off your stomach while wearing that, might-as-well-be-wearing-nothing bottom."

"Okay, geez."

After sharing a laugh, both women closed their eyes and lay basking in the sun. About twenty minutes later Victoria sighed. "I'm bored. I'm sad that I missed the show earlier."

"Sorry it's not more fun over here," Jillian replied sarcastically.

"I came over to see your boyfriend?"

"Don't call him that. He's probably still sleeping."

"Maybe I should go check on him?"

"Don't." Jillian put her hand up. "Just stay where I can see you."

"What did it look like, and did you touch it?" Victoria asked, lifting up her sunglasses. "You gave him a blowjob, didn't you?"

"No! Jesus."

"How did he really lose his erection? You can tell me."

"Erections come and erections go. I don't know the inner workings of all that equipment."

"Erections *come*." Victoria flashed her a grin. "Get it... *come*."

"I get it." Jillian scowled.

"Once they actually come *then* they go. At least that's been my experience and, sadly most of the time, they go before *you* come." Victoria gave her a knowing look.

"I think this one *went* on its own without *coming*," Jillian said with a smile.

"How big was it?" Victoria held her hands up about a foot apart then slowly brought them closer and closer together. "This or more like this." When she finally had them only a few inches apart, she made a face, "Don't tell me it was more like this."

Jillian squeezed her lips together, flapping her hand at her. "Stop it. He could be looking out the window."

"Give me some details."

"Would you knock it off," Jillian shot back. She pulled her sunglasses off and said sternly, "I'm not saying anything else about it. I didn't touch it or anything else that you might think!"

"Okay. Okay. Relax. I'll drop it."

"Good."

Chapter Fifteen

About thirty minutes later, Brian finally woke up and let out a big yawn, stretching his neck from side to side. His back ached a little, probably from sleeping out on that chair. Hearing laughter outside, he got out of bed and looked through the window toward the pool area.

Jillian and another woman were sitting in lounge chairs by the pool, talking and giggling. Jillian was in a less revealing bathing suit than the sexy one he had discovered her wearing the previous day, but the other woman appeared to be wearing the smallest suit he'd ever seen. The top looked like it was made of two small nipple-covering triangles connected with a thin string. The bottom consisted of a super-tiny, white rectangle that barely covered her front and connected with strings that tied on each side of her hips. He was far enough away that from his vantage point, it looked like she was possibly wearing no bottom at all. Jillian's guest adjusted her chair to a flat position and lay face down with her best asset pointing right at him.

Brian watched her, open-mouthed, as she changed positions. He adjusted his shorts. Looking down, he contemplated a trip to take care of his issue but thought it probably would be inappropriate to do that after watching Rob's mother and her friend. But... maybe another glance wouldn't hurt.

When he looked again, he found Jillian kneeling next to the other woman's chair holding a bottle of suntan lotion. The woman in the tiny white bikini lifted her shoulders from the chair and held herself up with one hand, while with the other she reached around and untied her top. The fabric fell from her full breasts, exposing them completely to him from the side. He almost became suspicious, as she seemed to remain in that position way longer than necessary and for no apparent reason. Tilting his head to focus on a nipple, he forgot his concern. Staring even harder at the breathtaking globes, his heart pumped faster, and his shorts grew even more uncomfortable.

Poolside, Jillian rolled her eyes while she waited to apply the lotion as Victoria's never-ending bikini top adjustments continued. It wasn't until her friend managed to somehow drop the bikini top onto the patio that she eyed her, suspiciously. Staring in disbelief, Jillian watched as Victoria reached over to try to collect the top. After picking it up, she dropped it again. This time, it was further from her and retrieving it required a longer stretch toward Brian's window. Following the second drop, Jillian looked up at the window and spotted Brian standing there.

Their eyes locked together before he quickly disappeared from sight.

Frowning, Jillian glared down at Victoria as she finally grabbed the top and settled down flat. Instead of applying the lotion, Jillian slapped Victoria once on her ass and returned to her seat.

"What the hell was that for?" Victoria asked.

"You know what that was for."

"I really don't."

Turning over, Victoria, seeming somewhat confused then secured her top while looking at Jillian.

"Show's over."

"What?" Victoria asked, trying to sound innocent but failing miserably.

"I saw Brian up there in the window and your *oh so obvious* routine of, 'I dropped my top, and I can't reach it. Let me stretch my tits over and try... oh, I just can't...'" Jillian said, acting out a mock-sexy stretch while pushing her breasts together with her hands.

"I don't know what you're talking about," Victoria pleaded. "I didn't push my breasts together like that at all."

Jillian looked over at Victoria's lap. "From here, it looks like you're naked from the waist down. I'm glad Rob's not here. Where would someone even buy a suit like that?"

"Online. I'll e-mail you the site name."

"Please, don't," Jillian said.

"I think Rob would somehow be able to handle seeing me in this suit. You don't think he's ever seen a woman in a small bikini before?"

"Not like that, he hasn't."

"I'm sure he's seen lots of girls naked, and—"

"I don't want to think about that. Plus, he really doesn't need to see his mother's middle-aged friends traipsing around wearing nothing."

"They have even more revealing bikinis than this on that site."

"That, I can't imagine. Does your entire ass need to be sticking out like that? We have young, impressionable men here. They really don't need to see that."

"How do you know what they need to see?" Victoria asked.

"Brian is hurting right now. He's in love with this girl, and she's toying with him, or something. He's going through a lot."

"In that case, this is exactly what he needs."

"I doubt he could handle you now... or ever," Jillian said.

A sexy, evil look crossed Victoria's face, and she said, "I would be gentle with him... at first, anyway."

They both relaxed into their lounge chairs. Jillian began to daydream about Brian, but not him out by the pool. But him as Dallas and in bed and attempted to rewrite the scene from the novel she had been unable to finish, but this time without ED or STDs or any other nasty, sex-destroying acronym.

Katrina peeled the sheet carefully off Dallas, exposing his muscular body and six-pack abs. She quivered when she spotted his cock straining against the taught fabric of his boxer shorts. She noticed the large head of his sex poking its way through the access flap. Katrina licked her lips, knelt next to the bed, and reached though the flap gently to extract him.

Pulling his gorgeous penis out, she wrapped her delicate hand around him. She glanced at his face; Dallas was staring dreamily at her. Slowly, teasingly she licked her lips, and then she...

Jillian sat up quickly.

A breakthrough!

There was no ex-husband drama clogging up her thoughts. Jillian stood. She had to capture this into her computer right now, before she forgot a word.

Victoria glanced at her. "Where are you going?"

"I just remembered something that, uh, I need from the store. I've got to write it down."

"What is it?" Victoria asked.

"Remember, you stay out of the pool."

Victoria glared at her as Jillian took off toward the house. Jillian didn't want to tell her the truth about the scene that she had in her head. Victoria would hound her until she spilled the details, and once she told her, she'd never believe that it didn't happen exactly that way between her and Brian.

Chapter Sixteen

Fighting his urges, Brian put on a sleeveless shirt and shorts and went downstairs to the home gym. The gym overlooked the pool and was better equipped than some professional gyms he'd been in. He started on the treadmill and discovered that he had a clear view of Victoria sunbathing, which made it more than a little distracting.

He watched as Jillian approached the house. She spotted him on the treadmill and waved. Brian waved back, and then he watched as Jillian returned to Victoria and appeared to be scolding her about something. Victoria looked away, frowning. After a pause, she looked back at Jillian and nodded reluctantly. As Jillian walked toward the house, Victoria removed her sunglasses.

She waited until Jillian had entered the house before she made eye contact with Brian and waved to him. When Brian spotted her, he smiled and waved back. Picking up a spray bottle, she began squirting water on her stomach, arms, and neck. Then she spent a lot of time dousing her tiny bikini top with the cool mist. Victoria's nipples began to harden and show through the fabric.

Brian couldn't tear his eyes away from her chest, as her breasts appeared like they were coming into focus on a developing Polaroid. That's when he lost his balance. Coming down halfway off the treadmill's belt, his foot twisted. When he tried to steady himself, he fell sideways on the belt, landing on his hip. He shot off the back of the treadmill, skidding onto the padded floor.

Victoria watched as he tumbled out of sight. With her eyes obviously widened in alarm, she sprang to her feet and tried to spot him on the floor.

Brian popped up quickly as if nothing had happened, and he lunged to turn off the still-running treadmill.

Victoria rushed to the gym.

Brian took a seat on a weight bench, as he was still a little dizzy from his fall.

Victoria entered the room. "Are you okay?"

He looked at her, surprised. "What? I just... Yes, I was all done."

"I saw you fall. Are you okay?"

"Fall?"

"Yeah, it looked like you took a big tumble there," Victoria said as she approached him with her nipples responding impressively to the super cold room.

Brian took a good, long look at her bathing suit top, which was now nearly transparent and just a few feet away. "I, uh..." was all he could manage as his focus lingered over her chest.

"You sure you're okay?"

"Yeah," he said.

"I'm Victoria, by the way. Jillian's friend."

Still mesmerized, his gaze wandered down to the bikini bottoms, which struggled to cover her. He swallowed hard, and then he looked up at Victoria's face as she eyed him excitedly.

When he saw her grinning, he snapped back to earth. "Oh, sorry. I'm Brian Nash. Rob and I..."

"Sure, Brian, I know who you are. I've heard *a lot* about you," she added with a sexy smile.

Brian's only response was a confused look.

Walking over to the leg curl machine, she ran her hand along the footpads. "You look like you work out a lot."

"A couple times a week," he bragged.

"Do you know how to use this machine?" Victoria asked.

"Sure."

"Would you mind showing me?"

Brian walked over and pointed out how she should climb onto the machine. Victoria did as he instructed and lay on her stomach; he helped direct her ankles under each pad. After adjusting the weight to the lowest setting, he assisted her with the first repetition by pushing on the footpad. As she brought her heels nearly up to her butt, Brian stared at her shapely backside, focusing on the tiny string, which disappeared between her cheeks. As she struggled with the exercise, he moved closer, pushing harder on the footpad to help her curl her legs to the final position, mere inches from her rear.

As he did this, he noticed her swimsuit—if you could call it that—had virtually disappeared, and she was on full display for him. He slumped against the footpad, paralyzed by the sight, wearing a goofy expression. His sudden weight on the apparatus prevented her from returning to the starting position.

Looking in the mirrored wall at him, she grinned when she saw his face. She allowed him to have a moment then her lips curled down into a frown. "Ouch, I think I'm done."

"What?" Brian asked, dumbfounded.

"Could you, uh...?"

He snapped out of it and stood up. "Sorry."

She brought the weight down, slowly slipped her legs from behind the pads, and sat up on the machine.

"How'd I do?"

"Great. Your form was... perfect," he said.

Moving to the bench press, he loaded two forty-five-pound plates onto each side, as Victoria looked on while stretching from side to side. This was a total of 225 pounds, of which Brian could normally do two repetitions. That was generally after a few warm-up sets at a lower weight. It was twenty pounds short of his maximum, but he was in the mood to impress Victoria, so he figured he would start there.

She moved to the yoga mat, about ten feet away, and watched Brian in the mirror as he lay back on the weight bench and prepared to lift the bar from the rack.

After adjusting his hand position, he glanced over at her as she worked herself into the downward-facing-dog yoga position, her string covered ass staring back at him. She held the position, and she looked nothing short of spectacular.

Brian exhaled deeply, lifted the weight off the rack, and brought it down to his chest. He heaved it back up for one good repetition. Feeling strong, he steadied the weight above his chest, preparing for his second rep, and looked toward Victoria again, just as she was adjusting to a position with her legs spread. At that moment, her bikini bottom came untied on one side and slipped from her hip, exposing a gorgeous view of half of everything she had. Brian's eyes widened. He brought the bar down to his chest a little harder than he intended, and he seemed powerless to push it up.

While Victoria remained preoccupied with grabbing the loose string of her bikini bottoms, he made grunting noises. Looking at him through her knees, she finally realized he might be in trouble. She quickly straightened and rushed to him, as the other side of her swimsuit bottom became untied and fell from her body. She stood next to him, shaking her hands in a panic, completely nude from the waist down and only a foot from his face.

Brian again struggled to lift the weight from his chest and failed, as he looked right into her bare midsection.

"Help me!" he finally blurted out.

She cupped her cheeks with her hands as she stared at him wide-eyed for a few seconds. Then lifting one leg over him, and straddling him—her naked parts just six inches from his face— she grabbed the bar with two hands and attempted to lift it away from him. He looked directly at her womanhood and froze. He didn't or couldn't attempt to help her at all. Instead, he stared as if he was in a trance. She struggled once more before losing her balance and falling back, landing right onto his groin and causing him to yell out in pain.

It was at that the moment that Jillian walked into the room. She spotted Victoria nude from the waist down, sitting on top of Brian as he fought to balance the weight on his chest.

Jillian rushed over. "Victoria, what the hell are you doing?"

"I'm trying to help him."

"Why are you naked?" Jillian asked.

"I'm not naked—not completely anyway," Victoria insisted.

"I told you to stay out of the pool."

"I didn't go in. I swear."

"Then why can I clearly see your nipples? Your top is soaking wet," Jillian said curtly.

"I, uh, was hot, so I used the spray bottle."

Jillian glared at her, obviously that was a clear violation of her no-using-the-pool rule. *Well, the spirit of the rule anyway.*

Struggling to speak, Brian groaned, "GUT HIR UF ME!"

Narrowing her eyes, Jillian leaned in close to him.

He repeated, "Get. Her. Off. Me."

"Oh." Jillian gave Victoria an annoyed look. "Could you get the hell off him?"

After getting to her feet, Victoria moved away from the bench, while Jillian got behind Brian, in the proper spotting position. She counted to three, and together they returned the bar to the rack. Still lying on the bench, Brian breathed deeply.

Jillian glared at Victoria. "Why were you giving him a lap dance?"

"I wasn't," Victoria shot back.

"And why aren't you wearing bottoms?"

"They fell off when I was doing some stretching," Victoria said casually.

"Maybe because you're not wearing anything close to proper workout attire?" Jillian looked down at the still uncovered Victoria, noticed she was hairless down there, and said, "My God, you're completely shaved?"

"You like it?" Victoria asked.

Jillian didn't respond, so Victoria looked at Brian who was, of course, staring right at it again.

He glanced up at Victoria's face, smiled, and returned his attention to the area in question. "Personally I prefer a 'landing strip,' but now you've got me rethinking that... I do like it."

Victoria smiled and Jillian wore a slightly confused expression as she whispered, "landing strip?"

"What was that?" Victoria asked.

"Oh, nothing," Jillian replied.

Both women's attention zoomed to Brian's shorts, which sported a bulge, as well as a big wet spot in the center.

Victoria nodded her head toward Brian. "Looks like someone got a little too excited."

Sitting up, he glanced at his shorts and said defensively, "I did not." He made eye contact with Jillian and said, "I swear."

Slowly they turned their attention to Victoria both shooting the bottomless woman a suspicious look.

Victoria made a face, looked down between her thighs, and then back to Brian's shorts, raising an eyebrow. "Okay, maybe that was me."

Victoria ran a hand down between her legs. Jillian looked on with a horrified expression and Brian watched, open-mouthed. Pulling her hand back, she said casually, "Yes, you're right—it was me. Sorry about that. I'm really, really weaa—" She stopped talking when she saw Jillian's dismayed look and then hurriedly added, "Sweaty. I'm very sweaty. It's hot out there. That, um, Florida humidity, and all." Victoria turned to Brian, "Sorry."

He simply looked at her like a lost puppy. "Don't worry about it."

Jillian folded her arms over her chest with her lips pressed into a thin line. Catching Jillian's expression, Victoria asked, "What?"

"I told you to put on the cover-up."

"There wasn't time. I saw him fall off the treadmill and rushed in to help."

Jillian turned to Brian. "Is this true?"

"I did sorta fall off the treadmill," Brian admitted embarrassedly.

Jillian grabbed a towel from a table and tossed it to her friend. "Would you please put this on? Why don't you do all of us a favor and go back out and work on your tan?"

Looking a little sad, Victoria held the towel for a moment before reaching down to pick up her bottoms. She walked from the room, not bothering to wrap the towel around her waist.

Brian rose to his feet. "Thanks for helping me. I'm not sure what happened. Usually, I can handle that much weight."

"I think I know what happened," she grumbled. "Sorry you had to see all of her like that just now. It was—"

"Oh, no, um... I saw it before when she was on the leg curl machine."

"What?" Jillian asked.

"She had me spotting her earlier on the leg machine and everything just sorta popped out—if you know what I mean—proving that you're totally right about that not being a proper workout outfit." Brian glanced out the window spotting Victoria as she headed to the pool. "She's a real firecracker."

"She's a Darren Star production."

"What?" He gave her a confused look.

"Darren Star, the creator of Sex and the City."

His eyes lit up. "Oh, Samantha. Yeah, I've seen an episode or two... maybe," Brian said a little hesitantly.

She chuckled, and then they both watched as Victoria unashamedly slipped the bikini bottoms up her legs and over her ass as she stood near the edge of the pool.

Jillian added, "Maybe a little more like Samantha on female Viagra." They smiled and shared a nod.

"Has she always been like this?" Brian asked. "I'm not complaining, just curious."

"Her husband died two years ago. She worshiped him. He was only forty-two, and they had a very active sex life."

Brian gave her a solemn look and asked hesitantly, "He didn't, uh, die while they were... doing it, did he?"

"Surprisingly, no," she said with a slight grin. Her expression sobered as she revealed, "It was a brain tumor. Ever since then, she's been living life to the fullest. She rarely says no to anything."

"I'll bet," he said. "That's not a bad philosophy. You never know what could happen."

They shared another nod both gazing out toward the pool while Victoria lay in the lounge chair, once again squirting down her bikini with the spray bottle.

"He left her with a lot of life insurance, an unfilled sexual appetite, and a little angry at the world. That's a dangerous combination."

When Victoria's nipples once again appeared through her suit, Jillian took off for the door. "Now I've really have to take that from her."

"Don't do it on my account," he said.

When she reached the door, Jillian tossed over her shoulder, "Rob could come home, and he doesn't need to see those."

Brian watched her go, disagreeing with her one hundred percent.

Chapter Seventeen

Brian rushed up to his room and went into the bathroom; he noticed the remnants of Victoria's lap dance were still slightly visible on his shorts. He pulled them off, took a close look, and then shook his head and smiled as he stood in front of the mirror. When he closed his eyes, he saw visions of Victoria as she bent over before him. As he stood staring blankly in the mirror, he didn't think about her long but started having all these fantasies about Jillian instead. Minutes later, when he finally pulled himself back to reality, he glanced down at his erection, which was fighting to break free from his boxer briefs. Ashamed, he looked up at himself in the mirror. How could he be fantasizing about doing that to his best friend's mother? He stripped off his clothes and showered, ignoring his massive erection. It would be a cold shower—a really cold one.

After the unfulfilling shower, Brian walked to the window and saw that Jillian and Victoria were still out by the pool. He decided he'd spend the rest of the day in the house rather than go out and risk joining them. Maybe that way he could avoid throwing himself into another potentially embarrassing situation. He felt Victoria was an attractive but dangerous woman who acted as though a giant meteor was four hours from destroying the planet, and she wanted to bang as many guys as she could before impact.

Rob returned from his day trip with Laura just before dinner and he spilled his guts to his best friend. He told him that Laura had been arguing with him most of the day about why he chose to bring Brian home with him, since it would undoubtedly lead to Rob and her spending less time together. She had said she planned to spend most of the week with Rob having sex, but he'd been back more than a day, and they still hadn't done it once. The trip they took that day was unavoidable, and Rob felt like he couldn't leave Brian all alone in the house for the second consecutive night. Laura demanded that he spend the night with her, because it was his birthday. She promised to find an attractive friend for Brian so they could double date, but on such short notice, Laura didn't have a chance to find anyone.

Rob swore to Laura that it would just be the two of them going out that night, but then he thought he had a better idea. Brian could be their designated driver. It would be his birthday gift to Rob. That way, both Rob and Laura could start drinking at dinner, get drunk at a bar afterward, and spend most of the night with Brian while he drove them around the city.

When Rob and Brian picked Laura up, Brian could tell that she was not at all happy to see him in the driver's seat, and it wasn't until she downed her third drink at the restaurant that she finally appeared to get over it. While Brian knew that the happy couple hadn't seen much of each other recently, he didn't know exactly how long it had been since they'd last had sex. Out of the corner of his eye, Brian could see that during dessert, Laura began feeling Rob's crotch under the table. She, either, didn't care that he noticed or figured he couldn't tell. Then after dinner, on the way to the bar, Brian was convinced that she performed a hand job on his friend as they sat huddled next to each other in the back seat. He couldn't see it, per se, but he could certainly hear it in Rob's cracking voice as they struggled to make small talk during the ten-minute drive.

Jillian began working on her manuscript around 10:00 p.m., but she couldn't get the term, "landing strip," out of her head. In her mind, she flashed back to Victoria's presentation down there. When she finally shook Victoria's prepubescent look from her head, she stripped and took a good look at her own neglected area. While she wasn't completely out of control, Jillian thought she was probably—at the very least—in need of an update.

When Jillian performed an Internet search for "landing strip" and found that the very first result was not an airport landing strip but a Wikipedia bikini-waxing page, she had to giggle. She marveled that even some of the most innocent phrases are slang for a body part or a sex act and can lead to some very un-kid friendly results. Eventually, though, she found exactly what she was looking for, including explicit pictures, and picked up advice on trimming and shaving that most sensitive of areas. She also viewed many pictures of variations on the landing strip concept and picked the one she found most appealing.

After collecting all the needed supplies, she took a hot bath and performed her hair design work. When she was done, she was pleased. It felt clean and new, and she felt instantly different, almost as if she were ten years younger. The experience inspired her to write a scene about Dallas spying on Katrina while she gave herself the very same sensual trim job. Jillian wrote for two hours and then lay in bed unable to sleep. After another thirty minutes, she took an Ambien, hoping it would do its usual trick.

. . .

At the bar, Rob and Laura drank and hung all over each other, while Brian had a miserable time, fully sober. Brian did down one birthday shot with the horny couple at the bar, but he spent the majority of his time sipping cokes and looking out the window. The bar was mostly empty and contained only a few moderately attractive women who didn't seem very interested in speaking to Brian. Neither did Rob and Laura, who were busy dry humping in a corner booth. Other than occasionally handing him a twenty and asking for another round, there was no other interaction.

When the couple reached seven drinks each, three at the restaurant and four at the bar, Brian pulled the plug. When Rob asked for another drink, Brian glared at him. "Why don't you let me drive you to her place so you two can just do it already?"

Rob looked at Laura, they gave each other a matter-of-fact nod, and the three of them climbed into the car less than two minutes later. The couple returned to the backseat, and Brian couldn't see either of them in the rearview mirror for the entire trip. They were lying back there, doing who-knows-what, and the sounds they made prompted Brian to crank up the volume on the radio.

Brian remembered the route back to Laura's, and when he reached her dorm's parking lot, he simply stopped the car, turned off the radio, and adjusted the mirror to avoid any glimpse of them. He waited, never looking back, while he heard some whispers, rustling, and giggling, and then the car door opening. He watched Rob and Laura zip and button clothing as they stumbled away from the car. A few steps away, Rob turned back to Brian, raising his hands as if to say, *"Sorry for putting you through that dude,"* and they shared a smile.

. . .

As Jillian waited for the Ambien to kick in, the phone rang. It was just after 1:00 a.m. on the East Coast, but her ex-husband, George, was on the West Coast and tended not to be terribly considerate. The conversation started out civil but quickly took a turn. When it did, Jillian carried the phone to the kitchen and poured herself a glass of wine. She drank about half the glass before she started feeling a little lightheaded, remembered taking the Ambien, and firmly pushed the glass out of her reach.

When Brian arrived back at Jillian's, he found her sitting at the kitchen island talking on the phone, wearing a short, silky robe, a glass of wine nearby. Stepping into the kitchen and realizing that she was in the middle of a heated conversation, he winced, stopping dead in his tracks. She waved back to him like it was no big deal. After grabbing a beer, he headed out to the pool and sat in a lounge chair.

The window was open, and he couldn't help but overhear Jillian as she said, "I'm not writing you another damn check. If you've blown all the money already, that's your problem."

Brian took a sip of his beer as Jillian said at full volume, "Okay, why don't you tell me where all the money is tied up right now? ...Oh, *now* you can't tell me. Maybe if you hadn't been performing *oral sex* on that pool in my girl. I mean, on that girl in my—you know what the hell I'm trying to say. Maybe you'd still be sponging off me, but since you did, the checkbook is now closed."

Then after a brief silence, he heard what sounded like a cell phone bouncing across a kitchen counter followed by breaking glass. Turning, he stared toward the sliding glass door with his eyes wide, wondering if he should check on her. Before he could act, she appeared at the door, and when their eyes met, she brushed the hair from her face and gave him a smile.

She walked unsteadily but managed to make her way to the lounge chair next to him and flopped down onto it. "Did you hear any of that?"

"Maybe I caught a word or two."

"Did you hear the oral sex in the pool part?" she asked.

"Yeah, sorry."

"Don't be," she said, "You didn't lick that pussy in the pool did you?"

"I haven't even been in the pool yet," he said while noticing how spectacular her legs looked in that short robe.

She giggled. "Did I just say *pussy*? I'm so embarrassed." She looked at him with wide eyes.

He nodded and grinned. "Don't worry about it."

"Sorry. I took an Ambien and had a half glass of wine before I remembered and, uh, I'm starting to feel a little GRRREAT."

"Do you need to go to bed?"

"No, I'm fine here. I'm good... Isn't Miami, like, the best weather on the planet?" Jillian asked.

Brian humored her with half a smile and then took another sip of his beer.

"I really hate that asshole," she said as she looked at the pool and then to Brian. "I think I've really screwed up my life. It's halfway over, and I drove George away, and I have nothing to show for being here."

He scoffed and then collected his thoughts. "You've accomplished so much. Look at this house, and Rob... he's a great guy. Your books are so good. People love your books."

"Have you read any?" she asked.

"Well, no, but I plan to soon."

"I hate my books—all that screwing and oral and anal sex. And all the money I make off writing that crap. I should be shot." She grabbed his sleeve. "Can I tell you a secret?" She started without waiting for an answer, "I write about all those beautiful people having amazing, mind-blowing sex. The penises that never go soft and breasts that are huge and orgasm this and orgasm that... and I've never once had any really, really freaking incredible intercourse sex."

He avoided eye contact with her as he said, "I, uh, find that incredibly hard to believe. You're so beautiful."

"No, it's absolutely true. But aren't you sweet!" Jillian said as she let go of his sleeve. Placing her hands behind her head, she stretched back, which lifted the robe so that Brian could see nearly all of her white, silky panties. She closed her eyes as she asked, "Where are Rob and Laura?"

"At her place, they *really* missed each other... a lot," Brian said, rolling his eyes.

She nodded with her eyes still shut. "They're probably doing it. They think I don't know about them doing it, but I've heard them doing it. They're like animals."

"Tell me about it. I think they were actually going at it in the back of the car while I drove them to her dorm."

"No shit," Jillian said and laughed out loud.

Brian widened his eyes and fought back the urge to laugh. Turning toward her, he swung his legs off the lounger as he contemplated what to do. Her legs looked good, and those panties were tiny and sexy. Brian enjoyed looking at them—and her, for that matter. But he felt he should probably stop staring directly at the beautiful panties, legs, and thighs of his best friend's mother.

After stealing one last glance, he breathed in deeply. "I think I'm going to go in."

Jillian's head bobbed and she was startled awake. She opened her eyes slightly then said, "Okay, I'm just going to sleep out here." With that, her head slumped back down.

Brian stood next to her chair. "You can't do that. Let me help you up." He reached out his hand. She opened her eyes, shook her head groggily, then took his hand and attempted to stand. She got halfway up before she began to fall, but Brian grabbed her around the waist.

"Thanks," she said.

After Brian lifted her into his arms, she wrapped her arms around his neck, causing her robe to rise, exposing her panties. She looked down at her underwear, grinned, and then looked at his face. "Well it's only fair."

Brian opened the patio door, while she clung to his neck with her eyes closed. He carried her through the door, closed it, and made his way up the stairs.

She repeated, "Yep, it is only fair."

He chuckled. "What do you mean? What's only fair?"

Jillian opened her eyes, and they looked at each other with their faces almost touching as she said, "That you see my underwear."

"Uh, why is that?"

He reached the top of the stairs, and carried her into the bedroom as she said, "You are really, really strong."

He placed her carefully on her bed and stood next to her, grinning. "Why should I see your underwear? Why is that fair?"

"You're right. It's not fair. You should see it without my underwear. Then we would be *even steven*."

His brows knitted together in confusion as she continued rambling, her eyes heavy, "I'm so sorry. I didn't mean to see your penis. I feel like such a pervert. Do you think I'm a pervert?" Then she closed her eyes and drifted off.

"I really don't understand. When did you see it, exactly?"

Her head jerked, and her eyes flew open. "Huh?"

"Um, when did you, you know..."

Taking a deep breath, she sat up straight and looked him in

the eye as she tried to compose herself. "When you were sleeping by the pool. It was out. I was only trying to protect you from the sun."

"What do you mean *it* was out?" he asked, suddenly alarmed.

She shrugged. "I guess it slipped out the bottom of your shorts."

He raked his fingers through his hair, cringing. "Sorry about that. I didn't mean—"

"Don't worry about it."

"Oh." His eyes brightened. "So that's why I found a towel over me."

"Yep and you guys were right. You are hard to wake up. Did I say *hard*? Oops, I didn't mean to say *hard*." She broke into a chuckle.

He smiled at her then covered his mouth as he fought back a laugh.

"Whoa..." She shook her head, leaving her hair crowding her face. After using her hand to brush much of it away, she pursed her lips and blew out hard to dislodge the last strand that had stuck to her cheek. "Oh, and my phone rang. I dropped it as I was trying to cover you, I think. I don't remember all the details, but I remember IT." She looked pointedly at his groin.

"You do?"

"Nice!" She nodded with her eyes barely open.

"Gee, thanks."

She flapped her hand in the air. "Yeah, it was poking right out there like a great big turtle, like it wanted to be set free, you know?"

He swallowed hard and nodded. "Um, it does that sometimes."

Grabbing him by the shirt, she pulled him close. "And you don't want to know how long it's been since I've seen *one*, and it's been even longer since I've seen a real *one* like yours." She snorted like a pig as she laughed then playfully pushed him away.

He smiled at her, even though she pushed him so hard that it nearly knocked him over. She looked around the room as if to be sure they were alone, then motioned with her index finger for him to come closer. He moved to her.

She grabbed his shirt and pulled him close to her face. "I want you to know I didn't touch it, or anything. Victoria wanted me to, but I didn't."

"She was there, too?" he asked, recoiling.

"Oh, no." She shook her head. "She was on the phone."

Relief, then confusion, then finally concern settled over his face. "Oh, okay."

"You kind of had an erection, also," Jillian said while nodding with her lips pursed, as if she was impressed. "Very *niiice.*"

"Oh, no." He narrowed his eyes, shaking his head. "I'm so sorry."

"Don't worry about it. I was the one *voyer-ing* on you," she said, laughing out loud. Still holding his shirt close to her, she added, "You really have one gorgeous penis. I mean, I've only seen a couple, but yours is just beyond perfect." She stared wide-eyed at him.

He gently removed her hand from his shirt and pulled back to a comfortable distance. "Well, that's just about the nicest thing anyone's ever said to me."

Jillian asked, "That Natalie girl you're after... she hasn't seen it yet, has she?"

He shook his head. "Not exactly."

"I didn't think so, or she would have followed you down here... Next time you see her, just drop your pants and show her that penis of yours, and yeah... she'll be..."

Falling slowly back onto her pillows, she closed her eyes. "Here, I want you to see my pussy. I shaved it for the first time. You were right. The landing strip is a much better option."

"Really?" Brian chuckled, a mixture of fear and excitement flooding his body.

"No one has seen it yet. I really need an opinion." She opened her eyes a little. "Plus, I'm going to feel guilty about the whole *seeing yours* thing until we do this."

"I really shouldn't," he said shaking his head slightly.

"Why the hell not? It's just a vagina. Have you seen one before?"

"Sure... A few, actually," he added defensively.

"So, what's one more?" While reaching down, she lifted her rear end off the bed and slid her panties past her hips and off her legs. She shoved them into his shirt pocket. She lifted her robe a little exposing her tiny landing strip of perfectly coiffed pubic hair she'd left behind. She waited staring at him wide-eyed.

He glanced at it briefly then said shyly, "It's nice."

"No, really look at it." Frowning, she pointed toward the area in question.

He forced his gaze to her beautifully trimmed areas, and his mouth opened slightly. Craning her neck, she looked down at it as well. He felt that familiar rush in his midsection as he watched as she began to touch the hairless areas next to the landing strip and even below that.

She said, "It feels weird. But a good weird, you know?"

Brian swallowed hard and nodded.

"It's so smooth. Do you want to touch it?" She looked him in the eye. "You can."

"I, uh, really haven't washed my hands since I've been out, so..." he stammered.

"Oh, okay. I feel so much better now that you've seen it," she said smiling. Suddenly, her eyes widened with alarm. "Do you think Rob would mind if he knew I saw your... and you saw my...?"

"I would say yes... and yes!"

"Maybe we should just keep it between yours and mine."

"What?" He held back a laugh.

She giggled, swatting her hand at him and shaking her head. "I mean, we should keep it between you and me."

"Oh, that's probably best."

"I mean, I think it's okay that we've seen each other's parts. You know, since we could never really do anything about it because of Rob and everything."

He nodded. "Sure. We'd end up on Jerry Springer on the 'My Best Friend Slept with My Mother' show."

"Exactly, and I don't want to be on that show. It might be fun to do what you'd need to do to get on that show, but..."

"It would definitely be fun," Brian said, about twenty percent humoring her and eighty percent meaning it like he never meant anything more.

"So, we're good. I can sleep now." Closing her eyes, she slumped into the pillow with her lower body still uncovered.

He took one last look at it, because—as Jillian had said—it was only fair. He shook his head, admiring the whole picture, and then he exhaled and pulled her robe down over her exposed parts. After covering her with the sheet and blanket, he pulled the panties from his pocket, grinned, dropped them on the bed, and left the room.

Chapter Eighteen

Brian woke just after 8:00 a.m. Looking out the window at the pool, he discovered it was a cloudless day. He decided to put on a bathing suit and go for a swim. After forty laps, he climbed from the pool, and walked over to the tennis court. He made his way around the court in awe. The net was in perfect condition, and he couldn't find a single flaw in the surface. It was nothing like the courts where he usually played. Public courts were always full of cracks that caused the balls to take unexpected bounces, and the nets usually sagged so badly that you'd need to wedge a tennis ball container under the cord just to prop it up. Spotting a cabinet in one corner of the court, he walked over to it.

When he opened it, he found a ball collector containing about a hundred practice balls and a ball machine. He smiled and wanted to use it right then. It had been years since he had used a ball machine, and he remembered what a great practice tool it was. Brian wanted to be sure that Jillian was awake before he used the noisy contraption and thought he probably should ask first, anyway.

After making his way up to Jillian's bedroom, he found her

still asleep. He got the idea to make her breakfast in bed as a sort of thank you for letting him stay in her incredible home; and it gave him a good excuse to spend a few more minutes with her while she wore practically nothing. He was developing more of an attraction to her than he was comfortable admitting.

As he stood in the kitchen, mixing up the pancake batter, all the things Jillian had told him the previous night really started to hit him. Why was he being so casual about it all? This was a big deal, right? She confessed to invading his privacy and watching him—pretty much all of him—while he slept. Not to mention, she did it all on purpose. It wasn't like she walked in on him by mistake while he was changing, or something. Sure, it may have been a spontaneous thing, but she wasn't drunk, or anything; she chose to push the door open and look. And last night, she had shown him her most private of areas. Granted, she was under the influence of the unpredictable combination of a sleeping pill mixed with alcohol, but wow! What the hell did it all mean? *I guess she's just lonely, all alone in this big house.*

Closing his eyes, he flashed back to being in her bedroom. *She's so free with her body and open about everything. Being open was so much more fun than the alternative.* Sure, it was a little odd, but it was a refreshing change from his experiences living at home with his parents. Even his conversations with this older woman were engaging and so different than the ones he'd had with girls at school. He had so much in common with Jillian. He looked forward to simply speaking with her again.

He opened his eyes, and a grin spread over his face. He loved hearing that she thought his penis was gorgeous. No other woman had ever said anything about it. It was only a compliment—an incredibly intimate compliment—so he wouldn't try to read anything else into it. Hell, she was an erotic romance novelist; she wrote about penises every day, and she probably talked about them constantly... *Okay, maybe not.* He decided he would try to sort all of it out later.

Brian made Jillian a fabulous breakfast. And yes, maybe arranging slices of kiwi on the plate was overdoing it just a little, but he wanted to impress her. He enjoyed cooking, and Jillian's kitchen was so well equipped and stocked that it made cooking even better.

He used to make breakfast for his family every weekend morning when he was still at home. He used the pancake recipe he had perfected over the years with his own personal twists. He made three for himself and took a bite to be sure they were up to snuff. He poured batter on the griddle to cook up three more for Jillian while he ate his quickly. With her pancakes cooked to perfection, he arranged them professionally on a plate. He placed the plate and everything else he needed on the breakfast tray he found and took it up to her.

When Brian poked his head into Jillian's room, he found her awake but still lying in bed curled up with her pillow.

"Hey." He held the tray up. "Can I come in?"

"Sure." She forced her eyes open and rolled onto her back. She didn't seem put off that he was in there with her. They both seemed comfortable with the situation, even though he was in her bedroom, and she was barely wearing anything. She ran a hand over her face, pushed some loose tendrils of hair behind her ear then focused on the tray. "What's all this?"

"I made a little breakfast."

She sat up, and he placed the tray over her legs. Smiling, she eyed the spread of the decorative kiwi, blueberry pancakes, bacon, scrambled eggs, juice, and coffee. "'A little breakfast' is a banana."

"I like to cook, and I wanted to say thank you for letting me stay here. I also wanted to ask, but I'll wait until..." he said trailing off.

"What is it?" She cut a bite of pancake and slipped it into her mouth. "Wow," she mumbled with her eyes wide and her mouth full.

He grinned and sat on the bed near the footboard.

She gazed at him, nodding her head with her jaw hanging open. "This is delicious. You used my pancake mix right? I can never get it to taste like this."

"Mix? No, I never use a mix. Pancakes are easy to make."

"Right." She scoffed. "Not for me."

"They're just flour, baking powder, sugar, salt, oil, milk, and eggs. I do have a few secrets that make them come out perfect."

Jillian took another bite. "Secrets?"

Brian leaned a little closer to her. "First, you need to turn the griddle on before you start and set it to 350 degrees. It needs to be the right temperature and preheated for at least five to ten minutes, or they don't cook right at all."

Gazing at her plate, she shook her head. "How do you get them to look like they came from a pancake house? Mine always look like a greasy mess."

"Do you use butter on the griddle?"

"Yes," she replied.

He pressed his lips together and nodded. "That's the problem, but I'll get into that in a second. I've had this same recipe for years, except now I add a little more sugar, and instead of just two eggs, I use two whole eggs and one extra egg white. It makes them extra fluffy." He looked at her, wishing he could take back the word fluffy, but it was too late. He tried to repair the damage by saying, "*Fluffy*—you probably think I'm effeminate, but I just—"

"No, you can say 'fluffy.' And I think serving breakfast for a woman in bed is one of the most masculine acts that a man can do," she said, as she took a sip of her coffee. She smiled at him. "Finish telling me your secrets."

"The real secret is, you put some butter on the griddle and coat the entire surface, but then you make two what I call 'test cakes' that you throw away. Cook the first one, turn it over, and move it around the griddle to soak up as much of the melted butter as you can. Then do the same thing with the second one. The first one will look like a train wreck, but that second one should look golden brown on the one side. That's when you know the griddle is finally ready."

She looked at him, shaking her head and beaming. "I'll definitely have to try that."

"Just make sure you get ninety-nine percent of the butter off the griddle. You only want the faintest hint that butter was once there—too much will kill 'em."

After taking another bite, she groaned satisfied. "Wow. Just wow."

"Thanks."

She put her fork down. "So what did you want to ask?"

"I noticed you had a ball machine out by the tennis court. Can I use it?"

"Yes, do you need me to set it up?"

"No, I can do it," Brian said, as he was already leaning off the edge of the bed.

"Knock yourself out."

"Cool, thanks." He rose to his feet. "I guess I'll let you enjoy your breakfast."

"Did you already eat?"

"I did."

"Oh, okay. Thank you for the breakfast. It's amazing." She skewered a kiwi slice and slipped it into her mouth as he headed out of the room.

. . .

Jillian finished her breakfast and moved to the back window to watch Brian as he hit with the ball machine. He was better than she had anticipated. She was awestruck as she watched him fire balls down the line and crosscourt, running the machine on its fastest speed. After staring at the muscles in his legs and arms as he worked the court, she decided she had to go out and join him for a closer look.

When she glanced toward the pool area, she spotted a beer bottle on the table by the lounge chairs. This caused bits and pieces of a memory to emerge. She remembered that George had called and that she had been angry with him. She recalled taking a sleeping pill before the call, and then, in the heat of the argument, forgetting about the pill and drinking some wine. She could remember speaking with Brian out by the pool, but everything after that was a complete blur. She thought a moment about waking up without her panties on, and she couldn't remember the last time that had happened. Smiling, she shook those concerns from her head. She had no other memories of the previous night, but she was almost positive that nothing happened between Brian and her.

Chapter Nineteen

Jillian spent a little extra time getting ready before going down to the court. She pulled her hair back and wore the sexiest tennis outfit she owned. The skirt was super-short, and she thought it really showed off her legs. When she went out to the court, Brian was sitting on the bench, and he'd already worked up a pretty big sweat. Approaching him, she smiled. "I saw you hitting. You're really good."

"You think? You'd probably kill me out here."

"Want to hit?"

"Sure, but I'm a little tired from the ball machine and everything, so take it easy on me."

It didn't take long for the two to discover that they got along just as well on the court as they did off of it. They both favored a serve and volley game, and their skill levels seemed to match up perfectly. Brian stole many glances at Jillian's body in that short skirt. He watched her bending over to pick up balls and stared as she walked away from him to the baseline. It was more than a little distracting. They played two sets, and unlike Jillian's previous experience with Mike, the overly, hairy jerk, Brian was a good sport on the court. He even called a few of her shots in that were clearly out, but they were close enough that she didn't argue.

She won the first two sets six games to four. During one long point in the first game of the third set, Brian rushed to the net and hit a near perfect passing shot. He grinned when he hit it, confident it was a winner. She took off after it and reached it ten feet outside the court. Once there, she stretched then grunted, as she smashed a running topspin forehand toward the back corner. He watched it almost in slow motion as it arched high and looked like it would certainly go long. She had hit it flawlessly and with so much topspin that it dropped like a rock mere inches inside the corner.

Standing there with his mouth agape, he stared at the spot, unable to move. As he watched the ball slowly roll away, he said, "Fuck me."

In response, she whispered something under her breath that Brian couldn't hear.

He slowly turned his head to look directly at her as she stood in the perfect finish position, with her legs stretched far apart and her racquet held high. She grinned from ear to ear. He just smiled at her, and she shrugged her shoulders. Then she popped her legs together and headed to the baseline with a spring in her step, all the while maintaining eye contact with him.

"Was that you grunting just like Maria Sharapova?"

She rubbed her forehead. "Was it that bad?"

"If it leads to shots like that, I say grunt away." He added jokingly, "I can't compete with that. That was *so* my point." He simply clapped his hand against his racquet a few times, which is the proper tennis etiquette when your opponent hits a shot of that caliber. Retrieving the ball, he shook his head. "Sorry about dropping the F-bomb."

"Don't worry." She waved her hand at him dismissively. "I got lucky. I usually can't hit on the run like that."

Brian won the third set six games to three. Afterward, they sat on the bench chatting about tennis and other topics, spending twenty minutes on the racquets they had played with over the years. She asked if he ever had any formal lessons. He told her he hadn't and mentioned that his backhand was always the weakest part of his game. He asked if she had any advice for him.

After leading him back onto the court, she suggested that he adjust his grip by rotating the racquet slightly in his hand. Then added, that she thought he should keep his shoulder down as he hit the ball.

She moved behind him to demonstrate and got close enough that she could smell him. He was completely sweaty, yet he didn't smell bad at all. She actually liked his scent. As Brian brought his hand back, she took hold of his arm and demonstrated the recommended changes to his stroke. With their bodies pressed together, and as they looked each other in the eye, they stood completely still for a few moments. Then suddenly, Jillian cleared her throat, let go of his arm, and took a half step backward.

She said, "So, um, that's how I think you should... uh..."

He wiped the sweat from his forehead, turned away slightly as he surreptitiously adjusted his shorts. Turning back to her, he smiled. "I'll try it." He bounced the ball, brought the racquet back, lowered his shoulder then blasted a shot over the net.

"You see?" Jillian said with a bright smile.

"Thanks for the tip. I'll work on that," he said, as he rushed over and sat on the bench, covering his lap with a towel.

Joining him on the bench, she grabbed her bottle of water and poured a little down the back of her neck. She placed the cold bottle to her forehead, glanced at Brian, and touched her face. She closed her eyes and flashed back to a minute earlier when their hot bodies pressed up against each other; the memory overcame her. After fanning her hand at her face, she poured a splash of water down her front, just as Brian glanced at her.

He watched, mesmerized, as the water slowly dribbled between her breasts. His eyes widened as his cheeks reddened and he turned away from her pressing the towel into his lap. Looking over his shoulder, he said, "Thanks for the match. Maybe we can play again some time."

"I'd like that."

He rose quickly to his feet. "I'd better go take a shower. It's really hot out here."

Heading toward the house, he walked with a slightly unusual gait and as she watched him go, she poured the remainder of her water bottle down her front.

Jillian stood outside the guest room, eyeing the door and longing to kiss him, to touch him, and to shower with him. She didn't have a plan, but she was desperate for at least one more glimpse. She figured she should probably make sure he had enough towels. That would be the proper thing to do, she thought. Although, a towel restock was usually better done when your guest was fully clothed. Regardless, it still needed to be done, she kept telling herself.

After grabbing a towel from the linen closet, she knocked lightly on the door and called Brian's name. When there was no reply, she slowly opened the door. She entered the room, heard the shower running, and saw that the door to the adjoining bathroom was open. She heard the uneven sounds of water hitting the shower floor that told her he was actually in the shower and not just standing outside, waiting for the water to reach the proper temperature. She tiptoed to the doorframe and peered through the inch-wide opening on the hinge side, which gave her a clear line of sight to the glass enclosed shower.

A towel was draped over the clear glass door and hung down just enough to block her view of Brian's chest and upward. The glass was clean and fog-free, and it provided her a perfect view of him as he showered. But he wasn't showering; he was touching himself. With his left hand, he had a death grip on the towel that hung over the shower door and he worked himself with his right. Jillian's gaze followed the bulging muscle in his right shoulder to the equally flexed bicep, down to his straining hand, as he really focused on his task.

As she watched him, she slipped her hand under her skirt to her completely sweat-soaked panties. She closed her eyes, and the Jaclyn West third-person narrative kicked in:

Katrina watched as Dallas worked his manhood in the shower. She wondered if he was thinking of her or of someone else. She leaned against the doorframe, her breathing labored as she longed to be in there with him and doing that for him. Slipping her right hand under her skirt, she ran her index finger over her cotton-covered pussy. Her eyes remained glued on his sex, as he pumped it faster and faster. She pushed a finger under her panties and—

Jillian yanked herself out of the fantasy when she heard Brian grunt loudly as he successfully completed his mission. Slumping against the door, exhausted, he squeezed the towel hard, pulling it down into the shower as it fell from his grip. As he tried to prevent it from landing under the spray of the shower, he reached for it, missed it, slipped a little, and ended up on his knees along with the towel on the shower floor.

He tossed the soaked towel into the corner of the shower, cursing and trying to wring it out. It remained worthlessly damp. Feeling sorry for him, she considered coming clean and casually walking a dry towel to him, but she decided that was probably a horrible idea.

Suddenly startled by a noise coming from the hall, she sprinted from the guest room, rushed into the hall and closed the door. As she continued across the hallway, she saw Rob coming up the stairs. When their eyes met, she slowed and stared at him with a blank expression.

He asked, "So did you guys do it?"

"What?" Stopping dead in her tracks, she awkwardly bounced up and down on her heels with her jaw falling open.

"How is he?"

She froze, unable to speak or breathe.

He narrowed his eyes. "Tennis. Did you guys play?"

Exhaling, she smiled. "Oh, yeah, we did play. He's really good."

"Is something wrong?"

She narrowed her eyes in a slight panic and then paused to compose herself. "Sorry. Your father called last night, and I'm still, uh..." George's call was the furthest thing from her thoughts at that moment, but it was as good an excuse as any to explain her strange behavior.

"Sorry about that. Are you okay?"

"I'm fine. I think, uh, Brian is in the shower. Would you see if he needs another towel? I tried to catch him before, but, uh..."

She trailed off as she handed the towel to Rob and headed past him down the hall.

"Okay."

"I really need a shower, myself." She walked into her bedroom and closed the door. With her hands covering her face, she slumped against the door; her body trembling.

Chapter Twenty

Jillian leaned against her door, feeling even more horrible than when she stared at Brian's exposed penis while he slept. What was she doing? What, exactly, was the plan? This time she had surely invaded his privacy, and she was sure that her actions must qualify as some kind of lesser sex crime. Walking across the room, she stripped off her damp clothes and stood before a full mirror, admiring the reflection of her newly trimmed area.

As she studied her new look, a shadow of a memory from the previous night took shape in her head. Was Brian in her room last night? Did she show him? Did she tell him about the other day when she saw him sleeping? *No way,* she thought. *I must have dreamt about the show and tell.* Sure, she had been out of it, but she wasn't on sodium pentothal, or anything. It was only a half glass of wine and one Ambien.

Jillian looked at her reflection in the mirror, still shaking from nearly being caught, but also turned on from seeing Brian do what he did. She ran her hands over her body. Looking at her pussy in the mirror, she slid a finger over what little hair remained. She decided she had to finish what she already started.

After rushing to the door, she locked it and then fell backward in bed with her hand between her thighs. She imagined it was Brian licking her down there as she closed her eyes, moaned softly, and touched herself.

Minutes later, in the hall, Rob and Brian walked past Jillian's room. Rob turned back, approached her door, and then knocked once. "We're going to lunch, okay?"

After a few seconds with no response, Rob turned then stopped when he heard Jillian yell back, "Oookayyy," in an odd voice that sounded like she might be trapped under something heavy.

Rob and Brian exchanged concerned looks.

Rob asked, "You okay in there?"

Jillian called back, "Oh sure! I'm, uh, just about to get wet. I mean, in the shower. Have fun."

"All right." Rob raised a shoulder, turned to Brian, and they headed downstairs.

The two walked to a restaurant in the mall that was only a few blocks from the house. It was a scorching day, and the choice to walk left them sweaty and hot when they arrived. They each ordered a burger and a beer and then another. Rob shared with Brian how Laura had been insatiable since he arrived, how she seemed different, and how she was more into sex now than ever.

"Are you doing something new?" Brian asked.

"I don't think so, just the same old stuff."

"Enjoy it while it lasts."

Rob ordered another beer for both of them and looked at

Brian apologetically. "I knew I'd be spending a lot of time with her, but I didn't think she would want to see me so much. She's wearing me out, dude. I slipped out when she fell asleep. I feel like a dick, though. I brought you here because you were depressed, and now I've abandoned you."

Brian looked at him as if he was crazy. "I'm having the time of my life. Your house is like a freaking resort. I played tennis today and took a swim, and, uh, your mother couldn't be nicer."

"Is she okay? She mentioned she got a call from my father last night."

"I heard some of it," Brian said, aware that he might be heading into dangerous territory.

"Was she all right afterward?" Rob asked.

"She was... She had just taken a sleeping pill. She was kind of out of it and pretty angry at first, but she seemed to have cheered up a little by the time she went up to bed."

After taking a sip of beer, Rob looked distraught. "Jesus! Now I've abandoned her, too."

"She's fine, really."

"Thank God you were there in case she overdosed or fell, or something."

"Yeah," Brian said softly in a guilty tone.

"I've got to tell Laura to back off a little, so I can—"

"Dude, don't worry about me or your mom. She's fine. Look, if I had a hot girl begging to have sex with me repeatedly, I wouldn't be spending time with another guy and my mother. Seriously."

"You sure?" Rob asked.

"I have some schoolwork to do, anyway, and really, your primary mission should be to have sex with Laura until your dick falls off."

Rob smiled at him. "Thanks man. For a while there, I wasn't

sure if I wanted to break up with her or not, but now she's changed, and I think it could really work out between us."

"Spend as much time with her as you want. This is the best vacation that I've ever been on. I can honestly say that I'm not thinking about Natalie at all right now."

Chapter Twenty-One

R
ob and Brian returned home, exhausted from the heat and buzzed from the beers they had enjoyed at lunch. Deciding to cool off in the pool, they put on their suits and went out to the backyard. There, they discovered Victoria sunning herself in a slightly more conservative bikini (for her, anyway) and reading a hardcover novel. A half-full martini glass sat on the table next to her.

Glancing at them both, she raised her sunglasses, and a smile crossed her face. She watched while they knocked into each other clumsily as they headed her way. When they reached her, they tossed their towels down on the lounge chairs on either side of her.

Rob said, "Hey, Victoria. This is Brian."

"Oh, we met... yesterday," Brian said.

"We worked out together a little," Victoria added.

"That we did," Brian said sharing a quick, knowing smile with her.

Rob asked, "What're you reading?"

"Your mother's classic, *Knight Rider*," Victoria said, with her eyebrows raised.

"The medieval one?"

She nodded her head and eyed them suspiciously, certain that they had been drinking. They turned and headed toward the pool, and Victoria focused on their lean, muscular legs as they walked away. After shaking her head, a little dizzied, she picked up her drink and downed it. She watched as they dove in and swam to the far side, then back. When they reached the wall, they launched themselves from the water and sat on the edge of the pool. Rob stood first and walked to his lounger. He adjusted his towel and lay back in the chair next to Victoria. Brian soon followed and fell back into the chair on the other side of her.

She looked to one side and then the other, and smiled as she eyed their well-defined calf muscles, trying to decide which of them had the better legs. Then she looked up at the sun, which had changed positions, and decided to move to get the best tanning angle and to show off her best asset. She stood, fully reclined the lounger, moved her towel to the opposite side, and lay face down with her feet toward the guys' heads. Rob and Brian each stole a glance at her shapely ass and shared a look then slipped on sunglasses.

Victoria knew she could easily have one or both of the young men— probably at the same time. She had promised Jillian that she would not corrupt them, but she never promised she wouldn't fantasize about it. As she settled on the lounger, the medieval setting and a Jaclyn West-like third person narrative began flooding into her head...

Miss Victoria sat in her white frock and gazed on the two knights fresh from battle. The three had been captured, tied to trees deep in the forest, and left for dead. The knights wore full, heavy chain mail, so Victoria could not see their faces or any other part of their bodies. *The trees were close enough together that she could almost reach out and touch them. The knights' hands were tied behind the trees, but her hands remained free, as she was only secured about the waist and ankles. Victoria struggled to pull her ropes free but was able to loosen them enough to reach her metal-sheathed companions with just her fingertips. As she stretched further, her frock opened, exposing her gorgeous, abundant cleavage. Both knights' eyes locked onto her chest, and their loins started painfully expanding in their metal confines.*

Noticing their condition, she sighed and reached out to help. She placed a hand on the waist of each pair of chain mail leggings and miraculously released the clasps that secured them. The leggings dropped heavily to the forest floor with a loud thud. Each knight exhaled deeply as the burden was lifted from his sex. Their manhoods swelled even larger once released from one garment, but they were still encumbered by their battle-stained white underclothes. Victoria tore away the remaining garments, freeing both massive prizes. She licked her lips and stroked both knights' unyielding swords in an equal but deliberate fashion.

While Victoria was playing out this fantasy in her head, she wrapped her hands around the legs of the lounge chair, gently stroking each rounded leg as if they were the swords currently starring in her fantasy.

Jillian arrived home, went upstairs, and looked down from the second story balcony at the three sunbathers. The first thing she noticed was where both her son and Brian were looking. Then, when she saw the apparently obscene gesture Victoria was making with her hands, she narrowed her eyes, groaned, and rushed down to the pool.

When Jillian reached them, she demanded that the young men go into the house while she had a private word with Victoria. Sitting back in the lounge chair, Victoria smiled at her. "What's up?"

Jillian waited until the door closed before she asked, "What the hell was that?"

"What are you talking about?"

"I saw you. What you were doing?" Jillian whispered sternly.

"I was lying down, and I was almost asleep, too." Victoria looked at her friend as if she were nuts.

"What were you thinking about?"

"Nothing." Victoria looked away uneasily.

"And what were you doing with your two hands, exactly?" Jillian placed her hands on her hips with her eyebrows raised.

"I wasn't doing anything."

"You were suggestively stroking the chair, just like you were..." Jillian glanced back at the house and whispered, "... jerking them off."

"How in the hell would you have any idea what I was thinking about? Are you reading minds now, too?"

"You were between the two of them facing toward their... doing that and shaking your little ass in their faces." Jillian frowned in disgust.

"I was not shaking my ass, and, again, how could you know what—"

"Were you or were you not jerking off my chair while two impressionable young men had their eyes glued to your ass?"

"Their eyes were really glued? Like, the whole time or—" Victoria smiled.

Jillian didn't bother to reply; she simply stared her down.

Victoria exhaled, defeated. "Okay, so I kinda got a little

caught up in a fantasy out here. I was reading your filthy *Knight Rider* novel."

Jillian continued to glare at her, so Victoria added, "Do you know how hard it is to release two knights' swords from their chain mail confines *whilst* you are tied to a freaking tree?"

"I, uh..." Jillian said, unsure how to respond.

"One handed and at the same time?"

"That does sound tricky, but—"

"All that work to get them free, and you interrupted right when it was getting really good!" Victoria glared at her.

Jillian shot her an accusatory look. "And who were the two knights?"

"I'd rather not say."

Jillian stood with her arms crossed, waiting for the full confession.

After a few seconds, Victoria said, "Okay, but you know full well what they'll be up to later, with or without me harmlessly teasing them out here. Wouldn't you rather they jerked it to the thought of a real, regular woman, rather than some Internet porn star?"

"You're a regular woman?" Jillian asked, taken aback.

"Yes. Yes, I am," Victoria replied quickly.

"I don't think regular women would consider you in their club. You look like a porn star."

"Really?" Victoria said excitedly.

"That's not a compliment." Jillian glared at her until Victoria's smile melted away.

"Come on, it was just a fantasy. I wasn't actually jerking them off, or anything. I can control my behavior... for the most part," Victoria said semi-confidently.

"Can you, really?"

"Okay, you obviously don't want me here," Victoria shot

back angrily as she stood and collected her things. "This is all your fault anyway."

"How is it my fault?"

"I've read so many of your dirty little books that I constantly have this third person erotic narrative playing in my head. Do you know what it's like to refer to yourself in the third person in your own damn fantasy?"

"I never use my name, but I know exactly what you're talking about."

"I actually used the term 'his sex' for penis. I mean who says that? It's a dick, a cock, a rod, even manhood is okay, but what is this 'his sex' thing? What the hell does that even mean?"

"I just try to mix it up a little," Jillian said blushingly.

"Well, knock it off with the 'his sex' crap." Victoria started walking toward the back gate.

"Don't go," Jillian said. "I would just prefer if you didn't involve my son—"

"You really need to smoke that joint I left with you. Maybe then you'd relax," Victoria interjected.

Rushing after her, Jillian whispered, "Look, I'm sorry. I overreacted. I guess if you want to come over and jerk off my chairs some more, I don't really have a problem with it."

"Oh, you have a problem." When Victoria reached the gate, she turned back and gave her a snotty look. "And I know you. So don't go writing this scene into one of your little books or anything, you giant hypocrite." With that statement, she exited the backyard and slammed the gate.

Jillian knew Victoria wasn't really mad, and she was, in fact, already writing a scene in her head based on this conversation. It wouldn't be the first time—or the last—that Victoria was the inspiration for a chapter here or there. She was a gold mine for erotic fiction.

Chapter Twenty-Two

Victoria returned to her house and sat out by her own pool. It was time for her pool guy, Kurt, to perform the weekly cleaning, and she always enjoyed watching him. He was gorgeous and happily married, but it was all harmless fun, she thought. Victoria changed into the white see-through bikini, the one that had so mesmerized Brian, and lounged, waiting for Kurt to arrive. Lying face down on her lounger, she decided to try to continue her fantasy where Jillian had so rudely interrupted her. She was still a little mad at her, and this would help.

Victoria lost the medieval story line, choosing to go with something a little more plausible, by bringing the boys into her pool. She loved doing it in the pool, near the pool, on the diving board—you name it. If there was a pool nearby, Victoria was horny. As Victoria drifted into the third person erotic narrative, she avoided any obscene hand movements. Although if one looked closely enough, one might have noticed, she was humping the chair, albeit only slightly...

Kurt arrived and jolted her out of the fantasy when he

tossed a hose over the fence and onto the lawn, but she didn't mind. She could return to it later.

Craning her neck, she discovered that he was shirtless. After exchanging a hello with him, she let her eyes wander to his muscular chest. When she finally returned to his face, she caught him staring directly at her string-covered rear end. Grinning, she let him have another moment before turning over and asking, "Mind if I take a quick dip before you start? It's so hot today."

"What?" He mumbled softly as his gaze dipped down to her cleavage.

"Mind if I get in the pool before you start?"

"No problem. Knock yourself out." He turned away then raked his fingers through his hair.

She slowly walked down the steps into the pool, just enough to wet her see-through top, and then she climbed back out. When she did, her hard nipples showed right through the white fabric. She watched as Kurt leaned into the pool to collect water for a test. At that moment, he made the mistake of glancing up at her. With his eyes widened, he lost his balance and fell into the pool.

After returning to the surface, he looked at her, smiling, and then lifted his strong body effortlessly from the water.

As Victoria watched him, she held back a laugh. "Are you okay?"

"New suit?" he asked.

"Yes, do you like it?"

"I'd say it's my new favorite."

Jillian arrived, walked to the pool area through the gate, and looked at Victoria, apologetically.

"I'm not talking to you yet." Frowning, Victoria folded her arms.

"I'm sorry. I shouldn't have come down on you like that, especially since I think I did something much worse. I, uh—" Jillian started to say but stopped when she saw Kurt nearby.

Victoria looked at Kurt. "He doesn't mind a little girl talk. Do you Kurt?"

"No, I've heard some things that would, uh..." he began, but ended by shaking his head.

Jillian plopped down in a lounger and looked at the newly built house behind Victoria's. The house was large and about a hundred yards away. The backyard had a clear view into Victoria's yard.

Jillian asked, "Did they move in up there yet?"

"Yeah."

"It's a shame about your view. Are you still going to have those tall trees planted to get back your privacy?"

Victoria grinned then looked over at the house. "The view is actually a lot better now."

"What are you talking about?"

"There's a hot guy who moved in there. I've been waiting for him to come over, but it hasn't happened yet. We've only exchanged waves a couple of times."

"Is he married?"

"Not sure. I think I'll take something over to welcome him to the neighborhood. Maybe I'll bake something," Victoria said.

Jillian gave her a skeptical look. "You can't bake."

"I'll figure some way to welcome him."

Jillian shook her head disapprovingly. "Okay, but be sure he's not married first."

Victoria frowned again. "Did you come over here to give me crap, or..."

"No, I came to tell you Brian made me this incredible breakfast in bed."

"Great, so you guys did it then?" Victoria gave her a broad smile.

"No. Would you let me finish?" Jillian snapped. "Anyway, after breakfast, we played tennis together, and he's great and a good sport, unlike Giant Pube Boy.

"Who's Giant Pube Boy?" Victoria asked.

"You remember, from a couple of weeks ago?"

Victoria looked at her, confused. Jillian matter-of-factly pulled out her phone, loaded up the picture, and handed the phone to Victoria.

"I do remember now, the blind date that ended up in your pool, naked." Victoria studied the picture, smiling. "I still can't see his penis. Where is it again?"

"It's in there somewhere."

Victoria glanced up at Kurt. "You've got to see this."

He walked over, looked at the picture, and then laughed. "Wow, that's a lot of hair."

As he walked away, Victoria asked, "You're trimmed down there, aren't you, Kurt?"

"You know it," he said, without looking back.

Jillian shook her head with a smile. "Anyway... so after we finished playing, he went to take a shower, and I kinda sorta went to ask him if he needed any towels or anything—"

"Towels?" Victoria said accusatorily.

"Yes, towels. Would anyone buy that?"

"No, but please continue. This is getting good."

Jillian whispered, "I kind of caught him jerking off in the shower, and I stood there and watched while he finished."

"Did you do anything... else?"

"Not really," she continued whispering. Then she looked

over at Kurt, who either wasn't hearing any of this or listening intently and trying to play it cool.

"You didn't join him?"

"No, I... uh... thought about it, but Rob came home and..."

"Oh, you should have played less tennis and done more fucking!"

Jillian took a moment to processes that possibility. "I think it would be a mistake. He's Rob's best friend and all, and nearly half my age, but God, is he sexy!"

"Life is short. You have to seize the opportunities you're given. It's not like you have a lot of them."

Jillian glared at her a moment, then nodded in agreement. "For arguments sake, let's say I do want to sleep with him, but I'm so out of practice that I've forgotten exactly how to do everything. What do young guys like?"

"I can give you the perfect plan to blow his mind and keep him coming back for more. Once you do this, he will follow you around like a lost puppy just begging for you to do it again."

Jillian looked at her expectantly.

"First, have him lie on his stomach, fresh from a good, long, hot shower. Then you—" She looked over at Kurt. "Sorry, Kurt, I don't want you to hear all my secrets."

She whispered the rest of the procedure into Jillian's ear. Jillian listened intently, asked a few questions, and looked turned on by most of what she heard and a little put off by the rest.

"And that does it?" Jillian asked.

"Like you wouldn't believe." Victoria said confidently. "You really would need to like a guy to do all that."

Jillian nodded along in complete agreement.

"You need a perfectly groomed guy, as it were. For example, no one is doing any of *that* to Pube Boy," Victoria added as they both shared a sickened look. "I once brought a young guy right to the edge four times before I let him come. He nearly jumped out of his skin. When I thought he had finally had enough, I did that last thing I told you about, and he, uh... He claimed it was the biggest orgasm of his life."

Jillian looked at her in awe.

"That's why I think there are so many divorces today—married couples just don't have enough really good sex. I'm not talking about five minutes of 'I'm-exhausted, we-have-to-get-up-in-five-hours, we-just-finished-watching-the-local-news, but do-you-really-feel-like-doing-it?' sex. I mean the up-to-bed-early-on-a-weeknight, take-a-good-shower, slip-on-some-lingerie, and really-go-at-it sex. Your basic blow-job, oral-for-her, sixty-nine, regular-old-fashioned, and then-maybe-a-little-backdoor, around-the-world sex."

Jillian watched her bleary eyed. "This *is* just one night we're talking about, right?"

Ignoring the question, Victoria grinned. "You go 'around the world' with your husband a couple times a month, and he won't be straying. You won't be finding yourself at an attorney's office, arguing over who gets custody of the dog."

Jillian looked at Victoria like she was really making some sense, and Victoria summarized it with this last gem, "Look, all I know is that it's really hard for a couple to ask for a divorce from each other when their genitals are buried in each other's faces."

Jillian looked sheepishly at Victoria. "Brian still seems to be hung up on that college girl. I don't want to do anything to screw that up for him."

"You'd actually be doing him a favor. You give him one good night, and he goes back to school full of confidence and sweeps that girl off her feet. She won't know what hit her."

"Maybe you're on to—"

"Someone needs to help him out. If you don't, maybe I should," Victoria said.

"Okay. I'll let you know, but keep your paws off until I figure this out."

"Deal, but if you do sleep with him, please record it and e-mail it to me."

After rolling her eyes, Jillian smiled at her.

Just then, a man in his mid-forties exited the back door of the house behind Victoria's and approached the grill. Jillian and Victoria watched as the tall, muscular man in the polo shirt and shorts bent down to turn on the gas in the tank and then stood to fire up the grill.

"What's he, like, forty-five? Isn't he a little too old for you?" Jillian joked.

Smiling, Victoria waved to him as she growled, "Very funny."

The man looked over, smiled back, and returned the wave.

"He's cute," Jillian said.

"Look at those broad shoulders... I should really learn to bake."

The man walked toward the house. Turning back, he smiled, waved again, and disappeared inside.

Victoria squirmed in her chair a little. "Are you hot? I'm hot... I wonder what Austin is doing tonight."

Jillian narrowed her eyes at Victoria, who was clearly in need of some male attention.

Chapter Twenty-Three

At Jillian's, Rob slept at home that night. He and Brian stayed in and watched movies. Finding his mind wandering during the films, Brian thought mostly about Jillian and how much fun they had playing tennis. He thought a lot about how freaking incredible she looked in her short tennis skirt. Natalie also crossed his mind once or twice. Was she somewhere thinking about him, or was she with some other guy? He wished he knew.

Jillian was somewhat relieved that Rob was at home, since it lifted the possibility of anything happening between Brian and her that night. It gave her a chance to think about everything and to continue writing, since she was on a roll. She had written a few pages after the previous day at the pool, but while the guys spent time in front of the TV, she wrote for hours—more than she had in weeks. Her recent fantasies starring Brian, her actual firsthand experience watching him, and her recent conversation with Victoria had filled her mind with more ideas than she could process. She spent the day jotting down ideas on Post-it notes, making notes in her notebook, and recording voice memos on her phone. After spending some time organizing her notes, she wrote well into the night.

When she finally closed her laptop cover just after midnight, she was so horny that she had to touch herself for the second time in less than twelve hours. Jillian had never before done that twice in a single week.

As Jillian was attending to her needs, Austin and his friend, Steve, also, in his mid-twenties, sat far apart on the giant L-shaped sectional sofa in Victoria's living room. Each nursed a beer while Victoria prepared in the bedroom. In the center of the room, Victoria had moved together two center sections from her sofa and had placed a crisp, clean, white sheet over them. The guys didn't say a word to each other as they sat waiting, tossing concerned glances at the covered sofa pieces, which sat directly before them.

When Victoria appeared, wearing a tiny, bright blue lace bra with matching thong, they both swallowed hard. She approached them, wearing a sexy smile. "I've been thinking about this all day."

Austin's eyes locked in on her hard nipples as they fought to break free from their sheer cover-up, and Steve stared at her with his mouth agape.

Austin said, "You look amazing."

Victoria smiled at the compliment. "Why are you two sitting so far apart?" The guys looked at each other, the concern etched on their faces, and then she added, "You'll need to be a lot closer together if we're going to do what I've been fantasizing about all day."

Steve and Austin shared an apprehensive look. Then Steve

adjusted the bulge in his shorts as Austin returned his gaze to Victoria.

She touched her face. "I've always wanted to see if I could fit two in my mouth at the same time... and maybe other places as well."

Steve's jaw dropped. "We're not, uh, bi or anything."

Victoria shook her head slowly. "You guys don't have to do anything to each other. You're here to please me." She unclasped her bra and revealed her breasts as she added, "Things... may touch a little here and there. Is that... okay?"

"Well, uh..." Austin began as Victoria pulled down her panties and started running her fingers slowly between her thighs.

Steve glanced at Austin. "I think that might be okay. I'm, uh, comfortable with my..."

Slipping her fingers inside, she closed her eyes for a moment and moaned. Transfixed, Austin and Steve watched unblinkingly as the bulges in their shorts grew.

"Well, what are you waiting for?" Victoria asked.

The two stared at her dumbfounded until she gave them a tired look. Then they jumped up and quickly stripped off their clothes. Victoria eyed Steve up and down, and then stopped in the middle to stare at his growing manhood. Licking her lips, she looked over at Austin. He was more than ready, as well.

Victoria kneeled next to the sheet-covered sofa sections and motioned for them to join her. Without looking at each other, her boy toys approached.

She led them into position on the sofa sections until they were seated, facing each other. Moving behind Austin first, she guided him until he was lying flat with his legs spread. Next, she moved behind Steve and coaxed him down on the opposite side. The parts she was interested in were a few inches apart as she knelt down between them. Their eyes locked on her body, mesmerized.

Victoria said, "Slide together. I want to... try a few things."

Austin and Steve looked at her skeptically.

"Trust me. You won't be disappointed."

The guys didn't look at each other as they spread their legs apart and moved together until their knees were touching, but they were still too far apart.

Victoria frowned. "One of you is going to have to put your legs over the other. Sorry, I'm new at this and..."

Austin looked at her alarmed. "Now, wait. I'm not—"

He stopped talking when Victoria leaned down and devoured him with her mouth. Shutting his eyes tight, he groaned. With her mouth still occupied, she reached over and grabbed Steve's erection. Pulling her mouth off Austin, she moved it to Steve's manhood and gave him a preview of what was to come.

Victoria pulled her head up to look at one, then the other. "I'll keep going, but only if you move closer together."

They never moved faster in their lives.

For the next forty-five minutes, Victoria experimented with her two friends and performed acts she had recently seen in an adult movie. While some of the things they tried worked better than others, it was the hottest sex she'd experienced in a long time.

When they were finally finished, Austin and Steve scooted away from each other to the edge of the sofa pieces, avoiding eye contact with one another. Victoria sat down between them, placing a hand on each of their knees. "That was fun."

The guys simply nodded in agreement.

She looked to one then the other and said, "You guys want to go for a swim?"

Chapter Twenty-Four

T he next day, Rob left Jillian's house early to spend the day with Laura. Waking around 10:30, Brian went for a swim. Jillian got up soon after and sat out by the pool. She made Brian pancakes from a mix, but she did follow his griddle tips, and they weren't bad at all. They ate the cakes while sitting side-by-side on the lounge chairs, and she stole a few glances at his bare chest and legs as they spoke.

"I have this dinner party coming up soon, and I want to make a special dessert. You have any ideas?" Jillian asked.

"I make a mean lemon meringue pie. I use, like, triple the egg whites so it ends up being this giant meringue layer on top."

She shook her head no, since egg whites kind of made her want to vomit. It was something about the texture.

"How about chocolate éclairs? They're a pain in the ass to make, but they're good," he said.

"I was thinking about more of a cake."

After pausing to think for a moment, his eyes widened. "I make this cake. It's kind of my own personal creation. I put it together from a couple different recipes. It's like a chocolate mousse ganache cake."

Jillian's face lit up at the thought of chocolate and the impressive sound of the name. "It sounds good, but is it hard to make?"

"It's really pretty easy."

"Do you make the cake from scratch like your pancakes, because that—"

"No way, cake from scratch usually isn't that great," he began. "At least I've never found a good recipe, or maybe I'm just not a good enough baker to pull it off. I use a mix."

Jillian smiled. "You had me worried there."

"You whip half the cream and fold cooled melted chocolate into it. Then you heat up the rest of the cream and melt semi-sweet chocolate into that, while stirring it constantly, until it turns into, like, this silky, rich mixture. Then, you just pour it over the top."

She looked at him, confused. "How, exactly, do you 'fold' something?"

"If you want, we could go to the store, get everything, and I could show you how to make one today. Then you could easily knock it out by yourself when you need to." She gave him a broad smile.

When they returned from the grocery store, Jillian prepared the cake mix as Brian sat on a stool at the kitchen island, watching her. She glanced up from the bowl. "So, who's your favorite men's tennis player—Federer?"

"I, uh, really don't like any of the recent players. They're all baseliners, and they hit these 140 mile-per-hour serves that no one can return. All the points are either aces or forty-shot-long, incredibly boring rallies. The pro game has changed so much. There are no true rivalries."

She nodded in agreement. "You are exactly right. So, who's your favorite player all-time?"

"You're going to think I'm a nerd, or something, but I'm a McEnroe fan all the way."

She gasped. "I love him! He's the reason I started playing."

"Me, too!"

She looked at him confused. "But wait, you weren't even born yet when McEnroe was playing."

"I was a toddler for some of his comebacks, but my father was a huge fan, and he had videotapes of all the big matches." He looked away, thinking, and then said, "My favorite is the Borg-McEnroe U.S. Open final of—"

"1980," they said in unison and shared another smile. Jillian moved a half step closer to him.

"I think I still have a few old matches on grainy videotape. Do you remember that match at Wimbledon that same year?" she asked.

"Yeah, Mac saved five match points before he finally lost. Great match." Staring down at the floor, he looked to be replaying the memory in his mind.

"I remember that."

He shook his head smiling. "Freaking Johnny Mac, he changed tennis forever."

After they came down from their Johnny Mac high, Jillian put the cake in the oven, and when it baked and had cooled, Brian walked her through the preparations of the simple chocolate mousse. He instructed her to cut each round cake layer in half to create four thin layers, and then watched as she placed the first layer on the cake plate, followed by a third of the mousse, another layer, more mousse, still one more cake layer, mousse, and then the final cake layer on top. The cake stood about nine inches high when they put it all together. Next, he showed her how to make a double boiler out of a metal bowl and a small saucepan, and supervised as she heated the cream while stirring it constantly. When it started to get warm, he had her add the semi-sweet chocolate.

As Jillian continued stirring the mixture in the bowl, she began to frown. "I think I must have done something wrong."

"Just keep stirring," he said, "When you make ganache, before the chocolate and cream really mix, it's supposed to look like a disaster."

She kept on mixing, and it looked horrible, with the different shades of white, brown, and chunks of chocolate all fighting against each other, and then all at once, it came together into the dark chocolate silk as he promised.

She smiled at him pleased.

Grinning proudly, he glanced at her face. "You see? Now take it off the heat."

Jillian removed the pot from the burner, and he told her to taste it. She reached in with a finger, tasted it, and smiled. She presented her finger to him; he swiped a bit off with his finger, tasted it, and then nodded. They shared another brief, passionate, moment as they stared at each other for a little too long.

Then Brian cleared his throat. "We'd better get that on the cake before it cools."

He walked her through pouring it and spreading it evenly over the cake. As she poured it, she drifted away to a place somewhere, wearing less clothing and pouring the chocolate over something more fun—like each other. He seemed caught up in something similar with his eyes glazing over. She snapped out of it first, and when he finally did, he helped her smooth the ganache over the cake by steadying her hand as he looked over her shoulder, their bodies pressed together. When they finished, the cake looked magnificent, and they put it into the refrigerator to set.

Brian looked into her eyes. "Do you want to, uh—"

"What?" Jillian asked, looking at him anxiously with her lips slightly parted.

"Hit some balls?"

She beamed. "See you out there in two minutes."

They both rushed upstairs as if the conversation had gone more like, *We've only got about an hour. Do you want to get naked and do it?* She stripped down to underwear seconds after entering her room. Jillian decided to change her panties to something a little sexier, since they would be on display—at least partially—when she bent over to retrieve balls from the court, and maybe she planned on doing a little more of that than was actually necessary.

Once they were on the court, the intensity level picked up right where they left off the last time they played. They both grunted during some key shots, almost to the point where someone only listening might think the on court couple was having some mind-blowing sex. From all outward appearances tennis became this intense sensual experience for both of them. It was adorable in a somewhat disturbingly lame way. It really was their sex replacement.

Brian took the first set, and they tied in the second at six-all. The bulge in his shorts may have been related to her panties being visible on several occasions—at least Jillian thought she witnessed a bit more swelling in that area than was needed for a game of tennis. She was wet almost the entire match, a combination of feeling the sexy underwear against her skin, along with her proximity to the guy she was at the very least incredibly attracted to, if not smitten with completely.

The tiebreak to decide the second set was long and grueling, and it was the climax of the match in more ways than one. In a tennis tiebreak the first player to get seven points wins, as long as he/she wins by at least two points. Brian and Jillian traded points all the way, until they each tied at sixteen points, which is equivalent to playing nearly six full games of tennis. When Jillian called the score, they both stopped and looked at each other.

She said, "This is exactly that Borg-McEnroe 1980 Wimbledon fourth set tiebreak."

He nodded. "And I'm McEnroe."

"Go ahead, be McEnroe." She grinned. "He may have won the tiebreak, but he eventually lost the match."

While McEnroe did win his memorable tiebreak 18–16, Jillian and Brian's didn't end in the same way. They continued trading points up to twenty all. Brian and Jillian were both playing aggressively and taking chances, even though they were visibly exhausted and sluggish between points. Brian had six opportunities to win the match, but each time, Jillian was able to erase the set point with a tough shot, a lucky bounce, or an error on his part. She didn't have a set point opportunity until she went up 21–20. That's when Brian hit a shot into the net.

Serving her first set point, she held her head high as she looked at him. "Don't get discouraged because you blew all those match points, but I'm going to put you away right here. You had your chances, but this is getting ridiculous."

Brian mock-glared at her panting as he struggled to catch his breath. "Bring it."

Jillian blasted a serve to his forehand, and he hit a good, deep approach shot, and then rushed to the net. She drove a shot down the line to his forehand. Brian dove, barely got his racquet on the ball, and hit a brilliant touch drop volley. He ended up splayed out flat on the court.

Rushing the net, she stuck her racquet forward and stretched with everything she had without looking. She caught the ball on the edge of her racquet, apparently just before the second bounce, and it flew over the net for a winner. He watched as she hit the shot, though his view was partially blocked by the net.

She looked at him breathless. "I'm not sure I got it, did you see?"

"Nice shot. It was clean." Too exhausted to continue, he rolled over, pulled his legs toward his chest, and looked at the scrapes on his knees.

She rushed to his side of the net. "Your get was incredible— like a young Boris Becker. Are you okay?"

"I'm fine," he said as he slowly got to his feet.

Jillian trailed behind while he limped slightly to the bench, and they rested there for a few minutes in a sort of pseudo post-coital, spent bliss. Then, they looked at each other wearing the same "I-can't-do-it-anymore" expression.

She sighed. "We'll have to finish this another time."

Glancing over at her, he simply nodded.

She took a sip of water as her eyes lingered on his muscular legs. "Um, what are you doing later?"

"Nothing, I think."

"We've got that cake for dessert, so why don't I make us some dinner?"

He smiled. "I think Rob is with Laura tonight, so that sounds great."

After she showered, Jillian left for the store. Rob came back and told Brian he needed him to come with him somewhere but wouldn't tell him where. Brian told him he'd planned to do some school work that night, and he needed to be back by seven. Rob agreed and waited for him in the car. Brian left Jillian a note, telling her that he was with Rob and that he'd certainly be back by 7:00.

Rob picked up two other guys and told Brian he had a surprise for him, but he wouldn't be any more specific. When they were still driving about an hour later, Brian checked the time and saw it was already after 5:00. He began to get concerned, but he didn't want to come off like a douchebag, so he didn't say a word. He tried to mimic the excited look on the faces of Rob and the other two guys, who obviously knew where they were headed.

When they pulled into the parking lot of the strip club, Rob announced, "This place is great. Some really hot girls here and they take it all off."

"Awesome." Brian forced a smile.

Inside the club, it was instantly clear that Rob was right. The girls were hot and naked, and there were gorgeous bodies everywhere you looked. Rob handed Brian a stack of singles and a few fives and told him to live it up. Rob told him he was hoping this might help snap him from his Natalie related funk. They had a few drinks, and Brian went through the motions for Rob's sake. At 6:30, he went to the bathroom and sent Jillian a text message:

I'm so sorry. Rob had a surprise for me. We're at least an hour away, and it doesn't look like we're leaving any time soon. Really sorry. I don't know what to say.

After Jillian read the message, she texted back that she understood. She'd gone all out that night buying steak and lobster and preparing some fancy side dishes. Frowning, she ate a small meal, put the side dishes in the refrigerator, cleaned the kitchen, cut a big piece of the ganache cake, and went upstairs to her bedroom. She enjoyed the cake as she typed away on her computer. In a zone again with her writing, she worked until just after midnight.

Rob dropped Brian off and headed back to Laura's to work off some of the excitement he'd generated at the strip club. Brian went into the house, opened the refrigerator, and saw the uncooked lobster and steak. He also noticed a slice of cake was missing from their masterpiece. Slipping up to Jillian's room, he found her sound asleep and stood watching her for a few seconds. The empty plate was next to the bed, and she looked too peaceful to disturb.

He took her plate down and cut himself a slice of cake. He placed the plate on the kitchen island, went into the great room, and selected one of Jillian's novels from the shelf. Returning to the kitchen, he pulled a stool over to the island and sat there savoring the cake and enjoying Jillian's steamy, erotic novel even more.

Chapter Twenty-Five

The next morning, Jillian entered Brian's room, dressed formally for an appointment. She discovered him sleeping with a copy of her novel, *Longings Lost,* lying on his chest. Smiling, she grabbed the book, placed it on the table next to him, and left the room. She wrote the guys a note, telling them she'd be out most of the day. Jillian's appointment was with the division head of her publisher's imprint. They met to discuss a movie producer's interest in adapting one of her novels for the screen.

After her appointment, Jillian checked her cell phone calendar; it reminded her of a date she had set up a few weeks before. She'd joined a popular Internet dating site a few months back and had finally accepted a request. After checking out the man's photo and trading a few e-mails, she'd agreed to the date. The dinner, scheduled for that night at seven at the Cheesecake Factory, was in the restaurant row adjacent to the mall, just a few blocks from her house. She'd forgotten about it until seeing the appointment on her Blackberry.

. . .

Brian spent most of the day alone at the house. He woke up late, read Jillian's note, sat by the pool, hit balls against the ball machine for an hour in the hot sun, and then went for a swim to cool off. Sitting next to the pool, he thought about Jillian. He wanted to apologize to her for not making the dinner, and he was disappointed that she was out all day. Rob called Brian and told him he would be with Laura most of the day but asked if Brian wanted to go see a movie that night. After agreeing to meet Rob later, Brian fell asleep by the pool then went inside.

When he spotted Jillian's car in the driveway, he searched the house for her and discovered the door to her bedroom was now closed. He took a shower then headed downstairs. When she came down, she found him in the great room watching television. She appeared standing before him, looking a little nervous but breathtakingly beautiful in her skirt and blouse.

"How do I look?"

With his mouth hanging open, Brian's gaze traveled up her body, but he failed to reply.

She grinned. "So?"

"Sorry. You look... fantastic. Where are you off to?"

"A date. A blind date that I set up weeks ago and completely forgot about."

Giving her an apologetic look, he stood and took a few steps to her. "I'm so sorry about missing dinner. I didn't know what Rob had planned."

"Don't worry about it. Did you eat?"

"No."

"Make those steaks for yourself if you want."

Looking herself over in the mirror, she frowned. "I look awful."

"You really look amazing." Brian titled his head as he checked her out from head to toe. His head snapped upright as she turned to him.

She smiled. "You're sweet. I really hope this guy isn't a lunatic, or anything." As she headed from the room, she called back, "Have fun tonight, and eat those steaks."

Watching her go, he shared the hope that the guy wasn't a lunatic, but he did pray that her date was a complete loser or at the very least not her type.

As Jillian approached the right turn into the parking garage, a red car, speeding from the other direction made a left turn in front of her, cutting her off. Slamming on the brakes, she avoided a collision. She pulled in behind the red Mercedes convertible, expecting some sort of apologetic gesture from the driver, but none came. The driver pushed the button for his ticket, got it, and when the gate flew up, he took off. As she drove around looking for a space in the crowded garage, she saw the red Mercedes again. This time, it was parked, and the male driver was heading her way. She rolled down the window, and as he neared the car, she said, "You realize you cut me off back there?"

The man didn't even bother to look at her. "Sorry, lady, but I'm late."

It had been a few weeks since Jillian had seen the online photo of her date, and although the man seemed somewhat familiar, she could not be sure, but she hoped that wasn't her guy.

Making her way to the bar of the restaurant, she scanned the room and was relieved not to find the guy who drove the Mercedes waiting for her there. Her date was to meet her at the bar at seven. Arriving a little early for a nerve-calming cocktail, she was on her second, fifteen minutes later, when a man approached the bar. He spotted Jillian, walked to her, and introduced himself as Matt. She instantly recognized him as the guy who had cut her off minutes ago, but she chose not to mention it —at least initially. They agreed to have a drink at the bar, since there was a thirty-minute wait for a table.

Matt ordered a third drink for her and one for himself. Jillian had not eaten anything in about seven hours, and she was starting to feel the effects of the alcohol in a big way. He was a self-centered pinhead who gave himself away not only with his rude driving, but by the way he complained about his drink, about the restaurant, about the wait, and about pretty much everything else in the place.

While still sitting at the bar, nursing her third drink, Jillian looked down and noticed the outline of a familiar object in the pocket of Matt's pants. She looked again, to be sure, but with the way he was sitting and the way his pants fit tightly, she could clearly see the unmistakable ring of a condom showing right through the thin fabric. Holding back a smile, she took a tiny sip of her drink and summoned some courage.

She gave him a serious look. "You know, you cut me off on the way into the garage. I was the one who spoke to you in the parking lot."

"Oh, sorry about that." Glancing at her face, he put on an apologetic smile. "It's been a long day, and I thought I was late so, again, really sorry about that."

She took another sip of her drink and ran her hand along the side of the glass. "But I saw you out there about twenty minutes before you made it in here."

"I had to pick something up in the mall."

"What?" Jillian asked.

He stammered, "I, um, just was checking on some contact lenses I ordered."

After taking a deep breath, she looked him in the eye and said in a harsh tone, "I'm going to guess that there were no contact lenses."

He grinned at her as if she might be kidding. When her facial expression didn't change, he frowned. "What are you trying to say?"

"Matt, I'm thinking that maybe... you went to the drugstore." She raised her eyebrows.

He chuckled nervously.

Tilting her head back, she looked down her nose at him. "Did you possibly buy some condoms, because you assumed that you might be getting really lucky tonight?"

He scoffed. "Did you follow me? Are you insane?"

She shook her head and simply pointed to his pocket.

He looked down, noticed the obvious ring, and gave her a smug smile. "I knew I should have kept them in the box. Would it make any difference if I told you they're Magnums?"

She gave him a sickened look. "Not a bit."

"Look, Jillian, I was running late, and I was going to bring them to the car but didn't want to be any later meeting you than I already was."

"That's thoughtful of you, Matt, but I think I'm just going to go." Then she got up and walked away, a little woozy from the cocktails.

Jillian left the restaurant and walked into the mall courtyard area. She bought a pretzel and a Coke hoping to sober up enough to make the three-block drive home. She finished her pretzel and as she walked, sipping her coke, she spotted Brian sitting on a bench outside the movie theater.

She walked up to him. "Hey."

"Oh, hey." He looked up at her surprised.

"What are you doing here?"

"Rob's meeting me for a movie." He turned to her, cocking his head. "That date didn't last long."

"No it didn't." She stumbled a little and he reached out, taking hold of her arm to steady her.

"You okay?"

"I had a little too much to drink on an empty stomach." She sat on the bench next to him.

"So, what happened?"

"Let me put it this way." Pausing a moment, she held back a smile. "What kind of guy arrives late for a date and has condoms showing in his pocket?"

"A giant asshole," Brian said playing along.

"Right, and what kind of giant asshole then tries to diffuse the situation by telling you the condoms are Magnums?"

"A giant asshole with a giant penis."

She smiled. "Right again."

"I take it there won't be a second date."

She blew out a dramatic huff. "You've got that right."

"Do you want to join us?"

"No, I think I'll just go home and boil up those lobsters."

Brian's phone rang. He checked the display and answered. "Hey Rob.... No problem.... Sure, I understand.... Okay."

After hanging up, he grinned at Jillian. "Evidently you aren't the only one with relationship trouble tonight. Laura found out about our trip last night to the strip club, and she's not happy."

"He took you to a strip club last night?" She shook her head with mock disgust.

After nodding, he looked her in the eye. "Why don't you come to the movie with me? I already bought two tickets, and you probably shouldn't drive home like this."

"You're right. I think I will." She grinned. "And I haven't been to the movies a little drunk since I was like seventeen. This could be fun."

"Let's get you some dinner first. We've got, like, twenty minutes."

"What are we seeing?"

"*Battle: Los Angeles*. Rob wanted to see it. It's a sci-fi action thing." Brian gave her an apologetic look.

"I've got a better idea. For a *science fiction* movie..." She wrinkled her nose. "...I'm going to actually need more to drink. Let's sneak in something. It'll be like high school."

Jillian waited on one side of the street as Brian dodged traffic to cross to the liquor store about a block away. When he returned, she placed the bottle of rum in her purse, and they went into the theater.

Chapter Twenty-Six

They took their seats in the nearly empty, large theater just as the previews began. Jillian ran to the bathroom but passed Brian the bottle of rum first. He poured about four-and-a-half shots' worth of the rum into his Coke and poured the rest, which amounted to about half a shot, into hers. He mixed them up a little with the straws. Wanting to catch up with her at least a little, he sucked down about a quarter of his giant, super-strong rum and Coke while she was away.

An older couple was many rows behind them in the last row, and four rows ahead of them sat two people. Jillian returned and sat next to Brian in the center of the theater. Brian set the popcorn bucket on his lap, and she held her drink. Slumping in her seat, obviously still a little woozy, she sipped from her Coke and said softly," Did you already put it in?"

"Yeah," he whispered.

"It tastes like nothing's in here."

He glanced away shyly. "It's, um, a really big cup."

Nodding in agreement, she reached into the bucket for some popcorn.

As the movie began, another couple entered the theater and

rushed to seats in the same row as Jillian and Brian but across the aisle. They were about nineteen, giggling, and obviously dating. Twenty minutes into the movie, Brian looked over and noticed they were making out heavily.

He nudged Jillian; she took a look, smiled, and whispered in his ear, "Get a room."

"They're like animals."

Jillian's sipped from her soda. Glancing over at Brian, she studied his profile as the light gently reflected off his face. Their bare knees were touching, and she closed her eyes and sighed. She reached into the popcorn bucket, grabbed a kernel, and tossed it into her mouth. She looked over at the amorous couple and saw, as a particularity bright scene filled the theater with light, that the guy was rubbing the girl's chest through her shirt. As they continued to make out, the girl's hand disappeared into the guy's lap. Jillian nudged Brian to look, and when he did, they shared a smile.

The combination of the rum and Coke, the sexy knee rubbing, her perfume, the couple practically having sex, and Jillian plunging her hand every five seconds into the popcorn bucket right over his sensitive groin area, had led to quite an uncomfortable crowding in Brian's shorts. He had to remove something from that equation, or he was going to have a real problem. He decided the popcorn had to go.

He whispered, "You want the bucket?"

"No."

"You sure you don't want any more?"

She shook her head with a smile, as she stared at the screen.

After placing the bucket under his seat, Brian looked at Jillian's bare knee, which was still touching his. She seemed to be pushing her knee more and more into him as the movie progressed. He looked over at the busy couple and saw the guy now had his hand under the girl's shirt, and the girl was busy working her hand over the guy's lap.

Several minutes went by, but the removal of the popcorn bucket had done nothing to relieve his situation. Looking over to be sure Jillian was watching the screen, he slid his hand into his lap to quickly adjust his straining erection. Whatever he did inadvertently freed his manhood from the confines of his boxers. That relieved some of the pain, but unfortunately, it also made the problem worse, since his dick was now free to expand, which it rapidly did.

Jillian, her eyes glued to the screen, reached into Brian's lap, feeling for the popcorn. She didn't find any, but her blindly searching hand landed on something hard—extremely hard.

Instead of quickly pulling her hand away, she let it remain in his lap, as he sat frozen and unable to breathe. He glanced at her from the corner of his eye, and she appeared unfazed by her find; yet she still didn't make any attempt to move her hand.

Thoughts swirled in Brian's mind. *What was she doing? Did she realize where her hand was and what exactly she was touching?* He took a shallow breath. Maybe Jillian believed her hand landed on his cell phone. At that moment, his erection involuntarily twitched. He glanced at her out of the corner of his eye but she wasn't reacting at all. Maybe she decided to play it cool and avoid embarrassing either of them, by casually leaving her hand in his lap with a plan to remove it when the time seemed right. *Yeah, that must be it.*

Glancing down at his hands, Jillian noticed his fingers were spread out and awkwardly gripping the top of each armrest. She fought back a smile.

Brian picked up the Coke, his hand shaking slightly, and took a long drink. He turned slightly to look at her again, and she still seemed unaware of her hand's current location. A bead of sweat rolled down his forehead. He held his breath as he attempted to will his erection to subside. Think of puppies or baseball or that paper he'd been putting off for the last couple weeks. None of it worked. His cock throbbed and he closed his eyes tightly as he pressed his lips together.

She turned to him catching the look of utter distress on his face. Her hand remained motionless as she grinned, cupping her mouth to direct her comment only to him. Leaning over so that she was an inch from his face, she muttered, "Sorry about that. I'm going to take my hand off your penis now."

His eyes shot open wide. "What?"

"I'm going to take my hand off your penis now."

"Oh, is it...? I didn't, uh, notice." He froze, pretending to look at the screen. "You want some popcorn?"

"No," she whispered, and she slowly pulled her hand away from him. When she did, he exhaled deeply and finally relaxed in his seat. After quietly trying to adjust his shorts again, he took another long sip of his Coke, holding it out for her. "Want some?"

She sampled his drink and choked a little, it was incredibly strong—much stronger than hers was. She smiled, shaking her head. Jillian said accusingly, "Yours is really strong."

Busted, Brian glanced at her. "I must not have mixed it up enough. It, uh, settled."

She sucked her lower lip between her teeth then turned to look at him. He met her gaze. "You okay?"

"I am." She nodded then said softly, "I don't think I ever properly thanked you for making me breakfast in bed. That was so sweet."

He whispered, "I'm sure you thanked me."

"Well, it was delicious."

"It was the least I could do."

She looked over at the couple still making out nearby. She

noticed that they were really starting to produce some noise with their activities. She nudged Brian and smiled.

After checking them out, he turned to Jillian and widened his eyes. "They're practically going at it over there."

"Disgusting," she said in a sexy whisper.

Seconds later, Jillian was on top of Brian, kissing him, passionately. He returned her enthusiasm, and they continued to kiss and grope each other from his seat. From a few feet away, they heard, "Get a room you two," and they stopped kissing, looking over to find the source. When they looked around, they saw the couple that had been practically screwing during the entire film, staring right at them while wearing silly grins. Both Brian and Jillian fired back evil looks.

Falling back into her seat, Jillian slumped down. "Maybe we should get out of here."

Brian looked at her and simply nodded.

They stood and quickly walked down the row, leaving their drinks and popcorn behind. As they approached the young couple, they found them still staring, and the guy said, "Couple of animals," as his girlfriend giggled.

Jillian glared at them both, before rushing with Brian to the lobby. Once outside the theater, Brian looked down and spotted the huge wet spot and sizeable bulge in his shorts. While Jillian looked left and right, he quickly adjusted his shorts and held his hand over the telling wet spot, as people walked past them on the street.

"I think it's closer if we walk home. The car is at the top level of the garage, and I don't think I should drive, anyway."

Before Brian could finish nodding, she turned and took off down the sidewalk. Two people never walked faster or with such purpose. Neither said a word. When they reached Jillian's front door, she searched her purse for the keys.

He leaned in close to her and put his hand on her neck. "If I don't get inside you soon, I'm going to die," he whispered and he felt her shiver. As she turned opening her mouth to respond, the door opened, and Rob appeared.

Brian quickly removed his hand from her neck, and Jillian looked at her son, alarmed.

Rob lifted his palms up. "There you are. I've been trying to call you."

Brian stepped from behind Jillian, looked down at his crotch, and then moved his hand to cover the stain as he stammered, "I had my cell off. We, uh, were at the movies."

Rob gave him an odd look.

Jillian smiled nervously. "We ran into each other. I was on a, um, horrible date, and he saved me."

Rob said, "I didn't hear you drive up."

"I... we... left the car at the mall. It was such a nice night that we decided to walk," Jillian said a little flustered.

Rob narrowed his eyes at his mother, shook his head, then looked at Brian, and blew it off. "Laura has this girl she wants you to meet. They're at the bar right now. Let's go."

Brian glanced at Jillian before settling his eyes on Rob. "I, uh..."

"Come on. She's waiting for you. She's really hot."

Brian paused to think then said, "Okay. I just need to go to the bathroom first."

"Hurry up. I'll be in the car."

Jillian and Brian entered the house as Rob went outside. She closed the door and then looked into Brian's eyes. "What are we doing?"

"I don't know, but it feels right," he said partially convinced.

"I think you... you better go. He's waiting." Looking down at his shorts, she focused in on the wet spot. "You'd better change."

He stared at her, unable to find the words. He needed to say something, anything, but what? "I... When—"

"Shhh." Closing her eyes, she put her hand on his chest.

Gently, he placed his hand over hers and felt the electricity of their connection for a few moments.

She opened her eyes. "He's waiting."

"Okay."

Brian ran up the steps as Jillian stood at the bottom watching him and letting out a sigh.

Chapter Twenty-Seven

At the bar, Rob and Laura introduced Brian to Dana. She was attractive, but Brian was too preoccupied and a little too drunk to notice or care. Closing his eyes, Brian drifted away with his mind reeling. *What the fuck's wrong with me? I can't stop thinking about Jillian. I feel like I'm... It's not like what I felt for Natalie, or is it? Am I just a horny douche, trying to get laid? I thought I was falling in love with Natalie, but was that only because she can bend herself up like a pretzel, and I'm lonely? Shit, I don't know. And now that I've seen what a real woman is like, it's... it's... Jillian is amazing, but I'm an idiot. There's no way she really wants to be with me. And it's obvious that Natalie's not ready for any kind of relationship—at least, not with me. Is Natalie just jerking me around? Or do I only think that, so I'll feel less guilty now that I've been chasing my best friend's mother around like a pathetic moron? I've got to stop. I've got to fix this. Fuck, I'm so confused.*

After glancing for the tenth time at Brian's bored expression, Dana rolled her eyes at Laura. Then she tried to make conversation with Brian, but it just wasn't happening. A few minutes later, Dana joined another group of friends, much to Brian's relief.

Brian looked at Rob. "I'm not in the mood for this."

Rob glared at him. "You're not still thinking about her, are you?"

"What?" Brian eyes rounded in alarm. "Who?"

"Natalie. Jesus, who else."

Brian ran his hand over his face.

"You've got to get over her, Dude."

"I know. I know. I'm just going to go. I can walk from here. It's not that far."

"Are you sure?"

"Yeah. Don't worry about me."

"I'm staying at Laura's tonight, but maybe we can do something tomorrow."

"Definitely." Turning away from his friend, Brian closed his eyes for a moment, wallowing in his own shame before he headed toward the door.

Brian ran most of the way back to Jillian's. When he was within a block, he slowed his pace to a fast walk so he wouldn't be panting like an idiot when he saw her. After entering the house, he searched and finally found her on the balcony off her bedroom. Silently, he stood watching her with his mind churning. He needed to talk to her; he needed to clear the—

He sniffed, picking up the faint but unmistakable smell of pot in the air. He raised an eyebrow and shook his head, grinning. With his concerns suddenly pushed aside, for the moment at least, he rushed out and plopped down in the seat next to her. "Do I, uh, smell pot?"

"Want some?"

He held out his hand, and she passed him the joint.

After taking a hit, he returned it to her and shook his head, a little stunned. "This is some strong stuff."

"Yeah." She looked at him seriously. "About what happened at the movie and what almost happened when we came back... I've been thinking that maybe this isn't such a good idea."

His eyes met hers. "I'm so glad you said that, because this is wrong on so many levels. I'm still not sure what's going on with Natalie, and you're—"

"Rob's mother," Jillian said with a serious tone. They both shared a wide-eyed nod.

Rubbing his head, he closed his eyes. "What were we thinking?"

She shook her head at him, took another hit, and handed him the joint. They both slumped back in their chairs and could relax, with the weight of their mutual attraction seemingly lifted.

A few minutes later, after sitting together in complete silence, sharing the joint, Brian and Jillian looked at each other and smiled, mostly stoned but oddly coherent. He laughed out loud for no apparent reason.

She giggled. "What is it?"

"The other night when your ex called, and you were so upset, and—"

"What is it?"

"No, I..."

"Tell me." She motioned with her hand for him to continue.

He exhaled deeply. "Do you remember exactly, everything that happened that night?"

"I think so."

"You were really kind of out of it. You took that sleeping pill, then George had you so worked up that you had a glass of wine, and..."

"I wasn't that bad."

"Not bad... Do you remember how you got upstairs? We were talking out by the pool, remember?"

"I walked up. I think," she said with more bravado than confidence.

"I carried you up. You were going to sleep out by the pool."

"I was?"

"When we got upstairs," Brian started, and Jillian leaned in a little closer to him as he continued, "You told me about that first morning when you came into my room, and I was asleep."

Embarrassed, Jillian covered her head with her hands. "I thought I only dreamt that I told you that."

He looked at her, on the verge of laughter, "You told me everything about it. How you saw it. How you pushed my door open. Exactly what state you saw it in. How you had Victoria on the phone and described it. All of it."

"And you don't hate me?"

"No, I think it's hilarious. You told me how it had been so long since you had seen one and even longer since you'd seen a real one and on and on. You were very flattering about it. It was nice to hear."

"Is that everything?" She made a face, dreading his response.

"Not quite." He held his hand out for her to pass him the joint. After taking a hit, he handed it back to her. "You—"

"Wait." She took her own long hit and held it ready for another possible emergency one.

"You... said that in order to make us... 'even-steven'— that was the totally, hip term that you used." He chuckled. "You needed to show me yours. Not only yours, but your newly-trimmed yours."

She looked at him horrified. "I did?"

Lifting his eyebrows, he stated, "Nice work. You really did a great job with it."

She exhaled, deeply. "So, we didn't do it after that, did we?"

"You passed out; I covered you up, and that was the end of the story," Brian said, pride mixed with a little disappointment in his voice.

She took a long look at him, "Apparently, Ambien and wine do not mix."

He raised his eyebrows in agreement. "I kind of like the effect it has on you, though."

"Look, even after going through all that, we've been just friends. I think we've exercised perfect self-control in a semi-inappropriate way." Jillian then gave him an odd look that said, maybe that came out wrong.

"So, friends it is." Brian gave her a big, over-the-top, high-off-his-ass nod.

"But we're, like, friends with... not benefits, but something else..." Jillian said as she paused apparently searching her mind for the right word.

"Like friends with... *partial* benefits."

She smiled. "Yes, *partial benefits*. I like it."

They paused, grinning at each other for a moment.

Suddenly, she wrinkled her nose. "It sounds good, but what exactly is it?"

"We need to figure it out... I think we just need to set up some ground rules first."

"Good idea—Rules?"

They each took a moment to ponder this, and then his eyes got big. "How about no touching?"

She shook her head. "That's a little too broad. I mean, what if I want to touch your arm? How about no touching... genitalia?"

"Genitalia." He laughed out loud. "So you want to use that word, huh?"

She made a face. "What should I call, you know, all the parts."

"No, you're right that's a good word." He nodded with a big smile. "I like that rule. And if I'm not mistaken, we haven't violated it yet." He cocked his head. "At least, I know I haven't."

"Neither have I. I only looked," she replied quickly. "So, good, it's settled, then. Rule Number One is no touching of each other's genitalia."

He pondered this a second and then took another hit off the joint. "Breasts aren't really considered genitalia, are they?"

He handed her the joint, and she took a deep hit. "Right. No, they aren't. Is that a problem?"

"Well, you probably don't want me to just grab them, or anything. That could jeopardize the whole F.W.P.B. relationship."

"F.W... what?" She narrowed her eyes perplexed.

"Friends With Partial... F.W.P.B," he said with a rolling hand motion and her face lit up with recognition.

Her eyes opened wide. "And what about your ass?"

"What about my ass?" Leaning closer to her, Brian asked eagerly.

"It would probably violate," she motioned to him with her hand, "as you say, the whole F.W.P.B. thing, if I touched your ass."

"Football players pat each other's asses."

She touched her chin. "So the ass is okay, but the ass..." she paused for emphasis with her finger moving from one imaginary word in front of her to the other, "...hole... is not."

"Exactly. You just can't go around touching someone there."

"Unless, of course, you're having sex with him... or her."

"And sex is certainly against the rules here." After Jillian gave him a big nod, Brian added, "And that would knock your ass... hole out of contention also."

"Clearly."

"So no touching of genitals, breasts, or ass... holes," he said proudly.

"I think we can put Rule Number One to bed."

They both sat back, thinking for a moment. After brushing the hair from her face, she sat up in her chair and turned to him. "No telling anyone about F.W.P.B. People are so judgmental, and they wouldn't understand it."

He met her gaze. "Just like *Fight Club*."

She looked blankly at him.

"The first rule of fight club is don't tell anyone about fight club... Brad Pitt."

"Right, right, right." She nodded.

"So, that's two." After taking a hit, she passed the joint to him.

"Okay, how about number three is no... kissing?"

"Just no... mouth kissing." She smiled at her contribution. "A cheek kiss is probably safe."

"Definitely." Brian narrowed his eyes as if they had missed something obvious. "No mouth kissing or kissing any of the aforementioned areas in Rule Number One."

"Why don't we just amend the first rule to be no touching or kissing of the mouth or any of those things defined in Rule Number One?" Jillian said, making a face which seemed to indicate she was half-proud of herself and half struggling with her logic.

He pursed his lips, trying to follow her reasoning. Then it came to him. "Two reasons. One: then it would be no touching of the mouth, and that doesn't seem to be a problem; plus, having three rules makes it seem like we really, really did our homework here."

She cocked her head, pushing a loose hair behind her ear. "Agreed."

"So, we have our rules?"

"We have 'em."

Brian stood and looked over the balcony at the pool. Jillian joined him, and there they remained for a few moments in silence.

He turned to her. "So, what the hell can we do?"

"Good question," she replied as they both tilted their heads skyward obviously pondering what they could do, given the semi-brilliant, yet somewhat restrictive rules. She dropped her chin and her eyes brightened. "I've lived here ten years, and I've never once gone skinny dipping."

"I've never either." He pondered this for a moment. "I don't think that violates any of the rules. It's really a perfect F.W.P.B. activity, because you really shouldn't swim alone."

"Swimming alone *is* dangerous."

Brian nodded in agreement. "Let's say you don't have a significant other, just like the two of..." He pointed back and forth between them, making eyes at her. "Then who else could you possibly skinny dip with?"

"You just wouldn't be able to do it." After holding her head high, seemingly proud of their accomplishment, her expression suddenly became serious. "But what if Rob comes home?"

"He's staying at Laura's all night." He gave her a big, wide smile.

Grinning at him, she pulled her shirt over her head, and tossed it on the chair. She shimmied out of her skirt and stood in front of him wearing another heart-stopping, matching bra and panty set.

"Do you have any more of that pot?" Brian asked.

"I do." She bounced on her heels, raising her eyebrows. "I'll get it and meet you in the pool."

He sat in the chair and struggled, trying to remove his shoes. Jillian unhooked her bra as she headed into the bedroom. Once his shoes were off, he stepped into the room and pulled off his shirt. He spotted her coming out of the bathroom bare ass naked and holding another joint in her hand, with her mouth wide open as if to say, *"Look what I found."* Smiling, she rushed out the door and into the hall.

Brian sprang into action. Hurriedly, he pushed his shorts down his legs where they got caught around his ankles. As he tried to free himself, he lost his balance and fell to the carpet. He flipped over, quickly pulled off all his remaining clothes, and started after her. Before he made it through the bedroom door, he heard her splash into the pool.

When Brian reached the pool, Jillian was floating on her back with the moonlight shining on her beautiful breasts. He stood, nude, watching her from the edge of the pool for a moment, and then dove in and swam under the water to the other side. When he came back to the surface, he found her by the pool's edge, lighting the new joint. She looked at him. "I think I'm really f'ing high, but I feel like I'm thinking so incredibly clearly right now."

He nodded. "I know exactly what you mean. This must be some special, new, clear-thinking blend of marijuana."

"I think you're right." She set the joint down on the patio and swam to the center of the pool to join him.

Brian gave her a serious look. "I'm sure compliments are fine, aren't they?"

Jillian shook her head enthusiastically.

"You have really freaking incredible breasts—like world-class, incredible breasts. And your ass, I uh saw it just briefly as you ran by, but really the whole package... how are you not married, again? It makes absolutely no sense and, uh..." His words trailed off a little shyly at the end.

"You *are* thinking clearly." Jillian grinned. "I think you are a wonderful young man, and any girl would be lucky to be with you. Natalie will realize that soon, I'm sure of it."

"Thanks." He smiled genuinely. "This partial benefits thing is great, because sometimes you just want to look at a really nice set of breasts. And you don't want to go on the Internet."

"Too creepy," Jillian said.

"You don't want to go to a strip club."

"Too sleazy."

He lifted his palms up and widened his eyes. "And you currently find yourself sans girlfriend."

Shaking her head sadly, she gazed at him. "Just plain sad."

"But with this situation, when the mood strikes, I could just say, 'Please, show me your breasts.' Not just any breasts; ones so beautiful that Picasso would have killed to paint them, by the way." Jillian nodded a thank you, and he continued, "And if I did ask, and you were in the mood, you would do it."

"Are you asking?"

"I am!"

Jillian swam over to the edge, grabbed the joint, took a hit, and then began to hoist herself from the pool, her curvy ass staring right at him for a few seconds. She stayed in that sexy position as she kicked her feet and struggled to lift herself from the water. Breathlessly, he watched her.

Turning, she sat on the edge to face him and then held her breasts together for his pleasure.

"Nice." Brian swam over to her, grabbed the joint, and took a hit. He put it back down, moved directly in front of her, grabbed one of her feet, and massaged it. "This is also, within the rules."

Laughing, she leaned back, obviously enjoying the rub as he studied her foot in the moonlight. "Jesus, even your feet are, like, perfectly shaped, your toes are exquisite, and..."

She gazed down at him. "I'm really starting to like this whole thing."

He rubbed her foot harder, more sensually as he wore a serious expression. "And when we play tennis, it's like we're... we're so in sync."

She looked at him, breathing heavily and nodding as if he were stealing the words right out of her mouth.

Brian gently kissed her foot. "Also, not rule-breaking behavior." He kissed each one of her toes while she stared at him desperately. Then he gently placed her foot back into the water, swam out to the center of the pool, and treaded water. After catching her breath, she slipped into the pool and followed him.

She treaded water alongside him with her breathing a little quieter now. "I've never been so connected, so attracted, and so in tune with another person in my life, and yet I don't need to actually have sex with you. I mean, I'd love to really screw your brains out right now, but..."

He gave her a casual look. "Oh, me also."

Jillian started again, "But since we can't, for obvious reasons, I'm so totally fine with this arrangement."

"We've only known each other, like, five days, but it seems like forever. I could go on like this for years and years."

"Yes, me too," Jillian said while spinning and treading water.

Brian mimicked her silly spin move. "That tiebreak we played the other day was like..." They each stopped spinning and gazed into each other's eyes as Brian collected his thoughts and then continued, "...sex. That last long point, where we were both focused and absolutely nailing the ball and pushing each other to the limit was like... our sex, you know? And when you won the point with that amazing shot, and we both just were trying to catch our breath, it was like we... we came together."

She looked at him as if she wanted to fuck the rules and him right along with them, there in the water.

He stared deeply into her eyes. "We don't have to fuck,

because when we play tennis, it's like we're fucking. When we play, it feels like I'm inside you, you know?"

"Uh-huh," was all she could manage to say.

They continued treading water, just staring at each other for a few seconds longer while barely breathing. Pulling himself back to reality, he shook his head quickly, and then moved away from her. He swam over to take a hit off the joint. He turned back to her and looked her in the eye. "I'm completely hard just talking about that tiebreak."

"Let's see," Jillian said breathlessly.

Brian quickly switched to the backstroke and his erect penis stuck out of the water in her full view as he swam toward her. He said, "Are we really that high, or is this whole partial benefits thing just about the best fucking idea that two people ever came up with?"

She nodded in silence, unable to take her eyes off his erection.

"My dick is so hard right now, but I don't really need to sleep with you."

"Uh, huh. Best... idea... ever," she said softly and sounding completely unconvinced.

"Do you have any more of that pot that I can take back to school with me?"

Before she could answer, the lights in the house blasted on. Her eyes went to the patio door. "Oh no."

Quickly Brian sank under water, and they both swam to the edge of the pool closest to the house. Rob appeared at the door, carrying a beer. Jillian pulled Brian over a few feet, under the cover of the diving board, as Rob walked out to the patio and sat at the table, about fifteen feet away. The naked couple held perfectly still and silently giggled just out of Rob's view. After putting out the joint, she waved the smoke away with her hand.

Rob took a sip from his beer, pulled out his cell phone, and typed a text message. When he received a reply, he let out a huge belch followed by a string of expletives, and then typed another message. He finished his beer in a few big chugs, then he farted loudly. The baked couple in the pool covered their mouths to keep from bursting out laughing. Rob stood and went into the house. He closed the door and when Jillian heard the click of the door lock, her smile disappeared. "Oh shit."

"Oh shit, what?" Brian asked.

"I'm pretty sure that he locked us out."

"What are we going to do?" Brian smiled his high still in full swing.

"He'll never believe that we're just two friends taking a late-night nude swim."

"No, probably not." He tapped his lip. "Do you have a towel or anything out here?"

"Nothing."

"Shit!"

They watched as the lights on the first level of the house turned off. Quietly getting out of the pool, she made her way to the patio door. She attempted to open it and every window on the back of the house and found them all locked. Smiling broadly, Brian admired the look of her body from his vantage point in the pool.

She looked back at him and snapped in an angry whisper, "Are you coming?"

Chapter Twenty-Eight

Naked and dripping wet, Jillian and Brian snuck around to the front of the house. Checking the front door and windows, she found them all locked. They rushed over to her other car, found it unlocked, and climbed into the back seat. Jillian leaned over into the front seat to reach the glove box and search for a spare key. While she did, Brian sat back and appreciated the view. He placed a hand on her ass, and she turned to glare at him.

He looked at her confidently. "I was nowhere near the, uh—"

"Is this really the time?" She gave him a tired look.

He rolled his eyes, as she closed the glove box and then returned to the back seat without the key. Sitting back, she put on a serious expression. "I know... Victoria has a spare key, and she only lives two blocks away."

She gave him the address and explicit instructions to return quickly with the key.

He opened the door, got out of the car, and quietly headed off. As he walked toward Victoria's, he was having a hard time keeping a straight face because of the lingering effects of the pot. He snuck down the street, completely naked and trying to stay out of sight, while repeating the address over and over so he wouldn't forget. "Fourteen Seventeen. Fourteen Seventeen." When he reached the correct address, he rushed to the front door, rang the bell, and waited without bothering to cover his groin. Victoria looked through the sidelight. When she saw it was Brian and that he was dressed very, very, let's say... comfortably, she ripped open the door and yanked him inside before he had a chance to say a thing.

Closing the door, she shook her head with a grin on her face, just admiring his body. He stood before her with his arms folded, wearing an impaired glassy-eyed stare. Her eyes finally traveled up to his face. "Does Jillian know you're here?"

"She sent me."

Victoria's smile widened. "Really?"

He added, "She sent me to get her spare key."

"Oh." Her eyebrows drew together in a frown.

Looking down, he noticed *everything* was completely out and quickly covered it up with both hands. "Sorry about that."

She glanced down and shrugged. "Don't worry about it. Why do you need the spare key?"

"We kinda locked ourselves out."

"Naked?"

"Well, yes, we were swimming, and Rob locked us out."

"You guys did it!" She shot him a big grin.

"No, we decided to just be friends. Only friends...it's way too complicated, and I'm still in love with Natalie—at least, I think I am. She can do this thing with her leg—"

"Friends who swim naked together in a pool?" she interrupted as she shook her head with her nose wrinkled.

"Exactly! We have this whole cool arrangement called friends—" He stopped himself suddenly remembering the rules. Turning a fake key on his lips, he shut them tight, his shoulders bouncing as he fought back a chuckle.

She looked at him as if he was crazy. Then her expression shifted and a slight grin spread over her lips. "So, Jillian said you were only going to be friends?"

"Uh-huh."

"Sorry, so to be clear, only friends. She used those words."

"Yes."

"Well, that's interesting and you're here"—she raised her eyebrows up suggestively—"and you're not wearing anything."

He bounced up on his toes. "Yep."

Victoria rubbed her chin in a play of amusement while staring at his pecs. "Where's Jillian?"

"Hiding in her car."

"Naked?"

"Yes, she is. I'm kind of in a hurry, since she's naked and all, so if I could just get some clothes and the key, I'll..."

"Relax, she'll be fine for a few more minutes." She waved a dismissive hand at him as she continued to look him over quizzically. "Are you drunk?"

"Not really. I mean, I had some drinks earlier, but I'm fine now." He broke into silly laughter for no apparent reason. "Yep, I'm more than fine."

"Okay..." She eyed him strangely then she cocked her head. "So, Jillian really is locked out and stuck in the car?"

He nodded.

She sighed. "Well, then let me get you all taken care of."

She took off and returned with the keys, a pair of the tightest, shortest shorts, and a half shirt. When she handed him the clothes, he scoffed. "You're serious?"

"That's really all I have," she said with a straight face.

With Victoria eyeing him up and down, he slipped on the tight shirt that barely covered his stomach then struggled to pull on the shorts. Once he had them fully on, an uncomfortable look appeared on his face, as the super-tight shorts were smothering all of his manly parts. When Brian shimmied uncomfortably, *he* popped out the side of the shorts. He looked relieved until he glanced down and saw it hanging there. Chuckling, he glanced at her. "I guess I can't go out like this."

She ran her thumb over her lower lip as she studied the problem area with her eyes glazing over. Finally, she shook her head then said, "Just shove it back in."

He tried twice, but each time it fell back out.

She grinned with her eyes still locked on it. "Do you want some help?"

Before he said, "Sure," she was already on her way over. She knelt in front of him and held *it* in her hands, admiring it as he stood there, looking straight ahead, and desperately trying not to laugh.

Biting her tongue between her teeth, her eyes roamed his body coming to rest on his manhood. "So, uh, you guys are only going to be friends?"

She looked up at his face and caught his nod. Smiling, she returned her gaze back down to it. "You're sure?"

"Oh, yeah, definitely." He laughed.

"What is it?"

"It tickles a little."

Victoria held his penis gently, sighing.

"Your hands are so warm."

She swallowed hard. "Is Jillian really locked out?"

"Yepper."

Exhaling deeply, she tore her eyes away from his groin and up to his face. "Will you let her in and come right back here?"

"I guess I could." He rocked back and forth slightly with his eyes closed.

Carefully sliding him back into the shorts, she directed *it* across his hip. She smiled; it looked like he was trying to smuggle a good-sized sausage. Victoria began adjusting him in the tight shorts, and it was starting to grow. Cocking her head, she took in the sight of him as she put a hand to her face. Suddenly his penis twitched and flopped out again. This time it was quite a bit bigger; most certainly from all her attention. Instead of trying to tuck it away again, she massaged it with both hands as he exhaled deeply.

"You do have one gorgeous cock." Closely admiring it, she licked her lips.

"Thanks," Brian said casually, as if he'd heard it a thousand times before.

She narrowed her eyes. "I don't think I can get it back in, because it keeps getting bigger."

"Well that's because you keep playing with it. Maybe if you stopped pulling on it," Brian mockingly scolded her as he patted her on the head like a dog while fighting back a laugh.

She looked him in the eye. "Are you high?"

After pausing, he grinned at her. "Maybe."

In an attempt to pull himself together, he exhaled sharply then slapped his hands on his cheeks. "I'm fine, but I really need to get back to Jillian. So, maybe you can *actually* help me get everything back inside, so I can go."

"Okay," Victoria let go of him, stood, and tapped his chin, narrowing her eyes. Staring down at the problem area, she cocked her head. "Why don't you put the shorts on backwards? I think they have more coverage in the back."

Brian slipped the shorts off and turned them around, and they did fit a little better in the front, but the back was another story. He looked down, a little more satisfied, glanced at Victoria, and she nodded her approval. Then he spun around for her to check out the back and asked how he looked. Craning his neck back, he tried to see his ass, but could not. In the back, the shorts were disappearing into his crack, and the bottoms of each cheek were sticking out. Brian looked a little like a woman heading out to the beach in St. Tropez. Smirking, she told him he looked fine. She reached out to give him the keys, but as he tried to take them, she would not let them go.

She continued to hold them tight. "You promised you would come back."

"I know."

"Just tell her you need to return the clothes and the keys."

Brian swallowed hard; there was something so incredibly sexy and yet frightening about Victoria—like if she had sex with him, he'd never walk again.

After releasing the keys, she took one last look at him in those shorts. "Hurry back."

"Okay."

He turned to the door, and she eyed his ass. "Brian, have you ever been around the world?"

Turning back to her slowly, he looked at her, baffled. "Uh, no."

She gave him a sexy smile. "When you come back, I'll take you."

He returned another confused look and then ran the hell out of there.

Chapter Twenty-Nine

Brian's high was wearing off just enough for him to realize he looked completely ridiculous in that outfit. He ran back to Jillian's in pretty much the same hiding mode in which he ran to Victoria's. Shocked, she watched as he rushed to the car, opened the door, and quickly slid in next to her. After breaking into laughter, she looked him over once more. "I can't believe that this is what she gave you to wear!"

"Is this not a good look for me?" Brian asked sarcastically.

"It's nice, but it's probably a little dangerous to be running around Miami in the middle of the night in that outfit."

After summoning their nerve, the pair rushed to the front door. Jillian opened it, and they quietly slipped inside. Brian shifted left and his hip bumped against a pile of mail and a magazine sitting atop the half-wall that separated the foyer from the living room. The items scattered loudly across the floor. The two shared a wide-eyed look.

Suddenly they heard Rob's voice from the second floor call out, "Mom? Brian?"

They both stood there with parted lips and one brow raised —Jillian naked and Brian dressed like a seventies roller derby queen. They were seconds from being discovered and no expla-nation could get them out of this. Flashes of ridiculous excuses floated through Brian's head. *Um, yeah, Rob, I was in the house and I'm a cross-dresser. And your mother... she is a nudist and she just happened to get locked outside the house and I let her in...*

Brian's eyes brightened. "Rob, I'm coming up. Stay right there."

"No, I'm coming down."

"Shit," Brian grit his teeth, frowning.

Hearing Rob's footsteps near the top of the stairs, Brian's eyes darted around in a panic. Wearing the guilt on their faces, both were trapped in the foyer with no way to escape. His eyes met Jillian's then he spotted the coat closet. Springing into action, he ripped open the door and shoved his naked friend-with-partial-benefits inside before shutting her in.

Looking up in the dim light, Brian saw Rob take the first step down. He bolted toward the back of the house calling out, "I'm heading to the weight room."

Once in the weight room, Brian sat down on the butterfly machine and began doing repetitions.

Rob entered and gave him a strange look that turned into a *really* strange look when he took in Brian's girly, super-tight outfit. "Dude, what the fuck are you wearing?"

"Oh this, uh, your mother lent this to me. All my stuff is dirty."

"Geez, if you need to borrow some clothes, just let me know."

Brian stood, and Rob's gaze went immediately to his friend's crotch. Rob covered his eyes cringing. "Seriously, let me get you something, because in that outfit, I can tell exactly what *every-*

thing looks like and believe me that is information I really didn't want to have."

Brian looked down, spotting the clear outline of his three-piece set in Victoria's shorts. He placed his hands over his groin as beads of sweat dripped down his forehead.

Rob narrowed his eyes. "My mother gave you those?"

Brian nodded quickly. "Yes."

Rob raked his hand through his hair, shaking his head. "She didn't actually see you wearing that did she?"

"No, she's not feeling well. She just handed them out to me through her door. I really haven't seen her much at all since I came back from the bar... you know."

Rob studied his face then asked, "Are you stoned?"

"What?"

"Dude, are you stoned?"

"Um, no. Don't be ridiculous. Where would I..." Brian stammered. "No."

"You sure? You're acting really strange." Rob shook his head, confused. "Why the hell are you working out at midnight?"

"Well, I couldn't sleep. I'm wired."

Sighing, Rob turned away. "Me too. Laura and I had a fight."

"That sucks."

Reaching up, Rob grabbed the pull-up bar and hung from it, stretching his neck out from side to side. "You know, we haven't really seen each other this whole trip. I still feel like I kind of abandoned you here all by yourself."

"No, I've been fine, really."

"Let's do something tomorrow, all day. There's this topless beach we could hit. Sometimes there are supermodels there."

"Sounds awesome."

"But seriously, let me lend you some clothes, because this outfit is scaring the shit out of me. I'm not sure if I'm more horrified that you're wearing that or the fact that my mother *might* have at some point." Rob performed five repetitions then dropped down to the floor. "Okay?"

"Sounds good." Brian nodded and breathed a sigh of relief. "I think I'm going to bed."

"Me too."

Brian turned away exposing his back side to his friend.

"Holy fuck." Rob gasped.

"What?" Brian turned back.

"Your ass cheeks, dude! They're like completely out."

Glancing at his reflection in the mirror, Brian cringed. "Wow, those *are* tight."

"You think!" Rob shook his head. "I don't have words."

"Sorry." Brian shrugged, taking a step back away from his friend.

Rob's gaze returned to Brian's groin and he rolled his eyes. "I'm not sure which view is scaring me more the front or the back."

Brian covered his junk with his hands.

"Let's never speak of this."

"You got it."

"I'm just going to walk in front of you." Tilting his head upward, Rob made a face as he headed for the door.

Craning his neck and glancing back once more at his reflection in the mirror, Brian took in the sight of his cheeks spilling out of his girly shorts. He shrugged, fought back a smile then headed out of the room.

Brian lay in his beds with his high wearing off just enough to realize that maybe the whole friends-with-partial-benefits thing was a bad idea. He thought it was inappropriate, at best, and completely dangerous, at worst.

He couldn't stop thinking about how close they had been to

actually having sex together. Jillian was gorgeous and sexy and everything, but he would never be able to forgive himself if he slept with Rob's mother. They were best friends, and he felt Rob would never do anything like that to him. Rob would never consider banging his mom. Granted, his mother looked nowhere near as spectacular as Jillian, but it still wasn't right. Brian was glad that both he and Jillian had decided to apply the brakes to their relationship, but that didn't stop him from replaying his night with her in his head until he fell asleep. He rolled his eyes and laughed thinking of his outfit and his run in with Rob. He ran his hands through his hair while the image of Jillian's body burned in his brain. He'd never be able to get it out. He wondered if she was thinking about him as well.

Chapter Thirty

J ust after eight, Jillian got up, went downstairs, and made a cup of tea. Brian came down minutes later. They shared an awkward look and then exchanged good mornings but didn't say anything else. After pouring him a cup, Jillian led the way to the pool. She wore a long, thick robe but still looked damn sexy; he wore a GSU college T-shirt and shorts. They both slumped into the loungers with their minds obviously racing about the previous night. Staring straight ahead at the pool, neither of them said a word.

They shared intermittent, uneasy smiles in each other's directions as their eyes met. Huddling in her comfortable robe, Jillian had her legs pulled up as she held the scalding tea an inch from her chin. She cradled it in both hands, almost shivering as if it was freezing outside, when it was really a mild 72 degrees.

He glanced at her. "Good tea."

"It's going to be beautiful day today. Low humidity," she said.

"Huh, really..." After sharing an uncomfortable smile, he asked, "So, where did you get that, uh, pot?"

"Victoria."

He lifted his eyebrows not at all surprised.

She widened her eyes. "Strong."

"Really, really, really super-strong."

"You're not yourself... at all... when you're smoking it."

Shaking his head, he took a sip of tea. "Even though you think you're thinking perfectly clearly, you probably aren't."

"Exactly, and the weird thing is you remember *every* word."

"Every word," Brian repeated as he nodded along with her. They looked at one another and shared a long, uncomfortable glance. After pausing, he placed his cup on the table between them and then swung his legs toward her. "Let me try to recap yesterday to see if we're both on the same page."

Jillian turned toward him, and her robe opened a little too much to where he got a glimpse of yet another pair of her sexy, spectacular underwear. He waved his finger at the problem area as he looked away shyly.

After correcting the problem, she closed her eyes embarrassed. "Sorry."

He looked back at her. "First the movie."

"Really inappropriate. I was actually only reaching for the popcorn."

"But it wasn't there," he said slowly.

She shrugged her shoulders. "Could happen to anyone."

"Oh, agreed. Second, I came back here, and you were smoking the, uh... and I shared the... uh... with you, and then we came up with the—"

"F.W.P.B.," she chimed in.

"Yes, that *is* the abbreviation we came up with for it. And there were several rules that went along with it."

"I remember all the rules." Fighting back a grin, she stared out at the pool.

He frowned. "Rules are important in life, but these rules,

although they seemed really inspired and brilliant last night, now just seem..."

She glanced at him. "Stupid? Ridiculous? Almost embarrassing, perhaps?"

"All of that." He nodded then exhaled deeply. "So where does that leave us, exactly?"

"Humiliated, ashamed, and wanting to crawl in a hole and die, with memories in our brains we'd love to forget."

As Jillian listed the items, he nodded along with each. "Why don't we just forget everything about yesterday?"

"Like it never happened."

"Problem solved." He picked up his tea. They both swung their legs onto the lounge chairs and returned to looking at the pool.

"We probably shouldn't ever play tennis again." Jillian stared at him with her eyes widened.

"Definitely not," he agreed.

"Although, we really are pretty well-matched out there."

"We are McEnroe and Borg... If McEnroe were a young, crazy, horny idiot and if Borg were a woman... a slightly older, wiser, amazing..." She smiled as he continued the seemingly endless list of compliments. "...unfairly sexy and gorgeous woman. Because let's face it, Borg was definitely the better looking of the two tennis champions."

She nodded in agreement just as Rob walked out onto the patio and looked at the two of them. "Beautiful day. Perfect tennis weather. You guys should play."

After glancing at each other in shock, Jillian and Brian turned their attention to Rob. Rob didn't wait for a reply; instead, he walked away as they stared at him, speechless. As he headed into the house, Rob reached back and inappropriately relieved what must have been a serious itch in a part of his ass, which was a clear violation of F.W.P.B. Rule Number One.

Chapter Thirty-One

Rob and Brian went to the beach and saw about two dozen topless women that day. No supermodel was there, as far as they could tell. They saw women of all shapes and sizes. Rob mentioned he preferred the curvier variety and Brian agreed that there was something to be said for curves, but could appreciate the less-curvy as well. They did agree that women of any size and shape, with enough confidence in their appearance to go to a topless beach, were certainly enjoyable to look at. They thanked the heavens above for supplying the fairer sex.

Despite the pleasant distractions, Brian spent most the day wishing he were back with Jillian, playing tennis or sitting by the pool or even having that awkward conversation and tea with her. Although Brian felt that he connected with her better than he had with any woman he had ever met, he felt like it was probably for the best that they ended things when they did. They both seemed to walk away with good memories before either of them did anything to hurt the other... or Rob. Even though they never had any real physical closeness, Brian considered it one of his most successful relationships to date as sad and pathetic as that sounded to him.

After enjoying the beach, Rob and Brian went out to dinner and then home to shower. Running late, they saw Jillian for only a moment and told her they were going to a party thrown by Laura's younger sister at her parents' house.

When Rob and Brian arrived at around 10:30, Laura was already there and on her second drink. She hugged Rob when he arrived, indicating that the trouble between them was either forgotten or dulled by the alcohol in her system. Rob began drinking, while Brian decided, again, to be the designated driver. Laura introduced Brian to a friend of hers named Maggie. Finding her attractive and interesting, Brian thought that she was the type of girl he could see himself dating. They spoke about school, but not about tennis, and she seemed to enjoy his company.

Just after midnight, Rob, Laura, Brian, and Maggie were chatting and drinking in the family room when Brian saw a girl who looked just like Natalie walk past the doorway and then out of sight. He looked at Rob to see if he'd noticed anything, but he didn't. Brian blew it off until moments later, when he saw her again. It *was* Natalie, and she was heading their way. She didn't appear to be looking at him at all. Completely focused on Rob, she didn't look happy.

She walked right up to him and said curtly, "Hello."

Rob looked at her and then froze for a moment. "Natalie... I want you to meet Laura—my girlfriend, Laura."

Laura eyed her suspiciously, and Natalie shot her a look before returning to Rob. Rob stammered, "Natalie's here to... see Brian. Yeah, they're, uh, dating."

Brian stared at Natalie, waiting. Turning to him, she flinched as if, until that moment, she didn't truly realize he was in the room. She flashed him a nearly genuine smile. "Brian, I've been looking for you everywhere."

Brian said, "What the hell are you doing in Miami?"

Natalie opened her mouth to speak, but Rob interrupted, "She wanted to surprise you, so she called me. I told her where we were and... Surprise!"

"Yeah." After pausing a moment, Natalie repeated less than enthusiastically, "Surprise."

Laura shook her head slightly with her nose wrinkled as she eyed Natalie. Suddenly, Rob offered to get everyone a drink, and Maggie headed off with him. While Rob was away, Laura, Natalie, and Brian stood in silence until Brian said to Natalie, "You just show up places, don't you?"

She gave him a confused look, and he elaborated, "Like my tennis match..." She smiled a little, and he joked, "You aren't going to disappear on me like you did then, are you?"

Natalie chuckled as she scanned the room. "Where's the bathroom?"

Laura pointed the way, and Natalie took off. After ten minutes, when neither Rob nor Natalie had returned, Laura and Brian headed off to look for them. First, they searched the downstairs without any luck, but when Laura and Brian walked into the master bedroom, they found the two of them kissing. Turning in shock to see Laura, Rob stepped away from Natalie. "It's not what it looks like."

Laura scoffed. "It looks like you were kissing."

"I mean, she kissed me, but I didn't... Nothing happened. I mean, I ended things before—" Rob pressed his lips together.

"So there was something to end!" Laura placed her hands on her hips, swaying a bit in her obviously intoxicated state.

"Just a little something, it meant nothing. I ended it before

Spring Break. I got scared, but now I know that I love only you. I didn't know she was coming down here."

Walking quickly to Rob, Laura swung to slap him and missed, losing her balance and falling to her knees in the process. Rob just stood, unmoving as Brian rushed to help her to her feet.

Laura narrowed her eyes. "When the hell did this start?"

After closing his eyes, Rob exhaled. "It, uh, started back in February. I was lonely, and she came over, looking for Brian." He motioned to Brian. "You were at the library and it just—"

Laura took a step toward her boyfriend, swung, and missed again when he pulled back.

Brian gently grabbed Laura to steady her. "Want some help?"

"Please."

Getting right in Rob's face, Brian glared at him. Laura took a step back, and Natalie watched the scene unfold wide-eyed and with her mouth hanging open.

Rob put on an uncomfortable smile. "Look, I know you want to hit me, but you won't, so let's just talk—"

Brian punched Rob hard in the face, and he collapsed to the floor, as Natalie looked on, mesmerized. Brian stood over him and said, "You're such a dick." Turning his attention to Natalie, he sneered. "And you're a monster. I'm such a moron. You had me waiting for you, waiting, while you were fucking him." He shook his head at her.

She stared back at him giving him no indication that she'd heard a word he'd said. Then her gaze went from Rob back to Brian and she sighed wearing a blissful expression. She seemed almost giddy from what had just transpired.

Grimacing, Rob held his face as he said to Laura, "Sorry."

Laura refused to look at him as she growled, "Screw you."

After shooting Rob a pitiful look, Natalie turned to Brian

with her lips parted. Their eyes met, and he waited for her to say something, anything, but she didn't utter a word. She simply stared at him, smiling. After a moment, he sighed, turned, and headed from the room. Laura sneered at her boyfriend before following Brian.

Chapter Thirty-Two

As Brian drove Laura to her dorm, he looked over to find her staring out the window in what appeared to be a daze. Turning to smile at him, she nearly broke into a chuckle. "You really nailed him."

He gripped the steering wheel. "I've never hit anyone before. It felt, uh, kind of good."

Her smile faded. "I can't believe he's been screwing that bleach-headed skank for months now. He admitted it."

"And I didn't see it either. I'm such a fucking moron."

"So, she can do this thing with her leg where she puts it over her head."

Brian's eyes widened. "How'd you know about that?"

"Oh, asshole mentioned it once," Laura groaned.

He nodded. "Oh."

"She's soooo flexible," Laura said in a mocking tone and then added, "You can't base a relationship on flexibility."

"You really shouldn't," Brian agreed self-consciously.

"I'm flexible, too," Laura said defensively.

Brian gave her a supportive smile then they each sat in silence. A few minutes later Laura fell asleep as they neared campus. When he parked the car, Brian touched her arm to wake her. "We're here."

Laura fought her way to consciousness, and he helped her to her dorm. Outside her door, he gazed wearily at her. "Can I take a bus back to Rob's from here, or..."

"Just come in for a few minutes. I'll have a couple Cokes and drive you back in, like, an hour or something."

After pondering his options, Brian reluctantly agreed. Once inside her room, Laura flopped on the bed. She rolled away from him, but he could hear her crying. He stood nearby, the awkwardness of the situation beginning to weigh on him.

He exhaled then gave her a sympathetic look. "It's really going to be okay. I think he's serious about how much he loves you. You guys were together for a long time. I know he's an ass and made a mistake, but he was telling me the other day how crazy he is about you. It almost sounded like he was getting ready to ask you to marry him, even."

"I would never marry him. He's been lying to me for months." She turned to him with her eyes puffy and a tear streaming down her cheek. "Will you just lie next to me for a few minutes? I promise. I'll drive you back soon."

Moving closer to the wall, she looked at him, waiting. After a few awkward seconds, he exhaled, and then climbed in bed next to her.

She asked, "Do you think he loves her?"

"No way. She has this power over men. I think he already sees that."

"I've never been with anyone else, you know. And now who knows how many girls he's been out there having sex with?"

He painted on a cheery, supportive smile. "I'm sure it was just the one. I would know if he was—"

"Right!" She glared at him. "You didn't know about this one." Brian conceded the point with his eyes. After taking a deep, calming breath, her mood seemed to turn on a dime as she gave him a gentle smile. "Sorry. I shouldn't take this out you."

He waved his hand at her as if he understood.

She placed her hand on his shoulder. "Thanks for staying with me. I really didn't want to be alone." She closed her eyes and quickly passed out. Brian turned onto his back and sighed, staring up at the ceiling for a moment before closing his eyes.

About thirty minutes later, Brian awoke in the middle of a vivid dream. It was a dream of Jillian giving him an amazing blowjob on the tennis court. When he reached semi-consciousness, he looked over and didn't see Laura next to him on the pillow. Instead, he felt something lower, and when he looked down, he saw Laura holding his penis.

"Hey!" He ran his hands over his face.

She looked up at him. "You really have one gorgeous cock." Pulling her eyes from his face, she moved her mouth toward it. Quickly, he moved away from her and fell off the bed, landing on his ass with a thump. He leapt to his feet as he covered his groin.

"Your cock is so—"

"I know. I know." Frowning, he tucked it away into his pants. "I keep hearing that. Sure, maybe it's nice and all, but it's just a dick, for God's sake. I—"

"What's wrong?"

"You can't start doing that without..." He lifted his hands in the air.

"Without what?" she said softly, raising an eyebrow. "I told you I've never been with anyone else. How do I know what I've been missing all these years?"

Sitting up in bed, she removed her shirt and bra, as Brian tried to avoid looking at her. "Aren't you attracted to me?"

He sat on her roommate's bed across the room and uncomfortably glanced up at her. "Sure, I am." He did certainly find her attractive, and she looked hot sitting up in bed with no shirt. "But I'm in a really weird place right now. I have, uh—"

"I know how we could both get back at Rob," Laura said in an evil yet sexy tone. "I haven't done *everything* with him, but we could do... everything."

"What?" He knitted his brow together half confused and half concerned about what she might be referring to.

"You could have my ass. Guys love that, right?"

He swallowed the lump in his throat. "Um, I..."

She cocked her head, pressing a finger to her lips. "Rob's always wanted to do that, and I've been holding back, you know, to save something for when we got married, but now there won't be any marriage with him, so..."

Looking away nervously, he stammered, "I, uh, feel a little... and I really shouldn't. You're great, and all. I mean, your ass is top shelf, and I'd love to, uh... But even though he's a douche, he's still kind of my best friend, or was, or... I don't know..." He closed his eyes, exhaling deeply.

She shook her head, her eyes filled with disappointment as she slipped her shirt back on.

"Sorry." He raked his hands through his hair. He thought he probably turned Laura's generous offer down mainly because he really wanted to be with Jillian. And how could he sleep with Rob's girlfriend at the same time that he also wanted to sleep with his mother and not be the absolutely lowest piece of shit on the planet?

"Just go." Laura rolled over then buried her face in the pillow.

"But I kinda need a ride."

"Get out of here!" she said loudly with her words muffled by the pillow.

"You'll probably thank me in the morning." He folded his arms across his chest.

Turning to him, she looked as if she wanted to decapitate him. He quickly left the room.

It took Brian almost an hour, using a combination of running and walking, to make it the approximately six miles back to Jillian's house. He used his key to go inside and found Jillian asleep in her room, but Rob was not in his. It was after 3:00. Brian was exhausted and flopped into bed, still fully clothed.

Chapter Thirty-Three

At just after 8:00, Rob struggled to wake the soundly-sleeping Brian. He tapped him and then called his name loudly, but Brian did nothing more than toss and turn. Rob pushed him hard in the shoulder a few times to no avail, so he left the room. Returning with an alarm clock, he plugged it in and set the alarm to go off one minute later. He placed it right next to Brian's head and cranked the wheel on the volume all the way up. Then he stepped back and waited while wearing an evil smile. The digital clock advanced one minute, but nothing happened. Frowning, he exhaled deeply and then rushed to the clock while mumbling obscenities. He checked the alarm time, and it was set correctly. He spun the volume wheel all the way to the other side, and the alarm quickly shot up to a full blast of annoying buzzes.

Rob cringed from the noise, and Brian shot straight up in bed and looked around the room, confused. After hitting the off button, Rob placed the alarm on the nightstand.

As Brian fought to regain consciousness, Rob yanked him up by his shirt. "I can't believe you tried to sleep with her."

"What are you talking about?" Brian asked with his eyes only half-open.

"Probably this whole week you've been sneaking around, trying to fuck her behind my back, haven't you? You've been acting different. I knew something was up," Rob released his shirt, and Brian landed back against the pillow. Sitting on the bed, Rob held his head in his hands.

As he struggled to find the words, Brian took a deep breath. "Look, I can explain. It wasn't something that I—"

"I've so screwed this up. I was going to ask her to marry me, and..."

"What? Who?" Brian asked confused.

"Who the hell do you think we're talking about?" Rob asked angrily.

Brian stopped to knock a few more cobwebs from his brain, figured it out, looked relieved, and then casually said, "Oh, Laura. You have it all wrong. She was the one trying to have sex with me. I just—"

With fire in his eyes, Rob bolted upright, grabbing Brian by the shirt again. "What the fuck are you talking about?"

Brian's eyes shot open wide. "Look, I drove her home, and I didn't have any way to get back. So she said to come in until she sobered up, and then she said she'd drive me back."

Rob gave him a skeptical glare. "I want to know everything that happened, every detail."

"I think she was drunk and trying to make you jealous. Nothing really happened."

"Right."

Brian rolled his eyes. "Okay, maybe she touched my dick for a minute. I was asleep, and she just sorta pulled it out. That was it, really. She loves you, Dude. Nothing happened. I put on the brakes, and she realized she didn't really want to have sex with me. Really, she was only doing it to make you jealous."

After letting go of Brian's shirt, Rob walked across the room. Brian got out of bed, went to him, and then placed a hand on his shoulder. "That's exactly what happened."

"Really?"

Brian nodded, and although he did think that Laura was only trying to sleep with him to spite Rob or to make him jealous, he felt the little detail about her trying to give him a blowjob and the rather big detail about her offering him *other* things were better left unsaid.

Rob gave him a slight smile, and they stood together in silent reflection until Brian realized there was an unresolved issue they had yet to discuss. He narrowed his eyes, turned, and paced around the room. "Um, if we're done with the whole Laura thing, can we talk about the little matter of you fucking Natalie behind my back for who knows how long, while you knew I was crazy about her?"

Rob's jaw dropped as he looked at Brian. "I thought we worked all that out last night."

"Worked it out how?"

"When you punched me."

"What the fuck are you talking about? It's not worked out. When did it start? Who came on to whom first? Does she touch your dick? I know she has a thing about that..." Brian rambled all these questions quickly as he walked to the window and looked out.

Rob began, "I'm not sure how it happened. As I said, she came over to the suite, looking for you, and you weren't there and—"

Spotting Natalie sleeping on a lounge chair in the backyard, Brian pointed down at her. "There she is."

"Who?"

"Natalie."

Rob joined him at the window. "The details aren't important. Look, I ended things with her last night, and I really think she wants to get back together with you. She wouldn't shut up about the way you hit me and how you seemed so—"

"We were never together!" Brian shot back.

"Whatever, she wants a fresh start with you."

"Why? Because you dumped her?" Brian sneered.

"No! Maybe. I don't know. Does it really matter, anyway?"

"She likes to mess with guys. She gets all in your head, and I think she's really crazy." Slumping against the wall, Brian stared at the floor.

"Natalie and I had a long talk, and I think she really has changed. We ended things kinda mutually, and she told me she really likes you and is sorry about everything. She was just scared, and you reminded her of this guy from her past, but she says she's all over that now."

Unconvinced, Brian looked at Rob and then glanced back out the window at Natalie.

"She said she was going to try to find you last night. She wanted to talk to you."

"Really?" Brian's lips curled up into a slight smile. "She is pretty hot."

"She is, and I really think deep down inside, she's not a complete psycho."

Brian nodded casually. "It would be weird dating her when I know you've had sex with her. What exactly did you guys—"

"Do you really want details?" Rob asked. Brian shook his head no, and then Rob added, "Look, I promise you, we never went all the way. In the most technical terms, I swear on my mother's life, I did not put my penis inside her vagina, not once. That, I promise you."

"Okay, I believe you." At first, Brian was relieved, but then he looked at Rob, confused. After pondering it a moment, he shook off trying to make sense of what his friend had just told him.

"Good."

Suddenly, Brian's eyes widened with alarm. "Your mother's not here, is she? She isn't listening to all this shit?"

"No, she went out." Rob pointed out the window at Natalie. "Now go down there and figure this out with her. I've got to go fix things with Laura."

Chapter Thirty-Four

Brian frowned a little as he stood next to the sleeping Natalie. After studying her closely for a moment, he gently woke her up. When Natalie saw him, she stood, jumped into his arms, and wouldn't let go. His anger melted into a smile. She told him that she was so sorry, that she was an idiot, that she would never ever hurt him or cheat on him again, and she begged him to drive back to Atlanta with her right then. She said she would answer every question he had and be completely honest about all of it.

He agreed, and she hugged him again. As he held her, he looked over her shoulder at the tennis court, wondering if he was making a big mistake.

After packing his things, Brian left Rob and Jillian a short note about how he was leaving and how much he appreciated their letting him stay in the house. He also thanked Jillian for the great tennis matches.

As Natalie and Brian were about to drive off, Jillian pulled into the driveway and parked. Brian watched as she got out of the car. She didn't see him as she entered the house.

Brian went to the front door and found it locked. He used the key he'd forgotten to return and went inside. Walking into the kitchen, he spotted Jillian through the window, heading to the tennis court with his note in her hand. Rushing outside, he found her sitting on the tennis court bench.

When she saw him, she smiled. "I got your note. Thought you had already gone."

"I almost was... then I saw you drive up."

He sat down next to her. "I'm driving back to school with Natalie."

"I..." She sighed then shook her head before tucking a loose hair behind her ear. "I... I just wanted to make sure you didn't have the wrong impression of me. Out of the few days I've known you, I was loopy on Ambien and wine, drunk, and then high. If I have two glasses of wine in a week, that's a lot for me."

"No." He gazed dreamily at her. "No, I didn't think anything... It looked like you were having a rough week, and this whole thing that happened—or almost happened—between us probably didn't help."

A smile graced her lips. "I usually don't go running around outside naked and spying on young men while they sleep and shower."

"Don't worry about it, it's not a—" His eyes shot wide open and he gave her a curious grin. "What shower?"

"What?" she asked in a casual tone as if she were trying to cover her tracks.

"You just said you spied on me when I showered. When was that?"

"Didn't we already talk about that?"

"No, I'm pretty sure I would have remembered. When, exactly, was this?"

"Okay." She closed her eyes, busted. "After the second time we played tennis."

Pausing, he remembered the shower in question. After closing his eyes, he asked hesitantly, "Did you, um, catch the beginning... or the end of that shower?"

"How would I know? Uh—"

He cringed. "Was I focused on one particular... area?"

"Focused is a good way to put it." She nodded with rounded eyes. "I'd say you were really focused."

"That would be the beginning then." He dropped his face into his hands, mortified.

"I was honestly going to join you." She placed her hand on his knee. "I was so worked up on the court, but then when I saw you doing... *that*... I had to watch." Staring into space, she obviously relived the memory with her lips parted. "You are really good at doing that, you know. I was moved."

His face remained in his hands. Unable to look at her, he said in a tired, slow voice, "I've had a tremendous amount of practice."

She pulled his hand from his knee and smiled. "It really shows."

Straightening up, he looked her in the eye. "So you're telling me if I wasn't doing... that... we would have done it?"

"Oh, definitely," she replied casually.

"Okay so, I'm never doing *that* again."

"But Rob would have also walked in on us. Remember, that's when he came home."

"Right, right, right." He exhaled deeply as he shook his head. "So, I guess it was lucky that I was abusing myself like that."

"That's one way to put it." She grinned. Glancing at each other, they shared a laugh until Jillian put on a serious expression. "So she drove all that way and just showed up here, looking for you? That's kind of sweet, isn't it?"

"Well..." He looked away for a moment, embarrassed by the truth. He thought about telling her the whole story, but maybe to protect Rob or maybe so she wouldn't think he was such an idiot for following Natalie back to campus when she didn't even come to Miami to look for him, he chose to spare her the details. "Yeah, she did. It was sweet." He forced a smile. "I still think she may be completely nuts. I'm going to take it slow, but I think I just need to see what happens."

After pausing to collect her thoughts, Jillian turned to him. "Out of the thousands of women on that campus, there must be a least one who would appreciate an intelligent, attractive, thoughtful young man who can cook and who doesn't take advantage of women when they're... you know. You are a real gentleman. And if you don't meet someone while at school, there's a whole other world out there when you graduate. Don't let her break your heart. Make sure she's really into you before you open yourself up again. Really *into* you. Don't let her string you along."

He met her gaze. "And don't you go settling for some jerk, even if he does wear Magnums."

They shared another smile. Reaching down, he picked up a tennis ball and smelled it. "Am I crazy for liking the smell of these?"

Taking the ball from his hand, she sniffed it, closed her eyes, and smiled. "Especially right out of a freshly-opened can." After looking at each other as if they were sharing some sort of bizarre bond, she said, "We're weird."

"Tell me about it."

She rolled her eyes. "What's wrong with us?"

"I don't know." Pausing, he breathed in deeply while fighting back his emotions. "But I don't think I'll ever play again and not think of you."

"We'll always have that tiebreak." A single tear fell from her eye.

He gently wiped the tear from her cheek and exhaled sharply. "I'll never forget it."

"Yeah." She gazed out over the court and sighed.

"You know..." He grinned. "I'm starting to think that last ball may have bounced twice. That would have completely changed the, uh... I would have won."

She narrowed her eyes. "Maybe, but I don't think you could have played another point."

"I still had a lot more tennis in me," he said with his expression dripping with manufactured confidence.

Jillian laughed. "Right."

He shook his head as he glanced up at the sky, drawing in a deep breath. Returning his eyes to hers, Brian leaned over and kissed her on the cheek. She closed her eyes as his warm, moist lips touched her skin for the very first time. She desperately wanted to turn to him, to kiss him hard, but as quickly as the moment arrived, it vanished.

Pulling back slowly from her, he stood. "Well, I guess I'd better be going."

She rose to her feet and struggled to maintain her composure. After he handed her the ball, they shared one last smile. Jillian watched as he walked toward the house, her emotions getting the best of her, hoping he wouldn't look back. He didn't.

Chapter Thirty-Five

On the drive back to Georgia, Brian decided not to ask Natalie any questions or allow her to give him any details. He thought that for them to have any chance, he would probably be better off not knowing. And since they hadn't been dating exclusively, anyway, the worst that she did was lie to him, and even that was a stretch.

He told her he needed time to think about everything, but he spent almost the entire ride home thinking about Jillian and not about Natalie, Rob or the two of them together. He decided that he wouldn't jump into anything with Natalie. As physically attracted as he was to her, he vowed not to have sex with her until he was sure that she was really interested in him, that she wasn't just playing some game, and most importantly, that she wasn't completely out of her fucking mind.

The more he thought about everything that had happened since he'd met Natalie, the more he was convinced that she was crazy or, at the very least, the kind of girl who enjoyed watching men suffer. He didn't want to spend another minute wondering what she was doing, where she was, what she was thinking, and whether or not she was really attracted to him. Because maybe she only wanted to get him back on the hook just to have one more guy fawning over her.

When they arrived back on campus, she invited him to stay over, but he turned her down. That weekend, he did allow her to sleep in his room, where he was the one in control. When she attempted to unbutton his jeans, he stopped her, saying that he still needed time to get over all that had happened. He decided to give her a little of the same treatment that she had doled out to him for so many weeks. When they went to sleep that night, Brian wore only boxer shorts while Natalie slept in a T-shirt and underwear. He pretended to fall asleep quickly and was amused to find that she pulled the same types of tricks that he and probably many men pulled in bed, when "sleeping over" meant literally *sleeping over* and not something a lot more active or fun.

Whenever she found his hand near her crotch, she would press against it, undoubtedly in the hope that his hand would somehow spring to life, realize the prize that awaited its touch, and go to work. Granted, it's a little easier to jut your male parts out to a wayward hand then it is the female variety, but that didn't stop her from trying at least three times that night. He held his ground all night, giving her whatever the female version of blue balls happened to be called.

He woke first and looked at her as she lay next to him, sleeping peacefully, but he hoped completely unsatisfied. When he lifted the sheet to look at her, he saw that her panties were pulled halfway down her ass, and her shirt had risen, exposing most of her back. He figured that her underwear was pulled so far down that it had to have been a deliberate act on her part—some kind of ploy to seduce him in the middle of the night. He was sure she was hoping that a hand might travel from her back down to her perky little ass, discover that it was uncovered, and once it did, a finger would slip into that magical crevice and be powerless to do anything except venture further.

It was the female equivalent of the old male trick, where one's thing just happens to sneak out of the flap of one's boxers "by accident" in search of some fun. Brian was convinced that's exactly what the guy had in mind when he came up with the idea to add the flap to boxer shorts. Were guys really using that flap to go the bathroom, or was it put there purely to make the "surprise slip" possible? That slip could lead to the discovery by your partner and the "*It's-already-out-so-I-might-as-well...*" kind of mentality.

Exhaling deeply, he sat up looking at the exquisite small of Natalie's back, as it tapered invitingly into the curve of her hips. Maybe he was giving himself a set of blue ones as well. He felt that familiar surge of excitement rushing to his groin, and he slipped off to the bathroom and took care of the problem. It would have been easy for him to fall off the wagon and be seduced by Natalie, but that would have given her back the power, and he was enjoying having that all to himself.

After the bathroom break, he went to his computer and searched for a gift for Jillian. Wanting to say thank you to her for her hospitality, he searched for tennis-related gifts and found a DVD copy of the McEnroe–Borg Wimbledon final from 1980, the match with the long tiebreak that reminded them both so much of the one they had played the last time they were on the court together. He ordered two copies, one shipped to him and one marked as a gift and shipped to her. Brian typed a personal message to be included with the gift, and it took him twenty minutes of editing before he was finally satisfied with what he wrote.

Down in sunny Miami, Jillian was craving pancakes. She grabbed the pancake mix but then reconsidered. She put the mix back and found a recipe in a cookbook. Then she followed

Brian's advice about plugging the griddle in before starting and adding one extra egg white and more sugar, along with his tip about how to butter the griddle and make two test cakes. When she sat down to eat her three flawlessly-cooked pancakes with their perfect, golden brown air bubble marks, she sighed. After pouring on the syrup, she cut into the stack with her fork, took a bite, and smiled while thinking of him.

After breakfast, Jillian went to her study to write. She started a story about characters based on her and Brian, except the characters actually began a physical relationship starting with the night at the movies. The story pretty much followed the events as they took place up until they arrived back home from the movie theater. In her novel, when the woman opened the door, her son was not there, and the horny couple ran up to the bedroom and spent a glorious night together.

After writing for so long that her eyes ached from staring at the screen, she spent an hour hitting against the ball machine, and while she smashed balls over the net, she wondered what might have been if Rob hadn't been at the house when they'd returned. Would things have played out as amazingly, as they did in her writing, or would it have been a big mistake? When Jillian had exhausted herself on the court, she took a long bath, grabbed a light meal, and retired to her room to get back to writing. She spent the remainder of the week cranking out the story and hitting balls against the machine. Writing for about eight hours a day, she slaved over every erotic word in the filthy descriptions of the many long, steamy sex sessions that her two main characters enjoyed.

Natalie wanted to go to a movie, and Brian suggested they spike their drinks and really have some fun at the theater. She turned him down, saying it was too risky. She said they might be thrown out or get into some other trouble with campus security. They went to the movie anyway, but Natalie's knee never rubbed Brian's, not even once... or if it did, he didn't notice.

Over the next week, Brian found the pre-Natalie masturbation routine was working quite well, even as she kicked things up a notch. She took to changing in front of him while he stood in her room, pretending to read a magazine. Her panties became sexier with each passing day as his will became more steadfast. She had never before bought him anything, but that week, she bought him a teddy bear (tennis-themed of course) and a new can of balls. She bought herself a racquet and a sexy tennis outfit, and they set a date to play the following morning.

That night, they slept at Natalie's, and Brian decided to ask her about the mysterious event from her past, which had prevented her from being able to touch a guy down there. She refused to tell the story until he threatened to return to his dorm.

She reluctantly explained, "I walked in on my brother while he was... touching himself. I was about sixteen, and he was a year younger."

He hoped there had to be more to the story so he motioned with his hand for her to elaborate. "And...?"

"And... it was really traumatic!" She glared back at him.

Brian treaded lightly. "And... he just kept going in front of you, even after you walked in?"

"Oh, God no! He was facing the other way. I didn't even see it."

Brian made a face. "Then it happened again, and he kept setting up situations where—?"

"No, he avoided me for weeks."

After staring at her with a blank expression for a moment, he had to ask, "And that's the whole story?"

"Yes, that's the whole story!" She angrily shot back.

He gave her a sympathetic look, even though his mind was telling him that she was a freaking lunatic. "I completely understand." He realized it wasn't the ideal formative years' experience, but come on. "Can you, um, touch one now?"

"To be honest, it was only yours that I couldn't touch. This sounds crazy, but it's your haircut. It reminds me so much of my brother's that it was freaking me out."

He paused, unable to respond until he glanced at her to find she was staring and waiting for him to say something. "Oh, that isn't crazy at all. Hair can be a powerful... trigger. I, uh... I had that psychology class last year. We talked about that... visual triggers or something." He calmly smiled at her, but on the inside, his brain was screaming, "*Holy shit!*" After enough time had passed with them simply staring at each other in silence, he gave her a comforting pat on the shoulder. "I have to go to the bathroom."

He stood in front of the mirror, making crazy eyes at his reflection; he couldn't help but wonder if he was thinking clearly about all this. After splashing water on his face, he returned to Natalie's room. When he arrived, he found her under the covers, and her bare shoulders were showing.

Turning toward him, she batted her eyelashes. "I really want to have sex with you now."

He sat next to her on the bed, contemplating what to do, as she added, "I'm pretty sure I can touch it now."

"Oh, that's good," Brian said slowly.

"But I have to tell you something first."

He thought, *Okay this should be really good.*

"I'm a... technical virgin," she announced proudly.

"What's that?" He made a face as if he didn't hear her clearly.

"A technical virgin."

"What does that even mean?"

"I mean I don't have vaginal sex. I'm saving that for when I'm married."

He looked at her, trying to process all this. "So, what kind of sex do you have?"

"Obviously, all the other kinds."

He wrinkled his nose. "Could you be a little more specific?"

"Mostly anal and some oral. A lot of girls are now doing this," she said casually.

"Wow, that's really specific." After attempting to process it all, he had to ask, "So, how many guys would you say you've done, you know, with?"

"Four."

"Four," he repeated, jumping a little out of his skin. "And Rob?" He made a hand gesture as if to ask if they had also done this act together.

"Yes, Rob." She widened her eyes. "Is that a problem?"

"Rob's not the problem," he said quickly.

Leaning out of bed to her drawer, she pulled out a pack of condoms and a tube of lubricant, and then handed them to him. "Have you done this before?"

"No, not really."

"We can go slowly, since this is your first time. It's fun, and there's no chance of getting pregnant."

He paused a moment, trying to let it all sink in. "Slow would be nice." Sitting there, he contemplated his next move. He glanced at the condom box, and then an idea hit him. He smiled. "Oh, these are latex condoms. I can't wear those. If I do, my dick totally blows up big... but not in a good big way... at all."

She nodded with her mouth open slightly as Brian glanced at her, hoping she'd buy his excuse. "Plus I'm not feeling very well—my stomach hurts. Let's do this some other time. I'll bring the right condoms, and it'll be amazing."

"That sounds good." After giving him a disappointed look she slipped on her T-shirt and opened the covers to invite him in. "Will you hold me all night?"

"I will."

After stripping down to his underwear, he slipped into bed with her. She snuggled up to his shoulder and smiled. "I can't wait to finally play tennis with you tomorrow."

"Me either." He reached over, turned off the light, and with the mention of the word tennis, he began thinking only about Jillian.

In Miami, Jillian sat out by the pool, drinking a cup of hot tea and thinking of Brian. It was almost midnight, and she was reminded of their pot-induced skinny dip as she looked out over the water. It was a hot night. She stood and walked to the edge of the pool, dipping a toe in the water. It felt warm but more comfortable than the humid air. Reliving a pleasant memory, she grinned, and then removed her clothes and slowly walked down the steps into the water. She swam one lap, then climbed onto a big raft. She lay on it face up with the cool vinyl sending chills through her warm skin. The air temperature was so close to the water temperature that she really couldn't tell which parts of her body were in the pool and which weren't. It didn't occur to her that she was slowly sinking into the water, having bumped the raft's fill valve when she climbed aboard.

Kicking her foot lazily off the side of the raft into the water, she flashed back to Brian as he held her foot and gently kissed it that special night. The Jaclyn West narrative began in her mind, except this time she and Brian were the protagonists named in her story.

. . .

Jillian lay back on the float as Brian kissed one of her feet and then the other. Moving to the side of the raft, he began lightly kissing the top of her ankle, followed by her calf, as he ran his hands up her legs, toward her womanhood. She gasped and clutched the raft with both hands; just the feel of his lips on her skin could lift her from it, almost magically. Brian looked at her face and softly said, "I've been waiting for this moment since I met you."

Jillian brought her hand to his neck and pulled him into her as he began trailing kisses from her knee to her thigh and—

At that moment, Jillian's body was completely underwater as the raft lost nearly all its air. Her head remained above water for only another moment as she opened her mouth, still locked in her third person narrative fantasy. As she sank further, pool water filled her mouth. In a panic, she swallowed, leapt to the surface, coughed up water, and then gasped for breath. She looked around for Brian, but he, of course, wasn't there to save her. Climbing from the pool, half-sad and half-smiling, she remembered the joke they shared about how swimming alone is dangerous.

Chapter Thirty-Six

The next morning, Brian awoke to the incredible feeling of Natalie sitting on him and giving him the best massage he'd ever received. She worked his shoulders, back, legs, and ass muscles to the point that he was super-relaxed and lightheaded.

"I got you something," she said, "Well, thirteen things actually."

"What?" Brian groaned as Natalie continued to work the muscles in his lower back.

"A bagel and a box of latex-free condoms."

"When did you do all this?"

"While you were asleep." Natalie nuzzled next to his ear. "After tennis, let's come back here and just do it. I've got to have you soon or..." She gently took his earlobe into her mouth, which sent a shiver down his back. "While I was out, I started to rethink this whole technical virgin thing, and I think that if I was really in love with a guy, I could break the rule, you know?"

"That's—"

"We wouldn't even need to be engaged or anything, but if we were really serious, then..."

She moved off him, and he sat up to look at her, grinning. "This sounds like it just might be the best day of my life."

She giggled.

"You know, I've been..." He shook his head. "No, forget it."

"Tell me." She placed her hand on his arm.

"Since the first day I met you, I've been picturing you doing that thing... that thing with your leg pointed to the ceiling while you were completely naked. You think maybe we could—"

"Sure." She tipped her chin up. "I can get into almost any position you can imagine. I dare you to come up with one that I can't do."

He could imagine quite a lot, and when he saw that she had remembered he liked a sesame bagel, he smiled. After telling her he would meet her on the court, he walked back to his dorm, enjoying the bagel and wearing a smile that only a natural disaster could erase.

He thought things could be much, much worse than having a beautiful girl who was incredibly flexible, into wild sex, and great at giving massages trying to please you with everything she had. Then he tried to justify her version of the *virgin* thing. It wasn't like she had done it with, like, twelve guys, or anything. Rob certainly didn't count since he was, well, Rob. One of the other guys didn't count because it was certainly the Greek ex-boyfriend guy, and everyone knew that to a Greek guy, that kind of sex was about as common as a kiss. At least Brian thought he had heard somewhere that another name for anal sex was Greek. Anyway, so that left two, probably a drunken one-night stand—which could be thrown away—and just one more. So, basically, she'd had that kind of sex with just one guy, and that clearly was not a big deal at all. He spent the rest of the walk home trying to come up with impossible positions for Natalie's flexibility challenge.

. . .

Natalie sure looked sexy on the court; unfortunately, her game was anything but. And Brian could deal with that and be patient with her, but she had no interest in trying to learn the sport and that frustrated him. She complained about the sun in her eyes, and the strong smell of the new tennis balls, as well as how her hands now smelled because of them. She seemed like she was only going through the motions out there, and it reminded him of their dates together before Spring Break.

Next to them, a couple of college girls were playing a match. They were both heavy hitters. Brian and Natalie took a break and sat on a bench, watching them play. The girls grunted, not terribly loudly, but loud enough for others nearby to hear. After a particularly grueling rally, Natalie watched them, horrified. "What are they doing? Why are they making those noises?"

"They're just really into it and trying hard to win the point."

"I can't imagine ever being into anything enough to make a noise like that," she said while peeling the paper off her water bottle.

Without saying a word, he watched as she took a sip, made a face, and then tilted her hand closer to her nose. After taking a dainty sniff, she cringed.

He played those words over and over in his head; *I can't imagine ever being into anything enough to make a noise like that.* It reminded him of what Jillian had told him when he last saw her. She said to make sure Natalie was *into* him, really *into* him. He took a long look at Natalie, as she smelled her hands again with her face all contorted. Then he watched as she discovered a dirt mark on her palm and struggled to wipe it off. He really saw through her beauty to the self-centered little nightmare that she was.

Standing, holding his racket, he contemplated his next

move. After hearing another grunt—one that reminded him of Jillian's—he watched as Natalie rolled her eyes in response to the outburst. He stared at her, expressionless then said, "Um, I've got to go."

"Good," she replied as she stood and collected her things. When she turned to follow him, all she saw was the back of his head, as he was already out the gate and running toward his dorm.

Brian ran into the suite and then burst into Rob's room. They hadn't spoken much since Miami, and Rob looked happy to see him. Brian asked, "Can I borrow your car?"

"Sure. I'll need it later though."

"I definitely won't be back until tomorrow—at the earliest—and maybe not until late Sunday." Brian bounced up and down on his heels, struggling to contain his excitement.

"Shit, really? I don't know..."

"Look, you slept with Natalie, and I didn't kill you, or anything. I also had an open invitation to violate your girlfriend nine different ways, and I didn't. Don't you think you owe me this?"

"Wait, you didn't tell me that. All you said was that she came to her senses." Rob looked at him suddenly concerned.

Brian said, "Do you really need the whole story? I was trying to give you guys a chance. Just like I'm sure you never told Laura about the particular type of sex that you and Natalie enjoyed."

Rob swallowed hard. "What do you mean?" Brian's raised eyebrow look apparently told Rob exactly what he meant. "Oh, that. Yeah, Laura doesn't really need to know about that."

Wearing an evil smile, Brian held out his hand. "Maybe it's better that you don't know everything about her, and she doesn't know everything about you. And for that to continue, maybe you should just hand over the keys."

"You swear you didn't have sex with Laura—no sex of any kind with her?"

"I swear on the life of..." Brian struggled to come up with a name, a good name, and then he smiled. "Johnny Mac. I swear on the life of the greatest tennis player of all time. You know I wouldn't fuck around with McEnroe."

Rob tossed him the keys.

"Thanks, man." As Brian rushed from the room, he yelled back, "If I'm going to be any later than Sunday, I'll call."

Jillian walked out to the pool area, wearing a swimsuit and carrying envelopes, along with a package. Victoria was lying on a lounge chair in a bikini. After sitting down next to her, Jillian placed the letters on the table. She studied the package. "I didn't order anything."

Jillian opened the box. When she pulled out the copy of the tennis DVD, she smiled. Discovering the note, she read it as tears formed in her eyes:

Jillian, I just wanted to thank you for letting me stay with you in your incredible home. You mentioned you had an old, grainy copy of this great match, and I thought of you when I stumbled across it. I hope when you watch that fourth-set tiebreak (the best tiebreak ever) you'll think of ours (the second best tiebreak ever). I bought a copy for myself, and I know I will. There are many things about the trip that I'll never forget... I wish you the very best.

Brian

.   .   .

Victoria looked over and noticed Jillian's face. "What's wrong?"

Jillian took a deep breath. "It's from Brian." She turned the DVD so that Victoria could see it. Victoria looked at it, a little confused, and then Jillian handed over the note. Victoria read the note as Jillian sat back, thinking.

When she reached the end, Victoria smiled brightly. "You need to go see him right now."

"He's with Natalie."

"How do you know?"

"Rob mentioned it."

"Then why is he sending you gifts?" Victoria asked.

"He's just trying to thank me for—"

"Watching him jerk off and showing him your pus—"

"No! For staying here," Jillian interrupted.

Victoria read the note again. "He totally wants to have sex with you. It says it right here."

"Where?"

Victoria read from the note, "'There are many things about the trip that I'll never forget' dot dot dot."

Jillian looked at her confused.

Victoria widened her eyes sexily, as she repeated, "DOT DOT DOT."

"Yeah?"

"There are many things I'll never forget, AND I want to lick your pussy for, like, an hour. That's what dot dot dot means."

"Okay, yeah." Jillian rolled her eyes and put her hand out to get the note back.

Frowning, Victoria handed it over. "Why don't you go visit Rob and just see what's going on up there?"

Jillian simply returned a blank stare.

Victoria gave her a tired look. "Well, at least call him to

thank him for the gift."

"I will."

Victoria rolled her eyes, and Jillian repeated, "I promise, I will. Tomorrow."

"You should have slept with him when you had the chance, and then when you had that other chance... oh, and then when you had that second-to-last chance and then when—"

"All right." Jillian exhaled sharply. "I get it."

Victoria put on a deadly serious expression. "I've been reading that semen is really good for vaginal health."

Jillian glanced back, intrigued, as Victoria added, "It's something about the pH down there and how it brings it back in balance."

"Hmm," Jillian said casually.

"Not to mention the muscles in your..." Victoria pointed to Jillian's crotch. "...will start to deteriorate if you don't use them often enough."

Jillian scoffed. "Just worry about your own muscles."

"Oh, I don't need to. I can pull the cork out of a wine bottle with my—"

"How would you even..." Cringing, Jillian put her hand up. "Wait. Don't tell me. I don't want to know."

Victoria grinned as Jillian looked away in mock disgust. When she looked back, they broke into laughter.

"I was just kidding," Victoria said.

"Thank God."

Chapter Thirty-Seven

Brian made the ten-hour trip in just over nine hours. Lucky for him, he wasn't pulled over and only needed to stop once for gas. When he reached Jillian's house, he noticed five cars parked in the driveway. After parking across the street, he walked to the house and peered through a window. He saw a group of ten people, including Jillian and Victoria, eating dinner in the dining room. There were two women sitting on either side of Jillian, and he breathed a sigh of relief, since she appeared to be dateless.

When he saw Jillian stand up and head to the kitchen, he took off. Running to the back of the house, he reached over to unlatch the gate, and then sprinted toward the kitchen window. He saw Jillian pull a chocolate mousse ganache cake from the refrigerator and place it on the counter. He tapped softly on the window and then a little harder until she looked over.

Recognizing him, she smiled as she rushed to the patio door. When she opened the door, Brian pulled her outside and kissed her before she could say a thing. She returned the kiss, which lasted for a good thirty seconds.

She looked at him shocked. "What are you doing here?"

While struggling to catch his breath, he collected his thoughts. "I had to see you. I've wanted to kiss you for weeks. Since I left, I've been thinking about what you said about meeting the right girl, and I... don't want to meet the right girl. I mean... I've already met her. I don't want to just be friends or partial friends or whatever the hell that thing was. And it's not just because Natalie turned out to be a total psycho. It's been killing me to find out. I've... If we're even half as good together in the bedroom as we are on the court, then the sex might just kill me, but it's a chance I've got to take."

She just stared past him, seemingly thinking and not saying a word. Brian narrowed his eyes, glanced where she was looking, found nothing back there, and then turned back at her, concerned. "It would really help me now if you said something. I just drove nine hours, and if you want me to go, I will, but I, uh, really need to pee first."

"If you take one step away from this house, I'll tackle you."

Brian smiled, relieved. "Good, because there is no way I'm getting back in that car right now."

She stepped in closer to him. "I missed you so much."

"Me too." Placing his hand on her neck, he pressed his lips to hers once again. She moaned softly into his mouth. The kiss lasted a long, long time and she wrapped her arms around him. He pulled back from her and gazed into her eyes, pressing his lips together and cringing.

"What's wrong?"

"I just drove the last six hours with no breaks. I really have to pee."

"Sorry. Sorry." She bounced on her heels. "I have people over, and I'm just trying to figure out how I can sneak you upstairs." Suddenly, a broad smile spread over her face then she blurted out, "Hold on." Then she disappeared into the house, leaving him wearing a perplexed look. Moments later, she rushed back to the door and pulled him in. "When I say it's clear, go up the back steps to my room and wait for me there. Read a book, or something. I'm sure I can get them out of here in ten or fifteen minutes."

She walked into the house, checked if the line of sight to the stairs was clear, and then motioned for Brian to come in quickly. He rushed in and slipped upstairs.

After a visit to the bathroom, Brian spotted the DVD he'd bought for Jillian on top of her player, and he found his note next to the bed. Sitting on her bed, he looked around the room. He picked up a novel from her nightstand, checked the back cover, frowned and put it down. Her computer sat on the bed next to him, and when he grabbed it to move it aside, the screen brightened to reveal her latest novel. He took a closer look, reading from where the document was opened, and it began to sound very familiar. It was an erotic and accurate account of Jillian and Brian's movie theater adventure, except the names were changed to protect the guilty.

Downstairs, Jillian cut ten slices of cake and served them without coffee. She told her guests the coffeemaker was broken, and when one of the men offered to look at it, Jillian told him she threw it away. She was acting nervous, and Victoria looked at her concerned. The group was loudly talking and making over the dessert as Jillian barely touched her slice. When guests asked for tea, they joked that maybe all her pots were also broken. After giving them a fake laugh, Jillian rushed to the kitchen. "I'll be right back."

In the kitchen, Jillian stood at the sink filling the kettle. Victoria rushed up behind her. "What the hell is wrong with you? You're acting crazy."

"Brian's here."

"What do you mean?" Victoria wrinkled her nose.

"Brian is here... here." Jillian pointed downward.

"Where?"

"In my bedroom. He just got here five minutes ago."

"Why?"

"Because, evidently, we're no longer just friends." Jillian raised an eyebrow.

"Why aren't you up there?"

"I have a house full of people, and I don't want to be rude."

"Fuck being rude. When's the last time you had sex?"

Jillian shook her hands nervously. "I, uh, couldn't even tell you right now."

Victoria walked over to the cake, cut a slice, and placed it on a plate for her. "Take this upstairs to him, then come down in two minutes and act like you have a migraine."

"Seriously?"

"It'll work." Victoria nodded, shoving the cake into her hand.

Smiling, Jillian headed toward the steps.

Walking into the bedroom with the cake, Jillian spotted Brian holding her laptop with his eyes wide and glued to the screen. He looked up at her and smiled for only a moment before returning to his reading.

She moved to the bed. "What are you doing?"

"Hold on." He motioned to her with a finger without looking at her. "This is really getting good."

She frowned, shaking her head. "You aren't supposed to be reading that."

"You said to read something." He glanced at her. "Are you Anastasia? And am I Brice?"

"Um..." She cocked her head. "Maybe."

"We, I mean they... had a whole lot more fun when they got back from the movies without Anastasia's pesky son, Ryder, there." He smiled, and then returned to the screen.

She cleared her throat, but he again held up his finger. "Really, I'm almost there... or Brice is, anyway." Brian looked at her and winked, then returned to the screen as Jillian sat next to him on the bed.

"Do you like it?" She asked as she used the fork to cut off a bite of cake and put it to his mouth. He smiled at her, opened his mouth, and she slid it in. He savored the taste. "Wow, you nailed the cake. Good job."

"What about the story?"

"It's the best thing I've ever read." Returning to the book, he pointed to the screen. "Is this what we would have done if Rob hadn't been home?"

She focused on the text and read a bit before murmuring, "Uh-huh." Then she sensuously licked the remnants of icing from his fork.

He grabbed her arm as he finished reading a sentence. "This thing with Brice lying on his stomach and Anastasia doing that with his... Is that even possible? It sounds freaking amazing."

"What?"

Squinting, she read for a moment and then nodded. "Victoria says it's possible. She says she's done it, and they always come back for more."

"I'll bet."

Just then, she remembered Victoria. "I've got to run downstairs. Victoria is going to help me convince everyone I have a migraine." She made a strange face. "How's this? Do I look like I have a headache?"

"No, that looks like you have a head injury. Just rub your temple, keep your mouth open slightly, and look like you can't stand bright lights."

"Okay." Nodding, she got to her feet.

He pointed to the screen. "If we're going to do all this tonight, I really need to take a shower or two. I left right from the court."

"Good idea. I'll be right back." She rushed from the room.

Outside the dining room, Jillian took a calming breath. When she entered the room, she followed Brian's instructions and made her way back to her chair with her hand over her eyes, trying to shield the light from her face. Her guests were enjoying tea and remained lost in loud conversation. It was as if no one noticed she had been gone at all. Jillian and Victoria shared a wide-eyed look, and Victoria mouthed, *"THEY WON'T LEAVE!"*

Victoria said loudly, "Oh, Jillian, are you feeling any better?"

Jillian groaned in a labored voice, "No, not really. I'm so sorry about this."

"Well, everybody, I think we should be going, since—" Victoria began.

"What kind of tea is this?" A female guest interrupted, and then turned her attention to Jillian, waiting for a response.

After staring at the woman, dumbfounded, Jillian closed her eyes. Victoria stood, picked up her wineglass, banged the side of it with a fork, and announced, "Jillian has a bad migraine, and she would like it very much if we all left now."

Another female guest came to life. "Oh, I get them also. Do you keep a list of food triggers? I must stay away from onions."

Yet another female guest blurted out, "It's coffee for me and white chocolate. Oh, and tree nuts."

Victoria looked again to Jillian and exhaled deeply. "All right, everybody, get the hell out of here now!"

The guests all froze with their eyes glued to Victoria as she continued, "Jillian has a guy upstairs, a hot sexy guy, and she wants to, for lack of a better phrase, fuck the absolute crap out of him..." The guests focused on Jillian, who had her eyebrows raised, as Victoria wrapped up her speech with, "... all night long. And she wanted all night to start, like, ten minutes ago."

Rolling her eyes, Jillian said to Victoria, "I could've done that, but thanks for your help."

The guests didn't seem offended at all as they started collecting their things and making their way to the foyer. Jillian held the door, and the comments flowed.

"You should have told us sooner."

"We know how long it's been for you."

"This is great news."

When only Victoria and Jillian remained at the open door, Victoria smiled at her. "Any chance of a threesome? I've never had one, but I'm a very giving partner."

"You've never had a threesome?" Jillian gave her a skeptical look.

Victoria shrugged. "Well, not one with just one guy."

Jillian gave her a tired expression. "Get the hell out of here."

Victoria walked out the door, then turned back as Jillian was closing it and said, "Maybe tomorrow ni—"

Jillian leaned with her back against the door, relieved. Rushing to the powder room, she checked her face. She frowned as she looked in the mirror at her semi-frazzled appearance. After pushing her hair around a little, she shrugged, displeased, and then headed up the stairs.

. . .

When Jillian entered the room, she found Brian naked on the bed with his arms behind his head. He smiled at her. "Brice is really talented. He's able to perform three times in Chapter Thirteen alone, I think it was."

She walked over to him, thinking. "Four."

"Wow. Four."

Standing near the bed, she gazed down at his nude body. "I like having you naked in my bed like this. It feels like I hired you, or something."

"To get it four times in one night, you'd better be paying me."

She reached behind her back and unzipped her dress as he watched. She shimmied her shoulders, and the dress tumbled to the floor. Jillian stood before him in a white satin bra and panties set, and his heart skipped two fucking beats.

"You really have the sexiest underwear I've ever seen, and you look spectacular in all of it."

Smiling, she reached to unhook her bra. He held his hand up. "Wait." She gave him an odd look until he added, "Put the dress back on. Let's back up, and I'll show you what I would have done that night we came back from the movies."

She grinned, reached down to the floor, pulled the dress over her shoulders, and zipped it up a little. He got out of bed, stood behind her, and whispered in her ear, "I've been fantasizing a lot about it."

"So have I."

He placed his hands gently on her neck, and electricity shot through her body. His penis quickly responded and pressed into her lower back. Feeling it, she gasped.

He moved his lips close to her neck. "Remember, we were at the door before we were... interrupted."

Closing her eyes, she sighed. "Um-hm."

He took hold of her zipper and pulled it down all the way, as he kissed the side of her neck. She exhaled softly. He slipped his hands under the dress straps on her shoulders and slowly moved them aside until the dress fell to the floor. Returning his lips to her neck, he grasped her bra strap with both hands and expertly released it. He slid his hands around to her breasts and pushed the cups from her chest as he sucked gently on the flesh of her neck. Reaching back, she grabbed his hips, pulling him to her, his hardness pressing between the cheeks of her ass.

He slipped his hands to her panties and pushed them down. He pulled his lips from her neck, backed up a bit, and gazed at her curvy backside. "My God, you have an amazing body!"

Jillian gasped, shimmying her hips until her panties fell to the floor before turning to him. They wrapped their arms around each other and kissed, her mouth opening wide to accept his tongue. Their bodies pressed together with his erection slipping down between her legs. He brought his hands to her breasts as she took hold of his engorged penis with both hands.

Pulling away from him, she slid onto the bed. She moved to the middle and lay down; he joined her, kneeling between her spread legs. He leaned his head down to her and kissed her full on the mouth. She pulled him down until his hard, naked body was covering her. Wrapping her legs around him, she drew him even closer as he moved to kiss her breasts. He took a nipple into his mouth as she leaned her head back, breathless. She wrapped her arms around him and caressed his neck as he sucked hard on one nipple, then slowly moved to the other.

Tilting her head toward him, she began, "This feels great, but if you don't put it inside me soon, I'm going to..."

He looked up at her and smiled. He slid up and held his erection with one hand as he guided it to her swollen, wet entrance. Putting her mouth to his neck, she kissed him. She gently sucked in his flesh as he pushed down slightly and slowly slid inside her. She stared up at the ceiling, her eyes wide, as she softly gasped.

Pulling his head up, he moaned. She met his gaze, and they stared into each other's eyes as he pressed harder, slipping his length fully inside her.

He held still while catching his breath for a moment. "Why the hell did we wait?"

She shook her head with a grin, held his hips, then slipped her hand around to his ass, and ran her finger gently at the top of the crease. "You feel so good."

Brian smiled at her. "So do you."

She wrapped her legs around him tighter as he pulled back then began to pump in her slowly. They kissed again as Jillian spread her legs wide and held them up in the air as he continued passionately making love to her. Angling her hips downward, she adjusted her position until his erection was stimulating her in just the right place. She opened her mouth wide and slammed her eyes shut as he rhythmically pumped into her.

Reaching down, she grasped his shaft, guiding it into her harder. He got the message and lifted up on his toes as he drove into her faster. They looked into each other's eyes and were one. Focusing all his energy, he flexed his muscles, collapsing onto her, his erection pressing deep inside her, his girth filling her fully. Gasping, she exploded with a giant orgasm.

She wrapped her arms and legs around him. They held there a moment until he began to move slowly inside of her. Releasing her hold of him, he pumped faster and faster. He strained then came hard, yelling out loud. He pumped twice more, pushed into her as far as he could, then slumped on her, desperate to catch his breath.

· · ·

For the next few hours, they performed all the acts outlined in Chapters twelve through fourteen. When they finally fell asleep, it was just after 4:00 a.m. A few hours later, she woke him to execute one of the two acts described in Chapter Sixteen, and they followed the manuscript, more or less. For the first time in her life, Jillian's imagination came to life, and it was actually better than it read on the page.

Chapter Thirty-Eight

When Jillian woke on Saturday morning, Brian was still asleep. After showering, she put on a short, silky robe, went downstairs, and prepared a fabulous breakfast for him. When she entered the bedroom forty minutes later with the tray, she found him reading from her laptop again. She rolled her eyes, grinned, and placed the tray on the bed.

He closed the computer and then put it down. "Anastasia is really a naughty girl."

"She can be."

Gazing down at the plate of pancakes, he rubbed his hands together. "I'm starving. Those look good."

"I've been following your advice." Jillian got onto the bed.

They both knelt on either side of the tray and began to eat. After taking a bite, he nodded to her with a smile. "And Brice, I mean, me... I'm, like, amazing in bed. I can evidently go all night."

"Remember, it's just a novel."

"But it *is* based on the truth."

"Loosely," she joked.

He looked at her with a curious expression. "I'm in Chapter Twenty, and Anastasia's having what some people call... "backdoor" with Brice, and it's really hot. Is only Anastasia into that or are... you, as well?"

"Oh, that's just her." Jillian replied matter-of-factly, and she took another bite of pancake.

"You might want to reconsider. I've had a lot of requests for that lately. Evidently, a number of women think it's an area of my expertise, so..." He forced a mock smug expression.

Scoffing, she wrinkled her nose. "How many women are we talking about?"

"Let me think." He tapped his chin.

"Okay." She rolled her eyes. "It's that many?"

"Well, I don't want to brag or anything, but that would be a total of three in just the last week."

"Really?"

He looked to the ceiling, thinking, and then glanced back at her. "No, I lied..."

"I thought so." She nodded while holding back a laugh.

"It's been about ten days."

After looking away with her mouth wide open, she returned to him. "So you're saying... you're like an anal sex magnet?" She gazed at him, awaiting his response.

He finished a mouthful of pancake while holding a finger up and nodding. "I don't want to necessarily paint myself with that brush, but you could call me that."

Covering her mouth with her hand, she looked away, grinning, before settling her eyes back on him, her curiosity piqued. "Okay, I've got to know... who are the three?"

He sat up straight, lifted his hand to count them off, and began, "First, there was Laura." He touched his thumb.

"Rob's girlfriend?" Putting down her fork, Jillian leaned back against the footboard. *This is getting interesting!* she thought.

"Yeah. They were fighting. She wanted to use me for *that* to get back at him." He gave her a defensive look. "But it still counts."

"Then there was Victoria when I picked up the key." He touched his second finger.

"She asked you for it... really?" Crossing her arms, she shook her head.

"Victoria said when I returned the key, she would take me *around the world*. I didn't even know what the hell that meant until I Googled it. She's a bad girl but fun."

She nodded casually. "So, that's definitely number two. And, uh, three?"

After glancing at the ceiling while seemingly trying to decide the best way to share the story, he gave her a hesitant look. "Have you ever heard of a 'technical virgin'?"

She gave him a confused look. "No, what's that?"

"Let me finish one last bite before I tell you." He devoured a forkful before sitting back against the headboard. "It's a woman who remains a virgin by never having vaginal sex and only having the other kinds, including the frisky Anastasia's favorite act."

He raised his eyebrows as she returned a sour look. "That's makes no sense."

"It doesn't, but evidently, it still counts. Natalie considers herself still a virgin, even though four guys—and counting—have had intimate experiences with her... um, backside."

Looking at him as if she smelled something foul, she widened her eyes. "Wow, she *is* nuts."

"So, I'm just saying... I've had requests. I guess you could say, there's a waiting list of sorts. I could add your name now... but if not, I can't guarantee your spot." Brian held his head high while somehow maintaining a straight face. "The list could grow."

"I'll take my chances." Jillian rolled her eyes. "What makes you such an expert in this area anyway? I mean how many times have you done it?"

"Never. But the women must see something in me." She held back a laugh as he continued, "How about this—in case you change your mind in the future, let me check you out down there, just to make sure you qualify."

Getting out of bed, he stood in front of her feet.

"Qualify?" She stared up at him, perplexed.

He moved the tray to the floor and grabbed her feet. "Turn over." She looked at him suspiciously, and he added, "It's okay. I'm a doctor."

After lying back against the bed, she flipped over. He dropped down onto the bed between her legs. "It's really more of a trade school certification than a Ph.D." He grabbed the bottom of her robe and flipped it up out of the way, exposing her gorgeous, naked ass. "Wow, weren't you getting a draft this morning?"

"Not really." She shook her head with a grin.

Studying her from that angle, he smiled. "Have you ever considered doing any ass modeling?"

Jillian scoffed.

He continued, "Or stunt ass work for, like, an A-list movie star."

"No," she giggled.

"Because your ass is spectacular. Let's say they wanted Sandra Bullock to do a shower scene, and she had a thing about showing her ass... you could totally fill in for her."

"I hear she does her own ass work."

"Well, if she ever stops..."

Resting her head on the mattress, she smiled widely.

He shook his head in admiration. "It's really breathtaking... But wait—that's interesting."

"What's that?" she asked.

"I'm not 100 percent sure, but your parts look like they might be a little too close together. Has your primary care doctor or gynecologist ever mentioned anything about—"

"No!" she shrieked loudly breaking into a laugh.

"Well, maybe you should have that checked out next time you're, uh—"

"Are you done yet?" she interrupted.

"Not even close. Has anyone ever spent any real quality time getting to know you back here?"

"No. No one has." She wiggled her hips, then turned on her side, looking back at him.

"Please be still. I'm not done with you yet." He frowned.

"You're not?"

"Nope." He ran his hands slowly up her thighs then massaged the cheeks of her rear. She settled back down flat, melting with his touch.

"That feels really good." She purred.

"So you really don't know if incorporating any of this type of... *play* into your activities is something that you might be interested in at all?"

She replied softly, unconvincingly, "I already know that it's not something that I'd be—"

The second his lips touched the back of her knee, she stopped talking. After placing a gentle kiss there, he pulled up. "You smell amazing. What is that?"

"It's a body wash called Moonlight Path. I took a shower this morning while you were still unconscious."

Drinking in her scent, he crawled up her body, kissing along the back of her thigh. "That's a great name, since that just happens to be the path I'm on next."

She picked her head up from the mattress, thinking. Once she finally got his moon reference, she smiled and lay her head back down.

He leaned in and gently kissed her right ass cheek near her hip, and a bolt of electricity shot through her body. She shuddered a bit. "That tickles."

He said slowly, "Have you..." then gently kissed her left cheek, "ever wondered..." then back to the right, a little closer to her cleft, "what it might be..." then left again, still closer, "...like to have..." then right, still closer to her sensitive crease.

Jillian closed her eyes, opened her mouth in pure ecstasy as she gripped the comforter with both hands, and lifted her hips off the bed toward him.

He kissed her more gently just on the inside of her cheek. "...someone kiss you..." He moved to the other side, and his lips barely touched her as he finished with, "...here?"

She exhaled deeply with her rear end raised up slightly more off the bed. Lifting his head, he took in the sight of her. Her closed eyes, open mouth and her intense grip on the comforter made it clear she was thoroughly enjoying his attention.

He asked, "Have you?"

She said slowly in the sexiest voice ever, "No, that's... not, uh... Should you really be doing that?"

His eyes traveled down her body, stopping at her hips, which still held her position, seemingly begging for his kiss. "I could literally stare at you for hours like this."

She replied softly and as if she didn't believe it at all, "Then there's something wrong with you."

He moved his head back to her. Jillian's pulse quickened as he kissed her again on either side of her sensitive bottom. The tingles flowed all over her body with each gentle brushing of his lips.

Tilting his chin up, he whispered, "If you don't like this, maybe I should stop."

"Don't you dare."

Brian spent the next twenty minutes pampering Jillian and giving her an experience she would use later to expand Chapter nineteen. After that, they attempted to move onto activities they had just discussed, specifically Natalie's favorite act, and it didn't go well at all. Inexperience, nervousness, incorrect angling, and quite possibly improper preparation all led to a mini-disaster. Following the failed endeavor, they bathed together, and then returned to the bedroom and activities that were a little more in their comfort zone. As they relaxed in bed, glowing in post-coital ecstasy, they both agreed, that sometimes you just gotta stick with what works. *Well, at least until they knew each other a little better at least.*

They didn't hit a single tennis ball that weekend, but Brian did read the first draft of the unfinished novel. Jillian had written just up to the point where Brice left to return to college at the end of Spring Break.

Early on Sunday, Jillian walked Brian to his car. He wore the same outfit as when he arrived. They stood together by his open door, him not wanting to leave and her not wanting to let him go. He frowned. "I probably should have brought my books then I could have stayed a little later... Some clothes would have been nice, too, a toothbrush, even... anything, really."

She smiled. "I was thinking of coming to Atlanta the first week of April."

"I've got exams coming up, but I can drive down some weekend." He added slowly with his eyes bugged out, "It's. Only. Nine. Hours."

They shared a chuckle. Widening his eyes, he gave her a suggestive look. "Maybe when I come back, we can *not* play tennis again. This is so much more fun."

Chapter Thirty-Nine

For the next two months, Jillian and Brian saw each other only four times. Twice he flew into Miami, and twice she made her way to Atlanta, where they spent the weekend at a hotel ordering room service, playing a little tennis, and spending a lot of time in bed. Falling for him, she thought about what might happen after he graduated—about how they should probably stop seeing each other soon. There were a million issues such as the age difference, Rob, and the fact that Brian had a job a thousand miles away from her. Any of these could force them to end it, anyway— collectively it was a steep mountain to climb. But the more time she spent with him, the harder it became to talk to him about it all. She decided she would see him once more after graduation, and that would be the end of their relationship.

Reflecting on her failed marriage to George, Jillian considered all the things she might have done differently. During one quiet evening, she called her ex-husband for the first time since the divorce. She told him that she didn't hold him completely responsible for their breakup, admitting that part of it was her fault, saying that back then, she knew they were growing apart, and yet she did nothing to try to stop it. She told him she still thought he was an ass for cheating on her at the house, but she just wanted him to know that she shared some of the blame.

Two weeks before graduation, she had a surprise for Brian. She instructed him to go to the Atlanta airport on Friday morning and pick up a ticket for a flight. She would fly out from Miami and meet him at their destination airport. After informing him that he would return on a flight Sunday afternoon, she provided no other details.

Jillian's plane landed in Phoenix an hour late, so Brian met her at the gate. She had arranged that a driver from a car service would be waiting to take them to Scottsdale in a black town car. As they approached the resort, Brian recognized it from an article he'd read on tennis resort vacations.

Staring out at the hotel, he beamed. "No way, we're staying at the Phoenician?"

"I booked the Center Court Tennis Package."

"They have that Wimbledon Championship grass court. I read about it. I always wanted to play on grass."

The car dropped them off, and as they rushed to the front desk with their carry-on bags, she said, "I could only get the court today at four. It was booked up the rest of the weekend."

Brian checked the time on his phone. "We have ten minutes. If we change quickly, we can make it."

After checking in, they hurried to the room, arriving exactly at four. Once inside, they placed their bags on the bed, opened them, and began frantically pulling off clothing.

"I'm going to beat you on grass," he quipped as he pulled off his shirt. "I'll be diving all over the court, and I won't get a scratch. You won't be able to pass me."

She scoffed. "You *will* be on the grass a lot. But you'll be looking behind you at the ball."

She was down to just her panties, and he was in only boxer briefs when he made the critical mistake of looking at her. There she stood, tossing items from her suitcase, in search of her sports bra, with her gorgeous, uncovered breasts just steps away from him. Standing frozen, breathlessly watching her, he didn't make any attempt to find his clothes.

She located the bra. "Found it."

As she prepared to put it on, she noticed him staring and not getting dressed. Glancing at Brian in his underwear, she was sidetracked a little herself. "What are you—"

Before she could get the question out, he rushed to her, wrapped his arms around her, and their mouths flew open wide as they kissed.

Almost an hour later, Jillian rested blissfully with her head on Brian's stomach, as she lay perpendicular to him, gazing up at his face. "That was amazing."

"I might have been able to make it to the court if you'd found your bra quicker. I saw your, uh, and I couldn't—"

"I thought about wearing it on the plane."

Nodding in agreement, he smiled at her. "You know, it was pretty presumptuous of you to think you could just whisk me away to this fancy hotel and rush me right out to the court. I'm not your tennis whore, you know. I need to be wined and dined and... other things... first."

She bit her lip, fighting back a laugh. "Well, you got your *other* things."

"Yeah, but you didn't plan it that way. Sometimes I think you take me for granted." He looked away from her, mock-standoffishly.

After pausing a moment, she started, "Maybe..." She covered her mouth to stop a laugh and cleared her throat to compose herself. "Maybe I'll buy you something really nice later. Will that—"

"Like what?" He looked back at her, unconvinced.

Flipping over, she slid next to him with her head on his chest. "How about something new to wear on the court? A new pair of shorts, maybe?"

He gave her a pursed lip nod as if that wasn't going to cut it. She kissed his chest and then looked at him. "We could have a light dinner first..." She kissed her way up to his neck. "Then maybe you could put on your new shorts, and we could go to one of the tennis courts." After kissing him on the lips, she added, "... not the grass court, but one of the others, and then we could just see what happens."

"Okay," he grumbled.

They both held serious faces for a moment, but then became all smiles. She grinned. "When did you come up with this bit?"

"In the lobby. I was going to use it on the court, but it worked here, too, with a new opening. It was killing me to wait... It was a play on the whole thing. You know, if I was the woman, and you were the man and—"

"No, I get it, very clever." She shot him an arrogant look. "I think I played my part well."

"Oh, yeah, you were great. Do you think if people heard us, with our constant pseudo-sexual-slash-tennis banter, they would want to kill us?"

"Definitely. After five minutes, they would beat us to death with our own racquets," she replied with a casual nod.

"Personally, I love us," he said a little sarcastically.

"Oh, so do I. We are a lot of fun."

He looked at her with a grin. "So, can I get those shorts now?"

Rolling her eyes, she pushed away from him and slipped out of bed. He tilted his head, and with his gaze glued to her shapely naked ass, he watched her disappear into the bathroom.

Jillian called her editor, who somehow pulled the right string and was able to secure a special after hours slot on the grass court for them the next day. The blissfully, happy couple had a great match that he, in fact, did win. They spent the rest of the time eating, drinking, playing tennis on the hard courts, and having amazing sex.

Jillian's plane was scheduled to depart before Brian's, so he waited with her at her gate. When her section was called to board, they shared a long goodbye kiss. Afterward, she pulled away, gazed into his eyes and smiled. "I have a big thing planned for you for after graduation. I can't wait... I've been working on it for weeks."

Narrowing his eyes, he gave her an intrigued look. "Don't ruin it... I can stay until June 6th. I don't have to report to the bank until Tuesday now."

Her smile faded a little when she was reminded they would see each other for only a week before he had to start work. Together they walked to the empty gate. After handing her ticket to the agent, she turned to him with her smile only a faint memory. "Goodbye."

He gave her a quick kiss and smiled. "Hey, when you finally finish the book, e-mail me the last chapters. I'm dying to find out how it ends."

Nodding slightly with her expression unreadable, she

turned and then rushed away before he could see her tears. As she walked into the tunnel, she softly said, "Me, too."

As her plane took off, Jillian fought to hold back her emotions while thinking about Brian and their fabulous weekend together. She stared blankly out the window as the jet soared through the wispy clouds set against the backdrop of the azure blue sky. She took a deep breath and closed her eyes for a moment. She shook her head with determination then grabbed her computer from her bag. Opening her laptop, she typed the ending to their story with the tears sliding down her cheeks.

Chapter Forty

At the graduation for the Georgia State University Class of 2011, Jillian had two men to be proud of, her son, for whom she could openly celebrate, and Brian, for whom she had to cheer secretly. She saw Brian alone for only a few minutes during the couple of days she was in Atlanta. Brian's parents and younger brother, Jim, also attended, and the two families went to dinner together after the ceremony. Outside the restroom, Jillian and Brian shared some words and a quick kiss, but only on the cheek, which was within the F.W.P.B. rules. Back at the table, Jillian proposed a toast, which she prepared for the two new graduates.

She smiled. "I'm so proud of you, Rob. You've grown into a responsible, caring, and motivated young man, and Brian, although, I've only known you a couple of months, I feel, um..." She began to get choked up and her lip quivered as everyone at the table looked on. They all appeared touched by her emotion. After taking a sip of water, she started again, "Sorry. My baby boy is now a college graduate and it... um... I can't explain it..."

Rob rolled his eyes, and Laura squeezed his knee under the table.

Jillian sniffled. "Anyway, good luck to you both, and I kind of stole this off the Internet, so don't hate me... I'm a writer, and I should be able to come up with this stuff on my own, but this was so good I had to use it."

She held the note card with one hand and her wineglass in the other as everyone lifted his or her glass. "I hope your dreams take you to the corners of your imagination, to the highest of your hopes, to the windows of your opportunities, and to the most special places your heart..." She covered her mouth for a moment then struggled to finish. "... has ever longed... for."

Both of Brian's parents and his brother were tearing up a little, along with Jillian, Laura, and even Jillian's cheating bastard of an ex-husband, George. They lifted their glasses, all said cheers, and took a sip.

After pausing to collect herself a bit, she added, "I did change, like, three words in that, it was pretty perfect already, but I kind of had to make it my own."

Jillian and Brian shared a glance and a knowing smile. She noticed that he seemed to be fighting back his own tears. She wondered how much of her emotional reaction to this graduation she could attribute to her son growing up versus her coming to terms with the likely end of her relationship with Brian. She already felt bad enough and decided that was an area best left unexplored. She felt horrible that she had put herself in this position to begin with. But she thought if she could go back, she wouldn't have changed a thing.

With all that was going on, Jillian and Brian didn't get a chance to spend much time together that night either. The next day, as Brian drove back to Delaware with his parents, Jillian returned to Miami with her son.

Chapter Forty-One

A week later, Jillian picked up Brian from the airport. On the way to her house, they spoke about how she had sent Rob and Laura on the longest cruise she could find. Discovering an eleven-day cruise to the Caribbean, which set sail on the exact day of Brian's arrival, was a blessing for her, if not one hell of a graduation gift for her son. Neither said much else during the short drive, although Jillian did comment on the mustache that Brian had grown since graduation. It looked ridiculous on him, but she told him she liked it. She reminded him that she had that belated graduation present for him, and he told her he had a surprise for her, as well.

When they arrived back at the house, they went up to the bedroom. After tossing his bag on the floor, he grabbed her. "I missed you."

They kissed, and it grew heated as they began groping each other as if they hadn't seen each other in months. Placing her hands on his chest, she pulled back from him a little, flustered. "Me, too, but, uh, let's save this for later, after my surprise."

"Yeah, I'd like to wait until later also." He widened his eyes as he took a step back from her, trying to regain his composure.

She shrugged. "So, what should we do?"

After sharing a knowing look, he grinned. "Do you want to hit some?"

She ripped her shirt off, as did he...

It was late in the day and the sun was blaring onto the court at an annoying angle. They both wore sunglasses to fight it off, especially while serving. Jillian won the first set, and Brian took the second. The third set was tied six-all, and they went into a tiebreak.

After a quick rest and drink at the bench, he stood and pulled off his wet shirt to change it. She walked to the baseline as he picked up a new shirt. After pausing to think, he grinned, deciding to go bare-chested. He walked back to his side of the court.

When she saw his half-nude body, she made a face. "That's not fair. I'll be distracted."

"This," he began by motioning with his hand up and down his chest. "This is going to distract you?"

"It might."

"Take your shirt and bra off then. We'll be even-steven, as you say." Placing his hands on his hips, he wore a smarmy smile.

She returned a scowl. "You know I can't play like that. They'd get in the way."

"Not my problem. Just serve, and stop whining."

She was a little distracted by his sweaty muscular body, and he was up four–two in the tiebreak when they returned to the bench to get a drink and switch sides. As he walked back into position, she secretly stripped off her panties and tossed them into her bag. While walking to the baseline, she wore an evil grin.

He gave her a suspicious look. "What are you smiling about? You're three points from losing this."

"Nothing." She batted her eyes at him before turning away coolly. He shook his head, obviously now even more perplexed.

She walked back to retrieve a ball, put her legs together, bent over way too much, and flashed her naked ass to him.

He froze, gaping at the sight of her. "Are you wearing a thong? That is not cool."

"I might be," she teased.

"Maybe I'll just pull *it* out right here. How would you like that?"

"That would be against U.S.T.A. rules, and you would automatically forfeit the match."

"And a thong is not against the rules?"

"No, it's not." She stared back at him with her head held high.

He was obviously distracted while she played some focused tennis, winning four straight points and going up six–four. Smiling in preparation of her next ploy, she was just one point from victory. A ball sat on his side of the net, and he began walking to retrieve it. She held up her hand. "I'll get it. You'll need all your energy."

He watched with his brow furrowed, as she walked all the way to his side and knelt down to pick up the ball. After pulling her sunglasses off, she lifted her skirt up in the front and used it to wipe off her lenses. This exposed her fabulously trimmed female parts, which were just twenty-feet from him. He had an unobstructed view of her as she wiped the glasses for nearly ten unnecessary seconds.

Stunned, he watched as she dropped the hem of her skirt and walked slowly over to him.

She got close and said softly, "When your shirt was wet, you took it off..." Running her index finger slowly down his sweaty chest to his belly button, she smiled. "My underwear was soaked, so I did the same."

He stammered with his voice cracking, "This... uh... isn't fair."

She parted her lips as she moved within an inch of his face. "Good..." Leaning in, she gave him a passionate kiss while pressing her body into his. When she pulled back from him, Jillian finished her sentiment, "... luck." She turned and headed back to her side of the court, leaving him breathing heavily and uncomfortably adjusting his shorts.

Brian's voice cracked again as he shot back, "You're going down."

As Jillian passed the net, she yelled back, "I won't be now, and I certainly won't be later."

After processing this for a second, he gave her a pathetic look. "Really?"

She retrieved her racket and smiled. "Just kidding." She bounced the ball, prepared to serve, and then said confidently, "Match point."

"Bring it," he said as he continued to grimace and fight with his shorts.

She hit a solid serve to his forehand, but it was clearly playable. Grinning, he took a huge backswing to really nail it but swung badly. The ball hit off the side of the racquet frame, launched high into the air, and headed the wrong way.

They both watched as it traveled, almost in slow motion, out of the court and into the pool. He exhaled, defeated; she made a fist with her right hand in celebration, and they both headed to the net.

When they reached the net, she grinned. He gave her a frown and said while trying to maintain a straight face, "I'm going to check the rule book on that whole production. There's got to be some violation there." After shaking hands, they walked toward the bench.

He sat down as she tossed her racquet into the bag. Pausing a moment, gazing at his shirtless, sweaty body, she wanted him now and badly. He put his head down as he struggled to catch his breath. She looked him over once more and then glanced toward the pool. A smile spread over her face as she turned and headed off the court, pulling off her shirt and bra along the way. Looking up, he watched her with surprise. She stood still as she slipped off her skirt, stepped out of it, and then bent over sexily to remove her shoes and socks. He continued staring, mesmerized. She never looked back as she made her way to the water and dove in. Bending over, he fought to remove his shoes and sweaty socks. Then he shot up from the bench, ripped down his shorts and underwear and rushed to the pool.

When he reached the edge, Jillian was floating on a giant ring with her legs spread as she looked up at him, grinning. "I've always wanted to try something."

Smiling, he dove into the pool and swam underwater until he reached her. He came up inside the ring float, between her spread legs and took a quick breath. He extended his tongue between her legs, which left her gasping and holding onto the float for dear life. After exploring her for a few seconds, Brian came up for air. "Is this what you wanted to try?"

"It is. How'd you—"

"I read about it in Chapter One."

She frowned slightly. "No more talking."

He went back to work, and after about seven minutes of focused effort, she experienced a mind-blowing orgasm. After switching places, she happily returned the favor. When she was finally finished with him, she left him exhausted and panting as if he'd run a mile.

After recovering enough to speak, he said, "Wow. That was a great graduation present."

She shook her head a moment and grinned. "That wasn't it."

Chapter Forty-Two

Ten minutes later, Jillian and Brian were floating naked on large rafts in the pool. The gentle motion of the water, along with the exhaustion from both the tennis and the sex, had rocked them to sleep. Standing at the edge of the pool, Victoria stared down at them, grinning. She studied Brian's body for a moment before clearing her throat. "I can't believe you two are naked in the pool again."

The nude pair both awoke, startled. He lifted his head to Victoria groggily and instinctively covered his penis with his hands.

Flipping off her raft into the pool, Jillian turned to face Victoria. "What the hell are you doing here?"

Victoria smiled. "I came to borrow that little black dress. I have a date tonight with my neighbor." Then she glanced back at Brian and raised an eyebrow. "Nice penis, Bri."

Brian turned to Jillian, and then looked sheepishly at Victoria. "Thanks... again."

"Don't you knock?" Jillian asked.

"I did, but no one answered. So I used my key. I really need that dress."

Jillian swam over to the edge of the pool. Brian slipped off the raft into the water and joined her. They both looked up at Victoria as she sat down in a lounge chair.

Sighing, Jillian shook her head. "You can borrow it, but next time call first. If you had walked in here ten minutes earlier..."

"Oh, it would have been okay, because I've decided to become a sex therapist."

Jillian gave her a skeptical look.

"I'm going back to school. I only need fifteen credits to earn my master's degree. The University of Miami offers a program in marriage and family therapy. I'll be concentrating in sex therapy, of course."

"Of course." Jillian nodded. "That makes sense. You've been practicing unofficially for years."

Victoria cocked her head wearing a big smile. "It combines my two favorite things."

Holding back a laugh, Brian just had to ask, "What's that?"

"Sex and hot college guys."

Jillian and Brian both returned a matter-of-fact nod.

"I registered today. I'm taking one summer class and then a full load starting in the middle of August. I could give you two some pointers if you wanted to start up again. I could judge your technique and see if there's—"

"No, that's okay," Jillian interrupted. "I think we have it."

"I'll just tell you that you need to be careful in the water, because the natural lubricants in the body are water soluble, so prolonged intercourse in the pool can lead to irritation."

Jillian chuckled. "We'll keep that in mind."

Jillian made eyes at Brian as if to say, *I wish she would leave already!*

Victoria's face lit up as she asked Brian, "So, how'd you like your surprise? When she showed me, I was blown—"

"Victoria!" Jillian interrupted. "We haven't gotten to it yet."

"Sorry, I guess you've been too busy fucking in the pool."

Widening her eyes, Jillian motioned to her with her hand. "Well, thanks for stopping by."

Brian placed his hand to his chin. "So, it's something you show me. I wonder what..."

Victoria stood up and then headed for the door. Jillian called out, "That dress is on the left side of my closet. Don't... uh... get anything on it. If you know what I mean."

She turned back. "Oh, I think I'm going to take this one slow. He seems like a really good guy. Mature, hot, and just... perfect."

Jillian chuckled. "So does that mean you'll wait until after dinner to have sex with him?"

After glaring at her a moment in mock anger, Victoria smiled. "No, I mean I'm going to wait for a couple weeks, at least. I don't want him to think I'm just some big slut, or something. If this works out, I might give monogamy a try."

"You should," Jillian began. Then she looked at Brian, completely smitten. "Monogamy can be pretty amazing."

He took her in his arms, and they kissed, as Victoria looked on, grinning. "You two kids are so adorable."

Jillian turned away as she felt her emotions getting the best of her. Brian looked up at Victoria and smiled, but as the awkward moment lingered too long, he gave her a tired look.

"Okay, okay. I'm going." Victoria headed into the house as Jillian squeezed the bridge of her nose to fight back her tears.

After Victoria was gone, he pushed back from the edge and floated on his back. "What are the chances that she doesn't sleep with this guy tonight?"

After putting on a smile, Jillian swam toward him. "I hate to say it, but if he's as attractive as she says, I'd be surprised if she kept her clothes on much past the appetizers."

He nodded in agreement and slipped under the water for a moment before coming back up to find her treading water right next to him. He placed his hands on her shoulders. "So, what's the surprise? I can't wait."

Pushing him away, she swam to the other side of the pool. He watched as her back side rose out of the water right before him. He remained simply staring at it with his mouth wide open until it disappeared when she descended underwater. When she reached the edge of the pool, she climbed out, grabbed a towel, and began drying off.

"Come on. How about one hint?"

Turning back toward him, she gave him an evil grin. "You're just going to have to wait."

Chapter Forty-Three

After a shower, Jillian prepared a quick, light meal, and then they took a walk together to let their food settle. When they returned, she announced that it was time. She had him wait in the study while she went into the workout room. Brian found it a little odd that she would go into that room for his surprise, but at the same time, he was intrigued.

A few minutes later, she called his name, and he hurried to the room. Stepping through the doorway, he found her completely naked and in the famous Natalie-esque *leg thing* position. She stood on the ball of her left foot, and her right leg pointed straight up to the ceiling. Her right elbow rested against her right knee, her forearm ran along her leg, with her hand holding her ankle. In her left hand, she held a strap that came down from the ceiling for support and placed that hand over her right one.

Moving closer and seeing her in that position, his eyes shot wide open, as did his mustache-covered mouth. Blindly feeling for the weight bench and unable to tear his eyes from her, he finally found it and plopped down. "I can't believe you learned how to do the leg thing for me!"

"The proper name for this position is développé leg devant à la derrière."

He nodded quickly. "That name sounds better." Tilting his head, he gazed at her from a different angle. "How did you, uh—"

"I told you, I was a gymnast in middle school, and I worked a little with a coach for the last six weeks. It took a lot of practice, but it's been worth it. I'm so much more flexible now."

He straightened his head and then swallowed hard. "More flexible?" Looking away for a moment, he thought about the positions they had already explored together, he smiled dreamily.

He turned his attention back to her. "You look incredible." Motioning to her womanly parts, he wore a giddy smile. "I can see everything, and it's... wow... You look... there's not a word strong enough for how you look. I could watch you do this for hours."

Her body trembled slightly and her voice quivered as she said, "I can only hold it for, like, three minutes."

"Natalie said she could do it for thirty," he said with a smirk.

"Don't forget... Natalie lies." The grimace on her face grew with every passing second.

"Good point."

He looked up at the ceiling, noticed the strap, and then smiled. "Don't you think the strap is cheating a little?"

"Do you want me to do this or not?" Glancing at him, she frowned. "I'd like to see you do this naked, strap or not."

After obviously both processing the image of a nude Brian in that position, they cringed and said in unison, "Probably not."

"God, you look amazing!" He got up and walked over to her. Sliding in close, he tried to size up all the sexual possibilities while she was in that position. "I wonder if we could really do it like this."

"I've been thinking about it a lot, too, but if I don't put my leg back down, it's going to snap off."

He took a step back, then gently helped her return the leg to the floor. Slumping down, she scowled in pain while rubbing the muscle in her thigh. She straightened up, took a deep breath, and smiled. "Now, what's your surprise?"

He held his chin as he eyed her naked body, torn. "As much as I hate to say this, I really think you should be dressed for mine."

"Thank God. So it's not sex related."

"What, you don't want to do it again?"

"I do, but before we do..." She glanced hesitantly at him. "I hate the mustache. Shave it, please. You look ridiculous."

"You're kidding." After scoffing, he studied himself in the wall of mirrors. "I think I look older, maybe even thirty."

"You look like a seventies porn star." Shaking her head, she slipped on her underwear.

He sat back on the bench and watched her get dressed. "You know, watching you put on clothes is almost as much fun as watching you take them off. It was hot the way you shimmied that skirt back on."

When she was fully dressed, she checked herself in the mirror. After making some final adjustments to the skirt, she bounced up and down eagerly on her heels. "Now, what's the surprise?"

"Not here." Standing up, he motioned for her to follow as he headed out of the room.

He led her out to the pool area, where he had candles, glasses, and a bottle of champagne on ice waiting for them by the lounge chairs.

"When did you have a chance to set this up?" She gazed at the setup, blown away.

"While you were making dinner."

Holding her hand, he guided her to a chair. He lit the candles, opened and poured the champagne, and then handed her a glass. They each took a sip and placed the glasses on the table.

"So, what is it? Do you want to have sex right here or something?"

"Maybe later." He drew in a long breath and let it out slowly. "Okay, my company has a permanent position open in Miami, and once I get through the management program, they said it's mine if I want it."

"Do you want it?"

"It depends."

Getting down on one knee in front of her, he pulled a box from his pocket. She looked at him, holding her breath. He stared into her eyes. "I know I'm young, and I don't really know exactly what I want to do with the rest of my life... career wise or anything." Studying her face, he noticed he was losing her a little. "Sorry, I mean, I do know that I want to spend every minute I can with you. From the first moment I saw you right here on this chair and... then we spoke for, like, an hour on the tennis court... talking about the damn court surface," he added, rolling his eyes. He grabbed her hand, and they shared a smile as he continued, "I knew then I was falling for you. I'm absolutely head-over-heels, can't-stand-to-be-away-from-you in love, and I don't care who knows it. You are more alive and fun to be with than any of those young college women I've ever met."

He opened the box and displayed the gorgeous one-carat diamond ring. Her eyes lit up as she gazed at it. He pulled it from the box. "Jillian Grayson, will you marry me?" Smiling at her with hopeful eyes, he slipped the ring on her finger.

She gave him a hesitant look. "But I'm old enough to be your mother."

Slipping back to his chair, he did some quick calculations in his head. "You're still only thirty-nine right?"

"Yeah."

"So, maybe if you were sexually active when you were, like, twelve, which for both our sakes, I'm hoping you weren't."

She looked at him, confused. "What do you mean? I'm not a math expert or anything, but aren't you only twenty-one?"

He scoffed. "I turned twenty-six in January."

After trying to process this, she shook her head. "You and Rob both got fake IDs together."

"We did... I really didn't need it," he said sheepishly.

She shook her head, even more confused.

"Wait, I can explain. I have a late birthday, and I was held back a year because of some learning delay. After high school, I kind of fooled around a little before I started college."

She still didn't appear satisfied, so he added, "Look, I was a twenty-two-year-old freshman, and I didn't want anyone to think I was a giant loser, so I kinda lied about my age."

"And the fake ID?" she asked.

"Just part of the cover-up."

She said, "You have to be the only person on the planet with a fake ID that says he's younger."

After conceding with his eyes that it was completely ridiculous, he lifted his hands and opened his palms to her. "So, I'm, like, thirteen years younger. If you round it down, it's, like, ten."

Smiling at him, she seemed to warm to the idea a little. "But what about Rob? Do you think he would be scarred for life, or anything?"

"Don't you think he'll be a little more than understanding, since he had sex with Natalie and pretty much stole her away from me behind my back? I mean, what could he say?"

She fell back in her chair, shocked. "Rob slept with Natalie?

'Leg thing' Natalie?" Turning her head toward him, she stared, gape-mouthed.

"He didn't tell you that?"

"No, I'm learning all kinds of things today." She looked off toward the pool, trying to take it all in. Returning her gaze to Brian, she made a sour face. "'Technical virgin' Natalie?"

He nodded, and they sat together, staring at the pool for an awkward moment.

He turned to her. "Wait, did you give me an... Did you answer my question?"

"Um..." She met his gaze, sucking her lower lip between her teeth. "Sorry, I was just... I think I—"

"Wait, I know." He put on a bright smile. "How about I play you for it tomorrow? I win, and you marry me. You win, and I'll just be your sex slave for, like, the next fifty years or so."

"Either way, that sounds like you win." After pondering letting fate or their tennis skills decide, her worry melted away into a smile. "Okay, I'll take that bet, but only if you shave the mustache first."

Moving to her chair, he leaned over and kissed her.

The kiss lasted only a moment before she turned away, giggling. "Could you shave it now? It's just..." She rubbed the top of her lip, trying not to laugh.

He pulled back from her rolling his eyes. "All right."

Chapter Forty-Four

O ver at the Wilde residence, Victoria and her hunky neighbor, John, were making out furiously on the sofa. Controlling herself perfectly during dinner, Victoria didn't think about sex at all until she was about to serve dessert. That's when she found out that John was the head football coach at the university. He invited her to visit his office on campus. When she discovered his office connected to the locker room, she daydreamed about being there and walking through the locker room filled with naked, muscular football players. This completely knocked her off the wagon, and at her suggestion, he agreed to skip dessert. They moved to the sofa, and moments later, they were kissing.

They were fully clothed, but she was stroking his penis through his pants while his hands were all over her ass. After taking hold of his zipper, she exhaled deeply; reconsidering for a moment, then pulled her hands back and scooted away.

He looked at her breathlessly. "What's wrong?"

"I promised myself I would take it slow."

"You're right. You're right. This is moving too fast. I'm still getting over my divorce and everything—but you are so gorgeous."

"I'm so attracted to you, too." After standing, she moved a safe distance away to a chair across the coffee table from him.

Her eyes locked on the still-evident bulge in his pants.

Following her gaze, he gave her a sorrowful look. "Sorry about that. I... it's been a while for me, and I... uh..."

"God you're so... I hate to leave you like this."

"I'll be fine. I'll... Really, I'll be okay."

She paused a moment with her mind racing. "What if we could take it slow, but not? I mean, not leave here unsatisfied."

He looked at her, confused. "What are you talking about?"

"I have a friend who told me about this thing she... uh... they called it friends with... limited benefits, or something like that."

Looking at her, intrigued, he adjusted his still-crowded pants. "That sounds interesting."

"She was attracted to this younger guy. He's her son's best friend, and they didn't want to have sex, so they came up with this idea."

"What happened?"

"They were naked out in the pool and almost got caught by her son," she said casually.

"So skinny dipping is allowed?"

"It's within the rules." After pausing a moment to think, she frowned. "Oh, but we already broke one of the rules—no kissing."

He shrugged his shoulders. "But we haven't done anything else, so maybe we could just not kiss any more... for now. What are the other rules?"

She smiled as she went through them matter-of-factly. "No sex, of course... No mouth kissing, no kissing of parts..." She opened her eyes wide as he looked at her, a little baffled. To clarify, she pointed to her breasts and crotch. "No fun parts."

After his facial expression morphed into one of understanding, he nodded in agreement. "Well, that makes sense."

"No touching those same parts, and uh, no telling anyone about friends with limited benefits."

He looked away, smiling, and then back to her, puzzled. "If you can't tell anyone, then how did you find out?"

"She told me. That last rule is more of a guideline."

"Uh-huh."

"Should we maybe try it?" She smiled at him, waiting for his reply.

"I think we should. Do you want to go skinny dipping?"

"No, not really." She looked at him hesitantly. "What were you going to do when you got home?"

"Go to sleep, I guess."

"You weren't going to do... *anything* before that?" She stared down with a sultry gaze at his still semi-bulging groin.

Looking down at his crotch, he smiled. "Oh, maybe if I couldn't sleep, I, uh..."

She gave him a skeptical look. "Just maybe?"

He exhaled deeply and then smiled. "Well as soon as we stopped kissing all I could think of, was running home and jerking off while I thought about you. You are so beautiful and sexy. If you must know, I was going to do it as soon as I got into the house."

She grinned at him. "I was planning on doing the same." After bringing her finger to her lips, she widened her eyes. "Since we were going to do it anyway, why not do it here, in front of each other?"

He looked at her, obviously contemplating, with his mouth open as he adjusted his penis in his pants once again. "Do you think we'll be able to—"

"I promise I can control myself. I won't touch you or break any of the rules."

"I can control myself, as long as you stay over there."

"Okay, great." After spreading her legs, she brought a hand to her knee and touched it seductively.

He exhaled deeply as he squeezed his bulge through his pants. "So are we just going to do it? I mean, should I just...?"

She licked her lips then slumped down in the chair as she lifted the short black dress up and folded it to her waist.

His eyes locked on what her nonexistent panties should have been covering. He grinned. "You were planning on taking it slow, but you didn't wear underwear?"

"I had them on, but I got so wet during dinner that I took them off."

"Oh." Exhaling deeply, he quickly unbuttoned his pants, unzipped them, and unveiled his prize. She ran her finger slowly between her legs as she hungrily eyed him.

"You're so big."

"Are you really wet?"

"Soaked." After letting out a soft moan, she ran her tongue seductively around her lips.

"My dick is so hard." He stroked it up and down slowly. "You are so hot."

Lifting her legs up on the arms of the chair, she spread them wide. Her ass cheeks, fully exposed to him, curved down deliciously. He stared at her, mesmerized, as he continued to touch himself. Stopping, he squeezed the base of his cock wearing an expression that said he was about to come. "You have such a beautiful body, and your pussy is gorgeous."

She closed her eyes, imagining that John was tonguing her and whispered, "Thanks." With her fingers still busy, she opened her eyes and looked at his erection. After sighing, she held her hand still. "These rules they are..."

"What about them?"

"They're not like official rules, or anything. There's no

reason why we can't change them a little or make up our own rules."

"That makes sense. They are a little restrictive." He nodded wholeheartedly.

"I know, aren't they?"

They both gazed at each other's parts with open mouths. He shook his head with a grimace. "If you ask me, all these rules are kind of stupid, in fact. What did you have in mind?"

"What if we just had oral sex?" She raised an eyebrow. "We wouldn't go all the way, but we could..." Her words trailed away as she dipped a finger deeper between her legs.

He exhaled sharply and he narrowed his eyes. "What was that?"

"Oral sex—we could do just that. What do you think?"

"Oh." He nodded as a big smile spread over his face. "I think that's a great idea."

Popping up out of his seat, he rushed over to her. He got between her legs and gazed at her for a moment. She held her breath as his mouth slowly lowered to her. As John pressed his tongue gently into her folds, Victoria threw her head back and moaned. Blindly she reached her hand out and ran it through his hair before pulling his head closer into her. He obviously got the message and stepped it up a notch plunging his tongue into her harder and licking her feverously. Her eyelids fluttered away dreamily and she gasped.

Just as John came up for air, Jillian and Brian stood together in the master bathroom. She sat on the edge of her large soaking tub as he looked over at her with shaving cream covering his upper lip. "Can we do it with you in that deviant leg derriere thing position tonight?"

She didn't bother correcting him but frowned. "That really

hurts. I don't think so." Giving her a disappointed look, he turned to the mirror and began to shave his pathetic mustache.

She gave him a hopeful smile. "But I could get into the arabesque position, and we could give that a try."

He rinsed and dried his face and then pondered that while he met her gaze as she looked at him through the mirror. Turning to her, he smiled. "I have no idea what that is, but it sounds hot."

She popped to her feet, grinning. He tossed the towel on the sink and met her in the middle of the bathroom. There, they kissed; it was a long, deep kiss. Pulling back from him, she rubbed her finger gently over his smooth upper lip and smiled. "Much better."

They kissed again. With the heat rising between them, he ran his hands down to her ass and scooped her off the floor. Still locked in a kiss, she wrapped her legs around him. He turned and slowly headed to the bedroom.

Their sex that night was extraordinary and a lot like the McEnroe-Borg Wimbledon tiebreak; lots of sweating, long rallies and heavy breathing, and it went on and on for what seemed like forever. This time, though, there were two winners.

THE END...

Well, not really because these two have a lot more hilarious and sexy escapades ahead.

Thank you for reading Friends with Partial Benefits! Keep flipping to read an excerpt of the next book, **FRIENDS WITH FULL BENEFITS**. You'll laugh out loud as Jillian and Brian attempt to take their relationship to the next level while somehow still keeping Jillian's son Rob in the dark...

Never miss a Luke Young release, announcement or sale by signing up for my **NEWSLETTER**.

Hang out with me on social media: **Website Facebook**

Don't miss the Friends with Partial Benefits short film, which was adapted from one of my favorite scenes in this book. We shot it poolside out in Los Angeles on an unusually cold, thirty-four degree, December California night. Click **here** to watch it on YouTube.

More Books by Luke

Friends with Benefits Series

Follow the sexy and hilarious adventures of Jillian and Brian as they navigate the tricky waters of their reverse age gap romance in the seven-book complete series.

FRIENDS WITH PARTIAL BENEFITS

FRIENDS WITH FULL BENEFITS

FRIENDS WITH MORE BENEFITS

FRIENDS WITH EXTRA BENEFITS

FRIENDS WITH TOO MANY BENEFITS

FRIENDS WITH MULTIPLE BENEFITS

FRIENDS WITH REAL BENEFITS

The Friends with Benefits Prequel

FRIENDS WANTING BENEFITS

Discover the hilarious backstory of how Victoria and Jillian meet. When two very different couples, one who's just getting started and one who's apparently just getting finished... meet on a cruise, the better halves become fast friends.

The Friends with Benefits Bonus Book:

FRIENDS WITH BENEFITS BONUS BOOK - VOLUME ONE

Four stand-alone stories featuring your favorite "Friends With Benefits" characters. Some laugh-out-loud funny, some sexy and some, well, both...

Erotica by Luke Young under his Ian Dalton Pen Name

DESPERATE THOUGHTS

Uncover Victoria's secret in, Desperate Thoughts, the erotic prequel the Friends with Benefits Series! It's a dark and sexy tale of love, loss and letting go...

It's been fourteen months since Victoria's husband died and she's struggling to move on with her life. As the attractive widow tumbles into a clandestine sexual encounter with a much younger man, she's re-awakened sexually and motivated to pursue her desperately unfulfilled desires. With each new encounter the risk grows, along with the passion, until events spiral out of control and she's forced to choose between continuing down a path of self-destruction and finally letting go of the past.

Stand Alone Novels

BLAME IT ON EMERALD ISLE

Falling for a younger guy wasn't in the cards, but might be just what the doctor ordered...

Never quite getting over the loss of her college soul mate, and settled into a marriage of safety and convenience, Doctor Ally Larson fights a forbidden attraction during a much-needed beach vacation. If battling her own desires isn't disrupting enough from her getaway, dealing with her divorced, oversexed and quirky parents might just send her over the edge.

Torn between the memory of a man she lost, the sexy young man she desperately desires and her near-perfect husband, who she just can't get out of her own way to love, she's teetering on the edge of disaster. Who will she choose and will anyone survive the fallout?

Blame it on Emerald Isle is a guaranteed HEA reverse age-gap romance with an overworked heroine, sexy college baseball athlete, zany parents and the cutest dog ever. It's a vacation destination read, filled with laughter, a full range of emotions, tons of sexual tension and heat so hot you'll need SPF-1000.

SERIOUSLY MESSED UP

Eli Stevens has everything going for him. Married and successful, he's moving in the right direction, when suddenly his world shifts on its axis and he desperately needs to escape... After saving a pop star's life, he's given every man's fantasy as a thank you--a beach house and two incredibly hot women. From there, of course, nothing goes as planned...

CHANCES AREN'T

How far would you go for a second chance? Stunned by an impending divorce, Ben Hunter's life, which was barely working to begin with, suddenly takes a turn for the worse. After a series of extraordinary events, he's given a chance to fix all of it and in the process comes face to face with the last person he ever expected to see — himself...

CHOCOLATE COVERED BILLIONAIRE NAVY SEAL

Roll on the floor laughing while enjoying this contemporary romance parody. Heir to a chocolate empire, Brock Fullman joins the elite Navy SEAL team in order to avenge the death of his high school sweetheart. With his billionaire family one bad day in the stock market away from the dreaded "Mm Mm Mm..." word (Yes Millionaire... he's the only family member who can actually say it), he's torn between the woman he must marry to guarantee his family's future and the new woman he secretly loves. Out for revenge, will he destroy the company, his family, himself and all those around him in the process?

SO FAR GONE, GIRL: A GONE GIRL PARODY

You think you hated Amazing Amy... just wait until you meet Wonderful Winnie! Read the hilarious parody of Gone Girl. Get the ending you were hoping for and laugh out loud along the way.

What do you get when you take the amazing GONE GIRL story, replace the lame anniversary treasure hunts with deadly SAW movie-esque traps and have all the craziness investigated by lunatic detectives channeling the ones from the television show THE KILLING? You get an unputdownable and hilarious parody of EPIC proportions. Don't miss it!

SHRINKAGE

Be careful what you wish for because sometimes you might just get way too much of it!

Is it in yet? It's the phrase that no man ever wants to hear. Luckily, Tim Garrett has never heard those words. At least he has never heard them out loud despite being on the wrong side of the bell curve in the male endowment department.

Excerpt Of Friends With Full Benefits

Miami hadn't seen three straight days of drenching rain in more than a year. But as Brian waited to hold a tennis match with Jillian, with her response to his marriage proposal hanging in the balance, the rain came. It came hard. He was fine with the lack of acceptance of his proposal for the entire first day while they were joking about the match "rain delay;" by the second day, he was sure she would have accepted his proposal, but she hadn't. He didn't start to worry until Day Three, when neither of them mentioned the proposal or the match or any of it. Everything else was fine in the relationship—actually, it was perfect otherwise.

Perfect except for that one "little" thing—he'd proposed three nights ago out by the pool, and he still didn't have an answer. And when she didn't respond immediately, he'd tried to provide some levity by suggesting they play for it. He was really only joking; he saw it as just a formality. Even if she did happen to beat him when they played, he was sure she would still just say yes. But at 7:00 p.m. on Day Three, he was still waiting. It had stopped raining an hour or so earlier, but the court was still wet. Plus, Jillian's best friend Victoria had invited them over for dinner, and they were just about to walk out the door. He was in a slightly better mood since he'd learned the next day was going to be beautiful—perfect tennis weather. It was to be an unusual day for late June in southern Florida, eighty degrees with low humidity. He was psyched and ready to play.

Brian was behind the wheel of Jillian's car, and she sat in the passenger seat, holding a perfect-looking chocolate mousse ganache cake in her lap. They had baked it together that morning and not had sex afterward. They always had sex after they cooked together. There was something about being in the kitchen together and the sensuality of the whole cooking process that got her worked up, but not today.

Before pulling out of the driveway, he glanced out the windshield to the sky. "It looks like it's clearing up."

"Mm-hmm." She gazed out the window, preoccupied.

As they neared Victoria's house, he rolled his eyes and thought, *"Mm-hmm...mm hmm"*—that's it? Not, *"Oh good, we can finally get our big match in"? What the hell is she thinking?*

Out of the blue, Jillian announced, "I shaved *everything* for you today."

"Everything?"

"Yep." She flashed him a sexy smile.

"Wow, um, great..." Talk about changing the subject—that was the best segue he'd ever heard. The best by far.

"Let's get drunk tonight and just have sex; like, amazing sex. We'll walk home if we have to."

"Okay." He grinned excitedly, thinking that this was getting good. He had just been promised clean-shaven lady parts and drunken, wild sex. His favorite...

"I'm sorry I've been such a bitch lately. It's the rain. It makes me depressed. I think I have a touch of that thing where if you don't see the sun, you're in a bad mood. What's that called again?"

"I don't know, but I know exactly what you're talking about."

"That's why I live in southern Florida. It hardly ever rains here."

He nodded in agreement as he pulled into Victoria's driveway.

As he opened the door to get out of the car, she put her hand on his arm. "Wait." He met her gaze, and she gave him an uneasy smile. "We'll play tennis tomorrow. Then..." She gave him a wistful look. "I really want to play you."

"Oh, I know you do. I can't wait." A big smile spread across his face as they walked to the front door.

Victoria, Brian, and Jillian sat around the table in Victoria's dining room, enjoying a glass of wine after finishing a delicious meal that Victoria clearly had not prepared, because she never cooked. In fact, her oven was used mainly for storage. Instead, she had the meal delivered from a fine local restaurant.

"The food was amazing." Brian patted his full stomach.

"Yes, it was delicious." Jillian shook her head with a smile.

"It's not easy putting together a meal like this."

After they all shared a laugh, Victoria asked, "You guys feel like sitting by the pool?"

A few minutes later, the women sat on comfortable lounge chairs enjoying the beautiful night, while Brian prepared after-dinner drinks in the house.

Looking at the house directly behind Victoria's, Jillian's eyes widened. "You never mentioned how your date went with your hot neighbor."

"It was... okay."

"Did you keep your promise?"

"What promise?"

Jillian gave her a look. "About not having sex with him on the first date."

"Sure did."

"Good, so what does he do?"

"He's the head coach of the football team."

"At the U?"

Victoria nodded with a frown.

"That's an important job. Does he actually have any free time to date?"

"I think so, but I don't know." Sighing, Victoria stared down at the concrete patio.

"What is it?"

Victoria glanced up at her face. "It's just... I haven't had sex in over a month, and I'm not sure it's going to work out with John and me."

"Why not?"

"I think he has a premature ejaculation problem."

Jillian looked confused. "Did he tell you that?"

"No."

"Okay, then how do you know?"

"Well, he came, like, five seconds after I went down on him. That's how I know."

Jillian was staring straight ahead, looking confused, when Brian walked out carrying two cosmopolitans. He handed them off to Jillian and Victoria. "I'll be right back."

"But you said you didn't have sex," Jillian said.

"We didn't. He's pretty good at eating pussy, and I really enjoyed that part, but—"

"Let me see if I understand you correctly. He performed oral sex on you?"

"Uh-huh."

"You performed oral sex on him?"

"For five seconds."

"Okay, it was short, but his penis was in your mouth, right?"

"Right. So what's your point?"

"Sounds to me like you had sex."

"No, we didn't."

Looking at Victoria in complete bewilderment, Jillian's jaw dropped. Brian returned with his own girly drink, placed it on the table, and fell into a comfortable chair. "What the heck are we talking about?"

Jillian made a face. "Do you consider oral sex, sex?"

"Sure."

Victoria folded her arms across her chest. "Well, I don't."

"Who are you, Bill Clinton?" Brian scoffed.

"If that definition works for a former President, then it works for me."

Turning to Brian, Jillian asked, "Remember when Victoria said that she would not have sex with this new guy on the first date?"

"I remember."

"Well, he performed oral sex on her; then she did it to him, and—"

"Only for five seconds before he shot all over my face and in my hair."

"Yuck." Jillian glared at her as if that little detail was totally unnecessary.

"I had to wash my hair twice, and my eye burned for, like, an hour."

After Jillian and Brian shared a look, he looked back at Victoria. "Only five seconds, you say?"

"Not even."

He widened his eyes. "Well, in that case..."

Victoria looked at him, waiting hopefully for some support.

After pondering it for a moment, he nodded. "It's still sex. You had sex with him."

Dismissively waving her hand at him, Victoria shook her head. "Sex is fucking—penis-in-vagina fucking."

Jillian's eyes lit up as if she had the perfect argument to win the case. "Then, do you consider anal sex, sex?"

After narrowing her eyes to process that little nugget, Victoria let out a sigh. "No... I mean, yes. Oh, let's just drop it. We had oral sex, but I haven't had *vaginal*..." She scowled at both of them. "...sex in two weeks, and I'm horny. The closest thing I have to a sexual partner is a hot, middle-aged guy who shoots before you get your panties down." After staring at them again, hoping for something resembling understanding and getting nothing, she let out a long, slow breath. "I'm sad, okay?"

"I went almost a year without having sex once." Jillian announced proudly.

"Eighteen months for me... starting in my junior year, until I met..." He motioned toward Jillian with a couple quick head nods; in response, she grinned like a schoolgirl.

Victoria eyed them both with a condescending smile. "That doesn't comfort me at all. You guys were kinda like losers in the romance department. No offense."

Jillian sneered her way, and then they all took a big sip of their drinks.

After an awkward pause, Brian shifted gears. "So... Victoria, when do classes start?"

"My summer class starts in three weeks."

"What is it?" Jillian asked.

"It's called Advanced Sexual Problems. It focuses on case studies of couples whose sex lives are in desperate need of help. I got ahold of the syllabus and found out that I have to do a case study, either on a real-life couple or one described in the textbook."

"That sounds a hell of a lot more interesting than those finance classes I had to take," Brian said.

Victoria took another sip from her drink. "Do you guys have any issues in the bedroom that, uh, might help me come up with a topic? You could be a real-life case study. I'd love to get a head start."

Emptying her drink, Jillian shook her head. "Wow, that was strong. Let's see... um, bedroom problems." She curled her lip as they each wracked their brains for anything. Jillian shook her head. "No, I think we're all—"

"What about..." Brian's eyes widened. "No, forget it."

Jillian gave him a curious look. "What were you going to say?"

Motioning with his hand for her to let it go, he shook his head no.

"Come on." Jillian folded her arms across her chest and pouted. "What issue do you think we have?"

"You know that time we tried to do, uh... and it didn't..."

"What the hell are you talking about?"

He bit his lip, and then took a sip of his drink, before apprehensively looking back at her. "It's nothing, really."

Victoria smiled. This was getting good.

Jillian's expression softened a little. "It's okay, you can say it."

He leaned over and whispered in her ear. With enlightenment spreading across her face, Jillian nodded. "Yeah, that didn't go well. We should try again—like a year from now, or something."

Her curiosity piqued so Victoria asked, "What didn't go well?"

Unsure whether to share this information, Jillian eventually shrugged her shoulders at Brian. "You might as well tell her. She held your penis in her hand for, like, two minutes, for God's sake."

Victoria chuckled. "He told you about that?"

"He tells me everything."

Brian grinned. "Not everything."

"I was only trying to help him put... everything away," Victoria explained.

Rolling her eyes, Jillian gave her a half-smile. "Okay, yeah."

"So what is it? I'm dying to know."

"It's, uh..." He exhaled deeply. "Anal sex. We tried it, and... it didn't exactly go well."

Victoria's face lit up. "You two haven't had amazing anal sex yet? You've come to the right place. I'm an expert on backdoor pleasures."

"You must be proud." Jillian cracked a sarcastic smile.

"Don't knock it until you've tried—I mean *done* it successfully. You'll never have a bigger orgasm."

"Really?" Brian asked.

"Oh, yes, especially if you combine slow, gentle anal penetration with clitoral stimulation."

Jillian wore a sour expression. "Do we have to talk about this?"

"Oh, lighten up." Victoria dismissed her with a wave of her hand.

He moved to the edge of his seat. "But how does everything fit? I mean, is it really supposed to fit in there?"

"You'd be surprised. That area can open up a lot more than you think. Much more than the vagina, in fact."

"I didn't know that." After nodding mesmerized for a moment, he turned his attention to Jillian with his eyebrows raised.

Jillian made a face. "I don't want to talk about this. It's, uh..."

"Well, what do you want to talk about?"

"Can't we just sit here and enjoy the night?"

Brian lounged back in his chair, and they all sat in silence for nearly a minute.

While looking down at her empty glass, Victoria suddenly smiled. "You guys want to smoke a joint? I got some of that same stuff you both enjoyed that night in the pool."

The blissful couple shared a grin.

Twenty minutes later, the three were all half-baked, and Jillian had changed her attitude slightly about sharing details of their anal sex issue. In fact, she wouldn't shut up about it. Victoria listened, captivated, while Brian wore a silly grin. The combination of wine, vodka, and marijuana was creating a sort of mellow, sensual, open vibe at the small gathering.

"He was licking my ass, and it felt, uh... incredible."

"Oh, God, I love when a guy does that to me, and..." Victoria looked away with her words trailing off as if she were reliving the memory.

Jillian raised her eyebrows. "His penis is so thick."

"What?" Victoria whispered breathlessly, still caught up in the fantasy.

"His penis. It's very thick."

Victoria returned her attention to Jillian. "I know." Glancing over at Brian, she caught his proud look.

"It felt great as he rubbed it against me back there. Really incredible... you know, before he tried to put it in. But I moved my hips the wrong way or something, the head slipped in, and it hurt."

Brian put his hands behind his head and simply watched them, smiling and loving being the topic of conversation.

Victoria put her hand to her chin. "Did you use enough lube?"

"I think so."

"Did he prime you first?"

Giggling, Jillian looked at her in confusion.

"Did he use a lubed finger first to get you ready?"

"Oh, *primed*... that's a stupid word." Jillian looked at Brian for the answer.

He looked at them, insulted. "No, I didn't. I did not put my finger in her ass."

"Well, that's part of the problem," Victoria said smugly.

Jillian nodded at him. "See, this was your fault."

Pulling his hands from his head, Brian's jaw dropped. "Look, it was our first time. We were bound to hit a few speed bumps."

Victoria sat up in her chair and asked accusatorily, "And Jillian, when he tried to put it in, did you push out like you were trying to go to the bathroom?"

Jillian looked at her horrified. "I definitely didn't do that."

"That's very important."

"Really?" Jillian stared back at her with a furrowed brow.

"It's pretty much the most important part."

Brian gave Jillian a snotty look, and she shrugged her shoulders back at him. "Sorry. I'm not like your friend, Natalie. I don't do this with every guy I meet."

The three broke into laughter. After they composed themselves, they each took another hit. Jillian and Brian sat back in their chairs, particularly high but a touch depressed. Victoria studied their lost expressions and grinned. "Hey, you guys want to watch some porn? It will be educational. I've got this great backdoor scene. It's one of my favorites. It's so hot, and it just might help."

He widened his eyes at Jillian, and she looked to be on the fence. "Come on—it'll be fun, and we might just learn something."

End of excerpt - FRIENDS WITH FULL BENEFITS is available now.

Author's note:

I hope you enjoyed *Friends with Partial Benefits*. I've had this story in my head since a girl, I won't mention by name, actually broke my heart in college in pretty much the exact way outlined in this book. She really could do that thing with her leg and when I saw her do it at a party, I was hooked. Okay, so I was a shallow pathetic inexperienced loser... 'Miss flexibility' did end up secretly dating my suite mate and stringing me along. I really do think she enjoyed messing with my head just as much as Natalie did in the story. I did go on that spring break trip with my suite mate (while all this was going on), but it was Texas and not Miami. I was as clueless as Brian... Those two crazy real-life kids got married and I assume had like twelve kids together or something. Unfortunately, that's where the 'sort of based on a true story' part of the story ends and my imagination takes over. There was no hot mother, no 'technical virgin' story line, no super-fun Victoria or any of the other stuff you hopefully found hilarious. I do sometimes wonder if the girl in question can still do that thing with her leg because I really would... Sorry not sure where I was going with that.

Author's note:

And one note about tennis; McEnroe was the reason that I started playing. I rented the DVD of that match I quote in the book (the 1980 Wimbledon final) and wow has the game changed. Don't get me wrong; it was a great match. One of the best. But like so many other sports, the players are faster, the equipment better and today's players somehow hit the ball much harder now. I did enjoy watching all of McEnroe's finals during most of the eighties. He seemed to be in just about every one of them and I loved his style of play. I still miss those days and those rivalries compared to the ones from today.

I hope you'll read the rest of the series and learn what happens next. I'm having a blast writing it. Please check out the beginning of *Friends with Full Benefits* in the excerpt included with this book.

Luke Young

About the Author

Hey everyone! I'm romantic comedy, contemporary romance and comic fiction author Luke Young. I've written over sixteen books, including one Amazon number one in comic fiction and five Amazon and iBooks Rom Com Bestsellers. The best way to stay in touch with me for news and new releases is to sign up for my email list here: https://lukeyoungbooks.com.

You can email me at authorlukeyoung@gmail.com or on Facebook at https://www.facebook.com/LukeYoungAuthor. Please reach out and let me know what you think about my books! I love hearing from readers.

Printed in Great Britain
by Amazon

55817947R00160